Scratch the Surface

Scratch the Surface

A CAT LOVER'S MYSTERY

Susan Conant

BERKLEY PRIME CRIME, NEW YORK

THE BERKLEY PUBLISHING GROUP
Published by the Penguin Group
Penguin Group (USA) Inc.
375 Hudson Street, New York, New York 10014, USA
Penguin Group (Canada), 10 Alcorn Avenue, Toronto, Ontario M4V 3B2, Canada
(a division of Pearson Penguin Canada Inc.)
Penguin Books Ltd., 80 Strand, London WC2R 0RL, England
Penguin Group Ireland, 25 St. Stephen's Green, Dublin 2, Ireland (a division of Penguin Books Ltd.)
Penguin Group (Australia), 250 Camberwell Road, Camberwell, Victoria 3124, Australia
(a division of Pearson Australia Group Pty. Ltd.)
Penguin Books India Pvt. Ltd., 11 Community Centre, Panchsheel Park, New Delhi—110 017, India
Penguin Group (NZ), Cnr. Airborne and Rosedale Roads, Albany, Auckland 1310, New Zealand
(a division of Pearson New Zealand Ltd.)
Penguin Books (South Africa) (Pty.) Ltd., 24 Sturdee Avenue, Rosebank, Johannesburg 2196,
South Africa

Penguin Books Ltd., Registered Offices: 80 Strand, London WC2R 0RL, England

This book is an original publication of The Berkley Publishing Group.

PRINTING HISTORY
Berkley Prime Crime hardcover edition / June 2005

Library of Congress Cataloging-in-Publication Data

Conant, Susan, 1946-
    Scratch the surface : a cat lover's mystery / Susan Conant.—Berkley Prime Crime
hardcover ed.
        p. cm.—(Cat lover's mysteries)
        ISBN 0-425-20259-3
        1. Women novelists—Fiction.   2. Apartment houses—Fiction.   3. Detective and
mystery stories—Authorship—Fiction.   4. Cats—Fiction.   I. Title.

PS3553.O4857S29 2005
813'.54—dc22

                                                      2005041136

PRINTED IN THE UNITED STATES OF AMERICA

10   9   8   7   6   5   4   3   2   1

*To Carter, in loving memory of Clementine,
who gave us seventeen years of feline perfection.*

ACKNOWLEDGMENTS

My profuse thanks to Dru Milligan and Jolie Stratton, Ajolie Chartreux, who introduced me to the Chartreux cat; and to GRP Janvier Pandora Spocks of Ajolie (K.C.) and Ajolie's Shadow Dancer (Shadow Celeste), known herein as Edith and Brigitte. For support and advice, I am grateful to Jessica Park, who is my beloved daughter, my dear friend, and, as Jessica Conant-Park, my some-time coauthor. Jean Berman, Annette Champion, Laury Huessler, Renee Knilans, Phyllis Stein, Pat Sullivan, Margherita Walker, and Corinne Zipps generously helped with the manuscript and the proofs.

For answering technical questions, my thanks to Tina Paar, Jamie Wiley, and Bonnie Walker. Jean Berman generously helped with the manuscript. Special thanks to my agent, Deborah Schneider, and my editor, Natalee Rosenstein, for trusting a dog writer with cats.

ONE

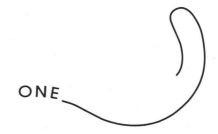

According to the newsletter of Newbright Books, Felicity Pride would visit the store on Monday, November 3, from six to seven to read from her latest mystery, *Felines in Felony*. In promoting the event, the store's proprietor, Ronald Gershwin, had described his friend Felicity in her own words: "The prizewinning author of the bestselling Prissy LaChatte series of cat lover's mysteries, Felicity Pride is a member of Mystery Writers of America, the National Writers Union, and Sisters in Crime. She serves on the board of the New England Chapter of Witness for the Publication. One of our favorite local authors, Felicity lives near Boston."

As Ronald knew, Felicity had last won an award at her high school graduation thirty-five years earlier. She still had the prize, a Latin medal embossed with the words *Labor omnia vincit*. From time to time, when Felicity came upon the medal in the top drawer of her bureau, she wondered about the truth of the motto. Was it really work that conquered all? And not love? On balance, the medal, however, brought consistent pleasure, proving as it did that she truly had won an award. As to Felicity's characterization of her Prissy LaChatte books as "bestselling," it was true that each addition to the series made the top-ten list at Newbright Books. What's more, all the books in the series ranked high on the sites of the major online booksellers in the sub-subcategory of mysteries about cats. Felicity often reminded herself that "bestselling" didn't necessarily mean the *New York Times*.

So, at ten minutes after seven on the evening of Monday, November 3, Felicity Pride had finished reading selected passages about Prissy LaChatte and her feline companions, Morris and Tabitha, to a smaller group than she'd have liked. These local events never gave her the crowds she drew at out-of-state bookstores and at conferences for mystery fans, but she could hardly have refused to do a reading and signing for Ronald, who, for all his oddity, was as close as she came to having a best friend. She had sold some books, and it was pleasant enough to sit in the cozy armchair at the back of the store and autograph *Felines in Felony* for the buyers who had lingered after the reading. *Felines* was, after all, a hardcover, which is to say that for every copy sold, her publisher's royalty department would credit her with a decent percentage of the book's satisfyingly high retail price. With that happy prospect in mind, Felicity glanced down at the title page of the book she'd just autographed. In bold marker, Felicity had drawn a line through the printed version of her name. Her horrified gaze, however, revealed that instead of merely replacing the cold, impersonal letters with her florid signature, she had written three mortifying words beneath it.

She snapped the book shut, slipped it behind her back, smiled at the woman who'd handed it to her, and said, "Well, I've botched that one. Let's try again. Are you sure you don't want it signed to you?"

"Just your name, please," said the woman, whom Felicity saw not as the plump, nondescript individual she was, but as a representative of the adoring public who clung with catlike claws to Felicity Pride's every written and spoken word. "I collect modern firsts," the woman explained. "They're more valuable without an inscription. At least while the author is alive. As you are, of course. Obviously."

Felicity waited for this unprepossessing representative of her worshipful readership to add some suitably flattering expression of happiness on that account: *Not just obviously but luckily!* Or maybe, *And thank heaven you are alive, because we devotees of Prissy LaChatte and dear Morris and Tabitha would be utterly bereft without you!*

To Felicity's disappointment, the collector of modern first editions remained silent, as did the four women who waited in line behind her. Had Felicity written the scene, all five women would have borne subtle and charming resemblances to cats of various types: perhaps a plump gray Persian, a petite marmalade, a sleek calico, a silver tabby, and a striped alley cat with facial scars. Felicity herself would have been a long, lean Siamese with a patrician bone structure and an air of elegance and savoir faire. In reality, there was nothing especially feline about the book buyers, and far from looking like a Siamese, Felicity was short and had a sturdiness of build and feature more suggestive of muscular human peasantry than of feline aristocracy. She was, however, tidy and well groomed. Her charcoal wool pants and cashmere sweater were neither too old nor too young for her age, which was fifty-three, and the blonde highlights in her straight, blunt-cut hair effectively covered any white strands that had the nerve to emerge from her scalp. Felicity would have been happier to live with head lice than with gray hair.

"Still alive," said Felicity, who was used to looking after herself. "Luckily for me. And I know what 'Just your name' means. You collectors! Some of you don't mind having the date added."

"Just your name, please," repeated the woman as she handed Felicity a fresh copy of *Felines in Felony* from one of the piles that Ronald Gershwin had stacked on the table next to Felicity's armchair.

The next woman in line was not buying *Felines in Felony*. Rather, she wanted Felicity's signature on a paperback copy of *Out of the Bag,* which had just been released in what publishers referred to as the "mass market edition." The term always struck Felicity as a wild overstatement, at least in the case of her own paperbacks, which sold well enough, she supposed, but could hardly be said to have "mass" sales.

The three remaining women turned out to be major fans who'd come to Felicity's reading together and deliberately waited at the end of the line for the chance to talk with her. Mindful that her readers irrationally persisted in seeing themselves as individuals and preferred, albeit unrealistically, to be so viewed by their favorite author, Felicity took careful mental note of their names when she inscribed their books. She subsequently made a point of addressing each of the women, Linda, Melody, and Amy, at least once by her first name. Although mnemonic devices had failed her in the past, she nonetheless tried envisioning Linda, who had a dark and mottled complexion, with ashes smudged on her face: Linda the Cinder. In the Boston accent that Felicity had labored to banish from her speech, the words rhymed. Melody, who wore a round-collared white blouse, was easy to see as a choir girl, her mouth open in song. *Amy* meant beloved. The association posed a challenge, since this Amy had a pinched face and a sour expression, but Felicity still succeeded in imagining her in the arms of a Hollywood leading man from a thirties movie, his dark hair slick with grease, his eyes heavy with passion.

Amy immediately ruined the image by digging into a large purse and producing a fat little album packed with snapshots of her three cats, whose names Felicity made no effort to remember. "And Tabitha," said Amy, pointing to a blurred picture of a black kitten, "is my baby. She came from a shelter, but I'm pretty sure she's part Siamese. She has that look, doesn't she?"

"Definitely," said Felicity. "She definitely looks part Siamese. And is she named for Prissy's Tabitha? If so, I'm very flattered."

Amy blushed and nodded. "I got my other two cats before I discovered your books, or one of them would be Morris."

Linda—Linda the Cinder—then asked what Felicity had come to think of as the second of the Two Inevitable Questions, the first being, "Where do you get your ideas?" The second was: "Do you have a new cat yet?"

Lowering her eyes, Felicity gave her Inevitable Answer. "I'm just not ready yet. My Morris was . . . my own Morris was irreplaceable. All cats are, of course. I know that it seems as if my grief is prolonged. But the fact is that I'm still in mourning for Morris. He was the inspiration for my

books, you know, and, really, writing about Prissy and *her*
Morris and Tabitha is my way of keeping my own Morris
alive."

Felicity had repeated the myth of her very own Morris so
often that by now, her grief for her fictional muse was genuine, as was her fondness for Prissy LaChatte's Morris and
Tabitha, who were adorable, intuitive, and frolicsome. Best
of all, when Felicity had had enough of the creatures, she
was free to turn off her computer or to set aside her manuscript. Prissy's cats were thus, as Felicity had often written,
utterly purr-fect. Indeed, from Felicity's viewpoint, the perfect pets were those who existed only in her mind, on the
pages of her books, and—a matter never to be overlooked—
in the hearts of her devoted readership.

Linda stooped to wrap a consoling arm around Felicity's
shoulders. "You'll know when you're ready."

Never, Felicity thought. "Yes," she said, "I suppose I will.
Thank you. And, of course, Prissy's cats are mine, too, really." With an arch look, she added, "Prissy is very generous
about sharing them with me."

The three readership representatives gave gratifying
chuckles.

"That's why Morris and Tabitha are so real to us," Linda
said. "Because they're real to you. We like the other cat
mysteries—especially Isabelle Hotchkiss—but you're our
favorite."

"Thank you," said Felicity, who didn't trust herself to
comment on Isabelle Hotchkiss, author of the Kitty Katlikoff series and Felicity's principal competition.

"Have you ever met her?" asked Amy, who was holding a
copy of the new Isabelle Hotchkiss hardcover, *Purrfectly Baffling.*

"No one has," Felicity said, "as far as I know. She doesn't do signings, and she never goes to conferences."

"Isabelle Hotchkiss, a lady of mystery," said Ronald, who had suddenly appeared. As usual, he spoke in a low, apprehensive tone, as if he were saying something he shouldn't and were afraid of being overheard. With the same air of imparting a potentially dangerous secret, he added, "It's a pen name. A *nom de mystère*."

"Ronald, we know what a pen name is," Felicity said. In the female-sleuth novels Felicity read, the protagonist's best friend was usually a six-foot-tall woman with red hair and a manner so dramatic as to suggest mental illness. In disappointing contrast, Ronald was of medium height and rather paunchy. His thinning brown hair was gathered in a ponytail, and if his furtive manner hinted at theatrics, it suggested a small character part in an amateur production rather than a leading role in a professional performance. Ronald's sly and even conspiratorial style was independent of the content of what he said. If a customer at Newbright Books asked to be reminded of the author of *The Cat Who . . .* series, for example, Ronald typically shifted his eyes left and right, lowered his head, and murmured, "Braun, Lilian Jackson."

Their tête-à-tête with the author having been interrupted, Linda, Amy, and Melody told Felicity that it had been a pleasure to meet her and said that they could hardly wait for her next book.

"Thank you," she replied. "It's with my editor. It's called *Upon Our Prey We Steal*."

The fans smiled appreciatively and headed for the front of the store with Ronald trailing after them. Felicity removed the ruined copy of *Felines in Felony* that she'd jammed behind her back. Feeling no need to revisit the scene of her unintended crime of self-revelation, she did not open the book before slipping it into her tote bag. When she got home, she'd rip out the title page and burn it, and the next time she visited Newbright Books, she'd replace this copy with a fresh one from her own stock. Thus no one would ever know that instead of autographing the book in normal fashion, she'd written:

Felicity Pride

For deposit only

TWO

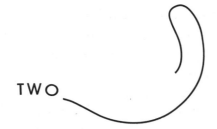

The name of Ronald Gershwin's store, Newbright Books, referred to its location near the Newton-Brighton line. The store, which sold both new and used books, was anything but new and bright. In the two decades since Ronald had opened the establishment, his redecoration had never gone beyond dusting and vacuuming. The fabric on the armchairs was threadbare, and the floorboards were worn to bare wood. As Felicity made her way to the front of the shop, she reminded herself to search for just the right moment to have a word about the decor with Ronald, whom she considered to have no business sense. Had the bookstore been hers, she'd have repainted the walls, tiled the floor, and added an espresso bar, if not a full café. She had, however, no more desire to run a business than she did to return to teaching, the day job from which writing had liberated her; whenever she sensed a drop in her motivation to continue the adventures of Prissy LaChatte, the prospect of returning to the classroom roused her ambition and set her fingers flying over the keyboard.

When Felicity reached the area near the cash register, Ronald was replenishing the stock of *Purrfectly Baffling* in a prominent display stand devoted exclusively to the works of Isabelle Hotchkiss.

After ascertaining that there were no customers in hearing distance, Felicity pointed at the rack and said, "Ronald, is *that* really necessary?"

"Probably not. Her books pretty much sell themselves." With a smile of redeeming sweetness, he added, "Her publisher gives her a lot of support."

"For talking cats!" Olaf and Lambie Pie, the feline stars of the Kitty Katlikoff series, spoke aloud to each other and to Kitty in a manner that Felicity found cloying. In contrast, Morris and Tabitha "communicated" with Prissy LaChatte via channels that had remained mysterious throughout all ten of Felicity's books. One never-to-be-forgiven reviewer of *Paws for Murder* had commented that the ability of the cats to transmit ideas was the only puzzling element of the supposed mystery.

"Isabelle Hotchkiss *is* very popular," said Ronald, whom Felicity credited with what she called "the social sense of a none-too-bright bivalve."

"Ronald, I know that."

"I've hurt your feelings. I'm sorry." After a pause, he asked, "How are you making out with your Russians?"

"They aren't *my* Russians. But thank you for asking. I finally found the contract, not that it'll do me any good."

Five years earlier, Felicity's agent, Irene Antonopoulos, had phoned with the exhilarating news that a Russian publisher wanted the rights to the first four Prissy LaChatte books. The amount offered as an advance was small, but Felicity was thrilled. Russia! Prissy had already been translated into German, but the Germans had evidently not taken to her, and the German editions had rapidly gone out of print. Besides, Germany wasn't exotic. It wasn't Russia! Felicity had savored images of Moscow subway cars packed with readers entranced by Prissy, Morris, and Tabitha. The contracts had been signed. Then Irene had called to say that the deal had fallen through. The Russian economy was in terrible condition. So sorry. Having announced her Russian sales in the newsletters of Mystery Writers of America, Sisters in Crime, Witness for the Publication, and several other organizations, Felicity was mortified.

Two months ago, her humiliation had turned to rage. She'd been on a mystery writers' panel at a local library when a young Russian woman had shown her a book with a title in Cyrillic characters and the words *Felicity Pride*. "I thought you might not know about this," the young woman had said. "My mother bought it in Canada. It happens all the time."

A search of the Web had confirmed the young woman's statement and provided a term that Felicity found consoling: *piracy*. "My books have been pirated by Russians!" she began to announce. "Pirated!" By comparison, it would have been nothing to report that her books had merely been translated. As it was, she made a great fuss with every writers' organization to which she belonged.

"The contracts," she informed Ronald, "are just the way I remembered. They're signed. And the edition I saw is exactly

what the contract says: two books published together in one
hardcover. But there's nothing I can do. My agent is all
sympathy, but she doesn't hold out any hope."

Before leaving Newbright Books, Felicity bought two
mysteries. She had been reading the genre since her Nancy
Drew days and felt justified in buying as many mysteries as
she pleased from Ronald, not only because she wanted to
support his business and enjoyed the books, but because she
liked keeping a tax-deductible eye on the competition. Neither of her purchases had anything to do with cats. As a
matter of principle, Felicity never contributed to the royalties of other cat-mystery writers. She took it for granted
that her rivals weren't foolish enough to buy her books new,
either.

As was her habit, Felicity took the long route home. She
had inherited her house from her maternal uncle, Robert
Burns Robertson, who, together with his wife, Thelma,
had died in an automobile accident the previous summer.
Uncle Bob and Aunt Thelma had owned the place for only
a year. It was one of twenty gigantic houses in a pricey
development called Newton Park Estates. The would-be
estates, which were organized as condominiums and gov-
erned by a condominium association, abutted the upscale
suburb of Newton, but, as the residents preferred not to
have mentioned, were actually in the Brighton section of
Boston. Neither Felicity nor any of the other residents of
Newton Park Estates ever referred to the neighborhood as
a development. Similarly, everyone avoided such phrases as
tract mansions and *McMansions*. Still, the houses were three
or four stories high, and all sat on very small lots. The late
Bob Robertson's sensitivity to derogatory remarks about
his splendid abode was the reason he had disinherited

Felicity's mother, Mary, who had made the mistake on her first and only visit to Newton Park Estates of remarking, "My father's house has mini-mansions. Isn't that what the Bible says?" Felicity's sister, Angie, had lost her inheritance by snickering at her mother's joke.

Together with the house, Felicity had inherited Aunt Thelma's car, a black Honda CR-V. Uncle Bob's Cadillac Escalade had perished with its owner. The all-wheel-drive Honda was a far more youthful, trendy, and economical choice than Felicity would have expected of the dowdy, elderly Thelma, who had been a pale-green full-size Oldsmobile type. Before the inheritance, Felicity had rented an apartment in a three-decker in Somerville and driven an ancient Chevy Nova, a vehicle that had relentlessly reminded her that *No va* was Spanish for *Doesn't go*.

On this Monday evening, Felicity's Honda not only went, but went where she wanted it to go, which was westward on Commonwealth Avenue and past the turnoff that would have taken her swiftly home. Following Commonwealth Avenue, she drove into Newton and followed a circuitous route that eventually wandered uphill to a neighborhood of narrow streets, spacious lots, and large houses of diverse styles and ages. The neighborhood, Norwood Hill, had grown over many years—it was anything but a development—and some of its houses were grand enough to be called mansions without prefatory mention of tract, Mc, or mini. In fact, the working-class streets leading to the Brighton entrance to Newton Park Estates were far better maintained than those in this prosperous suburb. The Brighton pavements were free of potholes, the sidewalks were wide, and the closely spaced streetlights provided bright illumination. In contrast, the little road in Newton that led to the Estates was bumpy. There were sidewalks in front of only a few of its houses. Tall Norway maples loomed overhead; in Felicity's opinion, the trees were overgrown and in need of pruning. Those in Newton Park were saplings. On Norwood Hill, the streetlights were spaced far apart, and some of the electric bulbs had burned out or were obscured by debris from sparrows' nests. Furthermore, the Norwood Hill Neighborhood Association had frequently written to the Newton Park Estates Condominium Association to implore the condominium owners to reduce traffic on Norwood Hill by using the Brighton route.

The knowledge that she was making her way home along a bumpy, dark, and hostile route bothered Felicity not at all. Although her talk and signing had drawn a small group, the fans had been enthusiastic, and, at a little local appearance, she was lucky to have had anything that might reasonably be called a "group." Her own *Felines in Felony* had been in the stores for a month, whereas Isabelle Hotchkiss's *Purrfectly Baffling* had just been released and was therefore bound to be selling well. As to the slip she'd made in autographing her book, the ridiculous mistake could be viewed as proof of her laudable determination to advance her career. On the passenger seat of the Honda were two promising new mysteries. In her refrigerator was a lovely salmon fillet. After cooking and eating the fish, she'd take a hot bath and curl up in bed with one of her new books. Life was far better than it had been in the apartment in Somerville with the old car that didn't go.

At the end of the dark stretch of Newton road, Felicity glanced at the prominent green sign that read:

Newton Park Estates
A Private Community
Residents Only

Despite considerable conflict between the Newton Park residents and those of Norwood Hill, the precise meaning of the sign had never been clarified. According to most Estates residents, the only people who had any business driving or even walking along its streets were condominium owners and their guests; all others were trespassers. The rule had proven impossible to enforce. Fire departments in both communities insisted on access, and the residents feared that if they pressed for a gated community, they'd find themselves gated out of Newton, with access only through Brighton. As it was, few Newton drivers passed through Newton Park Estates, and few people from either neighborhood walked there. Still, the green sign conveyed the message of exclusivity.

The developer of Newton Park Estates had taken care to give each of the twenty houses a distinctive appearance. Some had garages for two cars, others for three. The house colors included pale gray, pale green, pale beige, and pale yellow. Some yards had low picket fences; others were unfenced. The entryways differed from house to house. Felicity's house, located in the middle of the Estates, was pale gray with white trim. It rose to a height of only three stories and had a two-car garage. Its entryway was, however, elaborate, consisting as it did of a large glassed-in vestibule with a glass outer door, a tile floor, and, protected from the elements, a shiny oak front door with a brass knocker and glass panels on either side. One of the small luxuries of Felicity's postinheritance life was an automatic garage door opener attached to the visor of the Honda above the driver's seat. With a sense of pleasure in causing one thing in life effortlessly and reliably to do her bidding, Felicity pressed the button on the garage door opener as she turned the Honda into her driveway. In contrast to the old houses on Norwood Hill, which had long, steep driveways and garages inaccessibly placed in back of or under the houses, Newton Park had been designed for New England winters; short, flat drives led to garages attached to the sides of the houses. The concept of a service area screened from public view was prominent on Norwood Hill and non-existent in the Estates, where garage doors were, in effect, continuations of the facades of the houses.

When Felicity's lefthand garage door had obediently done her bidding, she drove what she still thought of as Aunt Thelma's Honda into the garage, which was clean, white, and empty except for a large yellow trash barrel, a green recycling bin, an orange plastic snow shovel, and a pail of ice-melting crystals. Felicity didn't participate in any sports that required the sort of equipment stored in garages; she didn't ski and hadn't ridden a bicycle since the age of eleven. After parking and locking the car, she ignored the door that led directly into the house, an entrance that she used mainly when she'd shopped for groceries or bought large items. As she'd done in taking the long route home, she took the long but appealing route along a stone-paved path, and up a slightly sloping bluestone walk and a flight of bluestone steps to the outer door of the vestibule. The house, like Thelma's car, seemed to belong to wealthy relatives. In using the front door, Felicity felt a bit like a visitor but also like the mistress of the house, a person who didn't have to use the servants' entrance but could enjoy surveying her impressive domain.

Although Felicity had brought with her to the suburbs the urban habit of always locking all doors, she made an exception in the case of the outer door to the vestibule. In late September, soon after she had moved in, two boxes containing her author copies of *Felines in Felony* had been delivered during a storm and, because the outer door was locked, had been left out in the rain. Since then, she'd always kept the door unlocked to provide refuge for materials sent by her agent and her editor, and packages containing items she had bought on eBay.

On that damp, chilly November night, the vestibule contained two bodies, one dead, one alive. The dead body was that of a small man in a gray suit. Wide strips of silver-gray duct tape covered his nose and mouth, as if someone had made a grisly effort to match the tape to his clothing. He was curled on his side with his head at an odd and uncomfortable-looking angle. His hair was gray, as was his only prominent feature, long, thick, bushy eyebrows. Snuggled next to the man's belly was a large shorthaired blue-gray cat, its eyes closed, its belly rising and falling in evidence of breath and thus of life.

Felicity froze in place. In her books, Prissy LaChatte managed to investigate murders without encountering the horror of corpses. In the rare scenes in which Prissy viewed a victim's remains, the decedent was usually on civilized display in a funeral home. Even then, Prissy avoided the casket. The corpse in Felicity's vestibule was in no condition for public viewing. To say nothing of the stench. Such was Felicity's policy in writing about death: Say nothing of the stench! As to the blue-gray cat, it had no place here asleep at her doorstep, dwelling as it did in a sphere of existence where, in Felicity's opinion, cats did not belong; in nasty contrast to the feline characters in her books, the cat was indisputably real. Indeed, the entire scene was one she would never have written: It was monstrous. And it was right here in her vestibule.

THREE

Edith dislikes anything new, but is accustomed to this mild grogginess and usually enjoys it. It wears off quickly, leaving her in the mood for a lovely nap. This evening, the slight dopiness that remains is unpleasant, as is this place, to which Edith has four principal objections. They are big ones.

First, she has never been here before. Her characterological mistrust of unfamiliar locations has been reinforced by experiences in them. In particular, despite her drowsiness, she feels a wordless, visionless apprehension that strangers will lift her up in the air and stretch her out, thus putting her at risk of falling. There is a lot of her to fall; she weighs thirteen pounds.

Second, this small space is cold. Her dense blue-gray coat, which was much admired by the lifting-in-the-air strangers, is supposedly an adaptation to a rough life in the outdoors. She is in no danger of hypothermia and is not afraid of catching a chill. Rather, she is used to being indoors and likes the warmth of sunny windowsills and beds equipped with comforters or electric blankets.

Third, this place has the repellent reek of litter in radical need of changing. Edith, who has high standards of personal hygiene, has spent her life in establishments with excellent litter-box service and expects no less even in alarmingly new and hatefully cold hostelries.

Fourth, Edith has had nothing to eat since ten o'clock the previous evening and is ravenous. She is also thirsty. Here, there is nothing to eat or drink.

Edith nestles next to the means to take her home, home being a familiar, warm, and clean abode where no one rouses her terror of falling and where there are always bowls of fresh water and dry food. Canned food appears often. Edith wants to go home, but the means is cold and getting colder. It does not respond to her.

FOUR

Although Prissy LaChatte's adventures were cozy rather than terrifying, it happened now and then that a character other than the brave, resourceful Prissy was startled into speechlessness, thus providing Felicity's sleuth with the opportunity to ask, *Cat got your tongue?* As Felicity stared at the scene in her vestibule, the cat had, indeed, gotten her tongue: A choking sensation in her throat suggested that she was incapable of producing so much as a moan, never mind an intelligible word. The cat in question was presumably the big gray creature nestled next to the small gray man.

In less than a minute, Felicity shook off her state of mute immobilization. After stepping out of the vestibule and allowing its door to close, she reached into her tote bag, retrieved her cell phone, and dialed 911. Her greatest fear was that the police would make her check the dead man for a pulse or otherwise touch him. If she herself were writing the scene, either Prissy LaChatte or her police chief friend would ask, *And what makes you think he's dead?* Alternatively, if the finder of the body did check for signs of life, in a later chapter either Prissy or the chief would lament the stupidity of the person who had tampered with evidence by ripping off the duct tape and uselessly applying first aid.

In any case, Felicity had no intention of touching the body, which she felt certain was just that, a dead thing. Still, she turned to face the glass door, peered in, and monitored the man for signs of movement, but the only motion was the rise and fall of the cat's abdomen. After reaching the police emergency number and giving her name and address, she said, "There's a dead man in my vestibule. I've been out. I just got home, and I opened the door, and . . . His mouth and nose are covered with duct tape, and his skin is gray. He isn't breathing. I don't know what to do! I need help!"

"Stay on the line." A male voice calmly issued the order. "We're on the way. Hang in there."

Still facing the glass door and still clutching her phone, Felicity mindlessly acted on a desire to distance herself from the horror by taking a few steps backward. If she had been living in the house for a long time or perhaps if it had felt like home, her mental map of the front entrance might have led her to turn around or come to a halt. As it was, she took one backward step too many and ended up tumbling down the low flight of bluestone stairs. For a few moments, she lay flat on her back, the wind knocked out of her. Light rain fell on her face. Newton Park Estates, never noisy, was completely silent. Felicity briefly missed Somerville, where a neighbor or a passerby would have found her by now and where there'd have been hundreds of people in shouting distance. The depressing thought crossed Felicity's mind that she had landed in her characteristic position in life: all alone on hard stone in the rain with no one to help her.

It was then that she remembered her cell phone. After struggling to her feet, she found it in the manicured grass beside the bluestone path, next to the tote bag she'd dropped. The phone was no longer connected to the police. She thought of calling Ronald but decided that he'd be useless. Neighbors? As usual, the nearby houses looked peculiarly uninhabited. Unlike the streetlights on Norwood Hill, those in the Estates had fresh lightbulbs and globes free of birds' nests, and no mature trees blocked the light. Furthermore, every residence in Newton Park had more than ample outdoor lighting, with an expensive fixture above or next to each front door, motion-detecting lights by each garage, and artistically arranged spotlights that directed attention to walkways, foundation plantings, and little weeping trees. All this brightness served mainly to reveal a complete absence of people. Lights shone in the windows of some houses, but the residents were wary of burglars and often left on lights to deter crime. Three of the houses were, as Uncle Bob and Aunt Thelma's had been, gigantic and extravagant pieds-à-terre, presumably for wealthy people with really big feet. Those three places were almost never occupied, but lights on timers created the illusion that the owners were at home.

Felicity had met all the other owners at two condo association meetings but had forgotten some of the names and faces. The meetings had been brief and businesslike. When she had moved in, there'd been no welcoming get-together, and even her neighbors on either side, the Trotskys and the Wangs, had failed to show up at her door with the offerings of brownies or cookies she'd half-expected. She first met the Trotskys one trash day when she'd placed her recycling bin at curbside, and Mr. Trotsky had angrily accused her of putting it on his property. The Wangs spoke almost no English but had introduced themselves in a friendly way, and always smiled and waved when they saw Felicity. It seemed unkind to reciprocate by summoning them to help with a murder, but they were far more approachable than the Trotskys. For once, Felicity, who valued privacy, simply hated being all alone. Consequently, instead of using her phone to call Ronald or to redial 911, and thus risk being asked to touch a dead person, she walked slowly and carefully down her walk, along the street, and up to the Wangs' front door.

With four stories and a three-car garage, the Wangs' house was considerably larger than hers, and its front entrance had two light fixtures, a knocker, a mailbox, a mail slot, an intercom, and a doorbell, all brand new and shiny. As she pressed the bell, she realized that for all she knew, Mr. and Mrs. Wang, whose first names she had forgotten, were Dr. and Dr. Wang and would take charge of the crisis as they'd presumably been taught to do in medical school.

When Mrs.—Dr.?—Wang opened the door, Felicity remembered the woman's first name, which was Zora. And the husband's? Tom? Bob?

"Zora," Felicity said, "I'm sorry to bother you, but there's an emergency!"

Zora was a little woman of thirty or so, with short black hair and no observable body fat. She nodded politely and gave a smile of complete incomprehension. Then she gestured to Felicity to come in. The front hall was the size of an assembly room. It had a bare fireplace and was empty except for a big vase of lilies on a Chinese table. There was a powerful smell of exotic food.

"An emergency!" Felicity repeated. She pointed toward the door through which she'd just entered.

"Dinner?" Zora asked. "Join us?"

"Thank you, but I need *help*!" The urge to shout at foreigners was uncontrollable. "A dead person! A person who is *dead*! Or hurt! *Emergency*!"

"Get Tom," Zora said. "Wait."

The tiny woman disappeared and reappeared with her husband, who was also very small and looked even younger than his wife. "Tom Wang," he said, holding out his hand.

"Felicity Pride." She shook the proffered hand and said, "There's a dead body in my vestibule. A man. Dead or injured."

"Police!" Tom Wang said.

"I've called."

"Call police!"

"I *have* called. They are coming. Can you come with me now?" She pointed frantically to the door.

Tom Wang addressed Zora in Chinese, and in seconds, Zora opened a closet in the hall and produced short jackets for both of them. They continued to speak incomprehensibly to each other as they donned the jackets. Outside, Zora paused to check the lock on the front door. She again spoke to Tom in Chinese. Leading the way, Felicity took fast but careful steps. When the three reached the bottom of Felicity's front steps, Tom marched up. Felicity paused for a moment. Zora was no bigger than a preteen. The corpse was no sight for childlike eyes. "Zora, wait here," she said. "You wait here."

When Felicity had finished speaking, she looked up to discover that Tom had opened the vestibule door and was now inside. She hurried up the steps to find him bending over the body and pulling at the strips of duct tape. "Hold good," he said. "Duct tape. WD-40. Duct tape. Good. Fix anything."

Felicity said, "Well, they won't fix death! He's dead, isn't he? I don't think you should touch anything."

"Dead," Tom pronounced. "Cold. Stink in here."

With no warning, he stood up, brushed past Felicity, opened the vestibule door, and shouted at the cat in Chinese. The animal had been huddled in a corner but responded to the shouting by making a dash for the open door and would have escaped but for Felicity's prompt action. Bending down while taking care not to drop her tote bag, she grabbed the cat and, finding it astonishingly heavy, wrapped both arms around it as if it were a heavy bag of groceries that would split unless supported on the bottom. Knowing nothing about cats that dwelled outside the pages of mystery fiction, she did not expect the animal to wiggle, scratch, and try to bolt, and was thus unsurprised when it settled itself in her two-armed grasp.

"This cat is evidence," Felicity said. "I'm taking it in the house right now."

Eager to escape the stench, she carried the cat down the steps, along the pathway, and to the back door near the garage. In this house that felt like Uncle Bob and Aunt Thelma's, there seemed to be doors everywhere: the front door, the door to the garage, this back door near the garage, and doors to more balconies and decks than she'd bothered to count. The house had an alarm system so complicated that she never turned it on. Squeezing the unprotesting cat with her left arm, she used her right hand to fish in her tote bag, find her large ring of keys, and open the back door. Once inside, she lowered the cat to the floor at the bottom of a flight of tiled stairs that led up to the kitchen. What had possessed her to summon the Wangs? Zora had been useless, whereas Tom had tampered with evidence. What would her adoring public think of her when it was revealed that she'd panicked at the sight of a body?

The thought of her public's reaction set her heart pounding. The cat! Her public, consisting as it did of cat lovers, would be concerned with one personage in this horrible drama, and that one personage would be the big gray cat. Where was it? Hiding, no doubt. Having followed it up to the gigantic kitchen, Felicity took a deep breath, opened a cabinet, removed a low crystal glass, and then opened another cabinet and extracted a bottle of single malt scotch. Even the liquor cabinet remained Uncle Bob and Aunt Thelma's, especially Uncle Bob's, and was so well stocked that it would remain theirs for a long time, Bob Robertson having been in the liquor business. Whereas members of other ethnic groups objected to stereotypes about national origin, Scots went out of their way, or so Felicity thought, to promote the image of Scotland as a land of tartan-clad pipers, single-malt sippers, and dancers of the Highland fling. As Felicity understood the phenomenon, Scottish chauvinism was such that it never occurred to Scottish-Americans that anyone could possibly think ill of the most intelligent and literate citizenry ever to grace the earth, the noble people who would, to a person, still be the Lairds of the Highlands if it weren't for the treachery of the scheming English. In any case, every one of Bob Robertson's liquor stores had had a neon sign showing a tartan-clad piper, and even now, after the chain had been sold to the DiStephano family, the pipers continued to brighten the night skies of eastern Massachusetts with what Uncle Bob had seen as a depiction of Scottish pride.

The taste of Laphroaig, combined with the happy image of her worshipful readership and her liberation from the stench of the corpse, gave Felicity a new perspective on the whole situation. Viewed with what she realized was good Scottish practicality, the position was this: She, Felicity Pride, Mistress of the Cat Lover's Mystery, had found at her doorstep the body of a little gray-clad man so mousey that he might almost have been something the cat dragged in. As luck would have it, with him was a handsome and undoubtedly photogenic gray cat that looked almost big enough to have done the dragging. Prominent in Felicity's musings was the memory of a painful fit of jealousy and self-recrimination she had suffered five years earlier when it had been publicly revealed that another famous mystery writer had, in her teenage years, served a brief prison sentence for having conspired in the murder of a friend's mother. What lack of foresight the young Felicity had shown! Ah, squandered youth! Determined to compensate for her adolescent failure to establish grounds for future free publicity, Felicity resolved to make the most of her present opportunity by slipping into the familiar skin of Prissy LaChatte.

Ambition triumphing over inclination, Felicity set the scene that her readers would expect, which is to say, a picture of greater concern for the live cat than for the dead man. Having received chastising letters about Prissy's error in giving milk to Morris and Tabitha, Felicity opened a can of albacore tuna, of which she herself was fond, and after mashing the contents in what she hoped was an appetizing manner, placed a dish of the tuna and a small bowl of water on the kitchen floor. In her books, the scent of cat food and the sound of a bowl hitting the floor always sent Morris and Tabitha scurrying in search of dinner; indeed, they often hung around begging Prissy for goodies. Instead of dashing to the kitchen and howling in glee before scarfing up the tuna, the large gray cat failed to appear at all. Damn the thing! Where was it?

"Here, kitty!" Felicity crooned. "Nice kitty! Here, kitty-kitty-kitty!"

Sirens finally sounded. Time was short if the drama was to open as Felicity had just scripted it. She ran from room to room—there were twenty-two—and eventually found the cat under a guest room bed. Flattening herself on the floor, she cooed in Prissy LaChatte fashion, "Nice kitty! Come on, kitty!"

Instead of emerging to "communicate" the solution to the murder, the cat hunched itself yet more tightly into a big gray ball of fur.

Undaunted, Felicity snatched one of the pillows off the bed, ran to the kitchen, and sacrificed her lovely clean pillow by putting it on the floor next to the dishes of tuna and water, thus creating as perfect a picture of the throughly pampered cat as she could achieve in the absence of the cat itself. Whether the damned cat liked it or not, it was going to assist Felicity in solving the murder that beneficent literary luck had deposited on her doorstep.

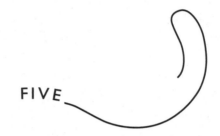

FIVE

Ears flattened, eyes simultaneously narrowed and closed, Edith huddles under the bed. Her expression is sour, and her heart rate is elevated; neither emotionally nor physiologically has she recovered from the shouting of the dangerous male. At first, the female, too, frightened Edith. The lifting-up-in-the-air females also dressed formally and exuded peculiar and unnatural odors. This female had, however, redeemed herself by squeezing Edith in a reassuring manner.

Still, the safe course is to remain under the bed. Edith has never before taken refuge under this particular bed, but recognizes beds as such and appreciates the cleanliness and warmth of her present situation. Also, although apprehension triumphs over hunger, she smells tuna in the air.

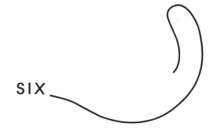

SIX

When pressed about the precise location of Newton Park Estates, Felicity and her neighbors described the area as "all but in Newton." It now seemed to Felicity that if her house truly were in Newton, cruisers and ambulances would have arrived a long time ago. Still, the scene she'd set in her kitchen proclaimed her as the caring and presumably noble rescuer of the poor, traumatized cat, and she was ready to face the public as represented by the Boston police and any emergency personnel who might show up. With luck, these representatives would include members of her very own public, which is to say, avid followers of the somewhat unadventurous adventures of Prissy LaChatte. Should anyone ask why the cat wasn't actually in view, Felicity had a plausible explanation ready: The poor animal, which had clung to her in its sorrow and terror, had, alas, been frightened away by the wails of the sirens. Cats were sensitive beings, she intended to explain. This one would return to her loving arms once peace was restored.

Having thus outlined the promotional aspects of her plan, Felicity was free to concentrate on fulfilling a secondary goal, which was the gathering of material for her next book. Mindful of certain critics' unkind remarks about the fanciful nature of her "crime" novels, she now resolved to take careful note of police procedure at the scene of a real crime. Eager to dress for her part, she put on a black trench coat and, stashing her keys in one of its pockets, set forth to present herself in a Prissy-like way while collecting useful details about official vehicles, law enforcement jargon, and other matters that she had often found herself glossing over or simply inventing.

To Felicity's satisfaction, three official vehicles drove up: a cruiser, an emergency medical van the size of a large delivery truck, and a sort of medical Jeep, as Felicity thought of it, a white sport-utility vehicle reminiscent of her neighbors' BMW and Lexus SUVs, their Lincoln Navigators, and, indeed, the late Uncle Bob's defunct Cadillac Escalade, but smaller than the recreational models and undoubtedly lacking such amenities as real leather upholstery and heated seats. In Felicity's books, political correctness dictated that there be at least one woman and one person of color among the officials at such a scene. Furthermore, the Fat Is Beautiful movement or whatever it called itself demanded that any character who weighed more than deemed ideal in the medical height-weight charts be a good guy; obese villains drew angry letters from readers, and, to play it safe, Felicity kept all of her characters lean or described them as appealingly heavyset or attractively plump rather than as overweight or just plain fat. To Felicity's annoyance, the police and EMTs who'd arrived were in blatant violation of her literary rules. The two police officers were male, the only people of color in sight were the Wangs, and the EMT who stood just outside her vestibule was a man who weighed more than she could begin to guess. There were apparently two or three other EMTs in the vestibule. She hoped that they were especially dark-skinned African-American women of inoffensively medium weight or, if heavy, gorgeous, charming, and medically heroic.

The main source of Felicity's dissatisfaction with the reality of her very own crime scene was, however, the absence of anyone of obvious importance. Ideally, there'd be a police chief remarkably like the one who confided his findings to Prissy LaChatte and solicited her assistance in solving cases that baffled him. Too bad about the "all but in Newton." The City of Newton just might be in the habit of dispatching its police chief to murder scenes, but Boston assuredly was not. Felicity's knowledge of police hierarchies beneath the level of chief was vague. What's more, her great and happy familiarity with British mysteries meant that she understood the titles and responsibilities of detective chief inspectors, superintendents, constables, and such far better than she understood anything about the ranks within American forces. Still, she knew a pooh-bah when she saw one, and there was, alas, none in view.

Prominently in sight and sound were a uniformed police officer of some sort and Felicity's trash-fussy Russian neighbor, Mr. Trotsky, who was shouting at the officer even more angrily than he'd ever shouted at Felicity about allowing her recycling bin to trespass on what was, in fact, condo association property. The object of Mr. Trotsky's rage was the police cruiser, which had two of its wheels on his lawn. Its front doors were open, its lights were flashing, and its siren was still screaming.

Undeterred, Mr. Trotsky was shaking a fist at the officer—constable? sergeant?—and yelling in accented but fluent English, "You know what my lawn service costs me? You wanna take a guess?" Answering his own question rather anticlimactically, he finished, "Plenty, that's what."

Mr. Trotsky looked nothing like the Trotsky of revolution and assassination. Rather, he bore what Felicity found to be an alarming resemblance to Joseph Stalin. He had the same heavy features, the same thick, dark hair combed straight back from his face, and the same oversized moustache. Felicity was certain that he cultivated the likeness as a way to intimidate people.

The policeman was apparently unintimidated. At any rate, he didn't move the cruiser.

"This is private property!" Mr. Trotsky hollered. "It's not a public street! That car is on my property, and it's compacting the soil. The grass is never going to recover."

Approaching the men and butting in, Felicity said loudly, "Then it doesn't matter whether it's moved, does it? If it's too late now?"

Turning to the policeman, she smiled, pointed at the cruiser, and held her hands over her ears. Having mimed her meaning, she shrieked, "Is the noise necessary? There was a darling cat left with the man in my vestibule, and the poor thing is very frightened. The siren isn't helping!" Backtracking, she bellowed, "I'm Felicity Pride. I'm the one who called."

The policeman nodded to Felicity and complied with her request by getting in the cruiser and silencing the siren. In one of her books, he'd have been astonishingly young or had an embarrassingly large nose or a marked stutter. In fact, he had to be thirty-five or forty. Worse, he was maddeningly ordinary, with no oddity of feature, speech, or manner to distinguish him from other characters.

"We'll want to talk to you, ma'am," he said.

"Of course you will," Felicity said. "And the cat is evidence. It . . . he, the cat, the very beautiful and sweet cat—strikingly beautiful and very lovable, irresistible—was in my vestibule with the man. The outer door was closed. The man and the cat were obviously left at the same time by the same person." After allowing a few seconds to pass, she added dramatically, "At *my* doorstep."

The pause failed to achieve its intended result: The policeman did not ask about the significance of *Felicity's* doorstep. Furthermore, Mr. Trotsky gave him little time to mull over the implications of her remark. Instead, he demanded, "You gonna move the car now?"

"This is a crime scene," the officer replied with an air of authority and dignity that surprised Felicity, whose low-ranking law enforcement characters tended toward the buffoonish.

As Mr. Trotsky was composing his face in an apparent attempt to increase his already hideous resemblance to Stalin, a silver sport-utility vehicle approached from the Norwood Hill end of the street and pulled up in back of the cruiser. The driver rolled down her window, and Felicity recognized a woman named Brooke whom she'd met at condo association meetings. Brooke, like her vehicle, was large, showy, and silvery. "What's going on here?" she called out.

In the cozy mysteries Felicity devoured, neighbors reliably nurtured the friends and relatives of the victim by brewing pots of tea, a beverage that they oversweetened and dispensed in warm kitchens. Sometimes they even insisted that the traumatized survivors couldn't possibly stay alone, but must move into guest bedrooms and be treated by sympathetic doctors who made house calls and dispensed sedatives or sleeping pills. Felicity was not, of course, a friend or relative of the little gray man. The only drink she wanted was a second shot of Laphroaig, she wanted to sleep in her own king-size bed between Aunt Thelma's luxurious sheets, and she had no desire to see a doctor. She was curious about the medications doled out in the English mysteries of the Golden Age of Detective Fiction and would probably have been happy to sample them—what on earth was in a *cachet blanc?* and how had aspirin lost the power to induce deep sleep?—but didn't want contemporary prescription drugs, all of which had modern and thus uninspiring names. Still, she longed to be offered any of the familiar comforts.

Replying to Brooke, Felicity announced, "Murder! Someone has left a dead man and a cat in my vestibule!"

"A dead cat?"

"No, the cat is alive. The man is dead."

"Who is he?"

"I have no idea. I've never seen him before. A little man in a gray suit. I've taken the cat in and given him some tuna. And water. And I've made a little bed for him. He's very frightened. Someone must have known that I, of all people, would make sure that he was all right."

Mr. Trotsky interrupted. "What about the no-pet clause? You're not allowed—"

"That means dogs," Brooke informed him.

"No *pets,*" he replied.

"Well, I didn't deliberately go out and get a pet," Felicity informed Mr. Trotsky. "It was left at my door. He. He was left at my door. And he's evidence in a murder. He's a very important cat. He probably holds the key to solving the crime." A Very Important Cat. Useful in her next book, perhaps? V.I.C.

"Probably has worms," Mr. Trotsky said. "Diseases. Did it scratch you?"

"No. He's very friendly. And sweet. Besides, he took to me right away."

"They always know who hates them," Brooke said. "Cats do. They have a sixth sense about it."

"I don't hate him," Felicity said. "On the contrary, I'm crazy about him, and I love cats. I write about—"

"Cats. Of course. Well, I hope it all turns out for the best," Brooke said, "but I've got to get some dinner and get to bed." With that, she drove off, leaving Felicity to wonder how a murder could possibly turn out for the best or even for the half decent. Brooke was probably too exhausted to know what she was saying. She and her husband, whom Felicity had never met, seemed to work eighteen-hour days and, understandably, to spend their weekends sleeping. Indeed, many residents of Newton Park left for work early in the morning and returned home late in the evening. Felicity assumed that they were slaving to pay their mortgages. Whatever the reason, the result was what often struck Felicity as an unpopulated or perhaps underpopulated neighborhood. If the murderer had driven up in an eighteen-wheeler and deposited scores of dead men and live cats on her front lawn, the chances were excellent that there would have been no one around to notice. With only a slight feeling of guilt, Felicity realized that in one respect, the murder actually was turning out for the best: For once, the neighborhood was filled with people.

SEVEN

Sprawled on her back on the unmade bed, Brigitte exposes her pale blue-gray belly to the musty air, which seems to her neither stale nor fresh but so familiar that it is taken for granted. She is named after Bardot but is no sex kitten. For one thing, even for a cat, she is flat chested. Also, she was spayed at an early age, and thus feels nothing for males and cannot attract them. Even so, her name, Brigitte, is pronounced in the French manner or in as close to the French manner as Bostonians can manage. Furthermore, at the age of two years, she is not a kitten except to the extent that her diminutive size and long, fluffy coat doom her to be eternally, if nauseatingly, known as Baby Brigitte. At seven pounds, she is only a little more than half as big as her absent companion, Edith.

Brigitte cannot be said to miss Edith but does find it dull without her, principally because provoking Edith is Brigitte's favorite means to banish boredom. In every tiff between the two, Brigitte is the instigator and the loser. To those who don't know Brigitte, it might seem stupid of her to tackle so hefty an adversary. Brigitte, however, understands Edith's gentle, pacific nature. Provoked beyond endurance, Edith strikes back, but she can be relied on to yank out great quantities of Brigitte's long, soft hair without inflicting flesh wounds. What's more, Edith never holds a grudge.

So, lolling on the sheets, Brigitte doesn't actually long for Edith's presence but suffers from the tedium that Edith's presence would relieve. Rousing herself, she leaps off the bed, flies to the kitchen, and attacks the dry cat food in the bowl that she and Edith amicably share. When she finishes, the bowl is almost empty. Brigitte is unconcerned. She has never experienced hunger.

EIGHT

Irked at the unliterary—and infuriatingly un-British—behavior of the police and her neighbors, Felicity longed to retreat to her kitchen to await the inevitable arrival of an important detective of some sort, preferably a chief superintendent, if the rank existed in the United States, as she suspected it did not. To fortify herself against shock, a condition commonly observed at crime scenes in British mysteries, she intended to pour herself a second shot of Laphroaig and broil a fillet of farm-raised Scottish salmon. Accustomed as she was to controlling the behavior of law enforcement personnel, she was chagrined to have the lowly policeman forbid her to enter her house.

"It's a crime scene," he explained.

"The *vestibule* is a crime scene, and I have no desire to go there. Ever again! I have already been in my kitchen, and I just want to go back."

"We'll need to check for signs of forced entry. Were your doors locked?"

"Of course. The doors to the house were locked. The outer door to the vestibule wasn't. And I have already been in the house! If the murderer were lurking there waiting to kill me, I'd be dead now."

"Do you have an alarm system?"

"Yes, but it was turned off. I never use it. I tried, but I kept forgetting the code or setting it off by accident. Please! I'm cold, and I haven't had any dinner."

As the officer was sympathizing, yet more official vehicles arrived, and for the next ten minutes, Felicity was temporarily distracted from her thirst and hunger by the sight of what looked increasingly like a movie set. Powerful lights flooded the area, and to Felicity's satisfaction, uniformed men taped off her yard with official crime-scene tape. Just as in a mystery novel, the police were securing the scene. Hurrah! Better yet, after Felicity had surrendered her house keys, a pair of officers armed with real, actual handguns entered her back door to search for the presence of what Felicity knew enough to call "the perp" or to look for signs that the perp had been inside. Meanwhile, other uniformed men walked around the house, presumably to check for signs of forced entry. At the outskirts of the hullabaloo, neighbors stood around in small groups. Noticing them, Felicity couldn't decide whether she was happy or embarrassed to have her house the center of attention. If the powerful lights had been mounted on media vans, she'd have been unambivalently delighted. Where *were* the media?

"I'm freezing," she told the officer. "And I really need to

use"—she lowered her voice—"the bathroom." What was wrong with her! She should have thought of that perfect excuse a long time ago. Maybe she really was suffering from shock.

After consulting with his colleagues, the officer gave Felicity permission to enter her house and returned her keys. "But don't go anywhere else. And please don't discuss anything you've seen with anyone. One of the detectives will want to talk to you first."

A detective! Felicity thanked the officer and made her way to her back door and into her house. After the damp of the November evening, the kitchen was as cozy as a British village mystery. The prospect of being interviewed by a real detective sent Felicity to the powder room off the kitchen, where she fussed with her hair and freshened her lipstick. Then, as she'd been eager to do, she poured herself a second Laphroaig, broiled the salmon, and congratulated herself on having attended a presentation for mystery writers about procedures for interviewing witnesses. An interviewer's first task, she had been told, was to establish rapport with the witness. The point was vivid in her mind because the example given, namely, remarking on the weather, had struck her as ludicrous. *Hot enough for you? So, what did the gunman look like?*

Seated at Aunt Thelma's kitchen table, she ate the salmon with French bread and a helping of leftover salad. Instead of depositing the salmon skin in the garbage disposal as she'd normally have done, she chopped it up and put it on a saucer for the cat, which had remained out of sight. Fish skin was evidently a safe food for cats if given as an occasional treat. At any rate, Prissy LaChatte fed it to Morris and Tabitha without provoking readers to compose the kinds of irate letters that Felicity had received after the publication of her first book, in which Prissy had foolishly overindulged the cats' love of canned albacore tuna. "If those cats don't start eating a well-balanced diet in a hurry," someone had written, "they're going to die of malnutrition, and where will you be then?"

Feeling and, indeed, sounding foolish, Felicity called, "Here, kitty!" Should she whistle? After placing the saucer on the tile floor, she picked it up and put it back in the hope that the sound of a dish landing on a floor would be familiar to the creature and would lure him out in time to play his part when the chief superintendent, captain, lieutenant, or whoever he was finally turned up. The cat, however, failed to come running for dinner in the gratifying manner of Morris and Tabitha, and when the back doorbell rang, as it soon did, all Felicity had to display in place of that crucial piece of living furry evidence in a murder were the pillow and saucers on the floor, and a kitchen that smelled unpleasantly of fish.

Opening her back door, Felicity was startled to see a tall and almost unbelievably muscular man with an exceptionally large head and thick, curly gray hair. In introducing such a character to her readers, she'd have described the color of his eyes as the blue of a Siamese cat's. There was, however, nothing truly catlike about the man; if he resembled any sort of animal, it was perhaps a Clydesdale horse. His muscularity was not confined to his body, but extended upward to his massive neck and jaw. Even his cheekbones were brawny. What surprised Felicity was not so much the man's monumental build as it was the memory of where she had seen him before and what he had been doing then: She'd noticed him at the Highland Games in New Hampshire a little more than a year earlier. He'd been tossing the caber, the caber being a log the approximate length and width of a telephone pole.

"Dave Valentine," he said.

Valentine or no Valentine, Felicity thought, *you look like a MacKenzie or a MacFarlane or a Campbell to me.* Then, having wondered what kind of name Valentine was and what it was doing on this Scottish Hercules, she realized with horror that her mind was, in effect, the pitiful victim of demonic possession; it had been so aggressively invaded and conquered by her mother that unless she immediately exorcized the maternal demon, she'd find herself quoting "Scots, Wha Hae" and offering this tree-trunk-hurling Highland giant a wee dram of Oban.

In triumph, she said, "Felicity Pride. Come in." The fresh air blowing through the door seemed to exacerbate the fish smell, and Felicity was suddenly and belatedly aware of the empty glass and the bottle of Laphroaig that sat on the counter near the sink. It was one thing to imagine inviting this Atlas of Inverness to take a drop with her, but quite another to have him catch her drinking alone. What's more, the damned cat was nowhere in sight. "Coffee?" she asked. "Something to eat? I could make you a sandwich."

Valentine shook his head. "No, thanks. I need to ask you about what happened. Are you doing okay?"

Was he looking at the bottle? Damn! The expert on interviewing witnesses had emphasized the need to inquire about the witness's condition and to take note of special circumstances. For instance, had the witness been drinking?

"I'm all right. More or less. But I'm worried about the cat. The one that was left . . . There was a cat in my vestibule. With the . . . with the man. I brought him in. The cat. I carried the cat in, and I've made a little bed for him, and there's food, but he's hiding somewhere." The scene was not playing itself out as Felicity had intended. Even to her own ears, she sounded frightened and uncertain, and instead of expressing overwhelming concern for the cat, she sounded irritated with it, as, indeed, she was. The sight of the Laphroaig bottle and the damned odor of salmon were beginning to make her queasy. "Could we go somewhere else?" This house of Uncle Bob and Aunt Thelma's was *her* house, damn it! Why was she asking permission to leave her own kitchen? "Somewhere other than the kitchen," she amended. "I had fish for dinner. I'm not afraid to be alone here." Not that anyone cared whether she was afraid, she reflected. Not that anyone had volunteered to take her in.

She led the way to the front hall. Through the glass panels on either side of the front door, she caught sight of figures moving in the vestibule. "Your men," she said, but hastened to add, "and women."

"A few," Valentine agreed.

He followed her into what had been Uncle Bob's study, not that her uncle had actually studied anything either there or anywhere else, so far as Felicity knew, since his graduation from Harvard more than a half century earlier. The inaccurately named study did, however, testify to her uncle's devotion to his alma mater, boasting as it did objects and furnishings emblazoned with the College shield and the word *Veritas*: a crystal carafe and drinking glasses, glass steins, and shot glasses on shelves that had been built for books; a leather chair for use at the desk; and, on top of the desk, a Harvard lamp. A brown leather couch and two armchairs were blessedly unadorned. The room looked to Felicity as if it had been copied from a movie set intended to depict a rich man's study that had, in turn, been copied from some British aristocrat's wood-paneled private office. The paradoxical effect of the successive copying was a sense of genuine warmth and comfort. Intending to use the study for writing, she had installed her desktop computer and printer on her uncle's large cherry desk. A complete collection of her own books occupied a prominent place on a shelf above the desk. To her disappointment, she had found herself writing on her notebook computer at the kitchen table, as if she were a housekeeper with literary ambitions instead of a published author who owned the whole house.

Felicity gestured to one of the leather armchairs. "Have a seat." Dave Valentine's presence made her absurdly aware of the big couch, which, she reminded herself, didn't even convert into a bed. Avoiding it, she took the other chair, but nonetheless felt aware of the man, as if she were seated a few yards from some powerful but safe animal: a tame lion. In leonine fashion, this animal wore no rings. In particular, she observed that the third finger of his left hand was bare.

Instead of immediately asking her about the body and the cat, Valentine nodded in the direction of the shelves above the desk. "You're the writer," he said. "*The* Felicity Pride."

As a means to establish rapport with the witness, referring to her books was dandy, she thought, far better than making small talk about the rain and fog.

"Yes," she replied modestly, "I write about cats."

"I know. My wife used to read your books."

But she stopped? Felicity longed to ask. *She developed an intense dislike for Prissy? Found a series she preferred? Developed early-onset Alzheimer's and became unable to follow a story line? Got religion and quit reading anything except the Bible? She got tired of going to the Highland Games and watching you toss the caber, so she left you for . . .*

Occupied with her unspoken questions, Felicity said nothing.

"I need to ask you a few things," Valentine said. "I take it you'd gone out."

Valentine, she thought, was doing well: Interviewers were urged to avoid leading the witness. "I was at a book signing. At Newbright Books. It's on the Newton-Brighton line. I left here at about five-thirty. And I got home at . . . eight? Somewhere around eight. I put my car in the garage, and when I got to my vestibule, there were the man and the cat. I knew he was dead. Or I thought so. And I couldn't stay there, obviously, so I went outside and called nine-one-one. On my cell phone. The call got cut off, and I . . . I guess I started to panic. I was worried that he might be alive, and I wasn't doing anything. So I went next door and got the Wangs. I'm sorry. It was a mistake. Mr. Wang went charging into the vestibule, and he touched things, he tampered with evidence, and he shouted at the cat. It nearly ran away. So I picked up the cat and brought it in. It's very traumatized. It won't eat. It's hiding somewhere."

"Cats do that," Dave Valentine said. "The man. Did you recognize him?"

"No. I've never seen him before." Seizing the opportunity to regain control of a plot that was escaping her, she said, "Or the cat. It's a beautiful cat. A very large gray cat. Someone left that cat for me, you know."

"Could be a coincidence."

"And there's the vestibule, too. There's a mystery called *The Body in the Vestibule*. By Katherine Hall Page."

Valentine shrugged. "Does anyone else live here?"

"No."

"Big house."

"I inherited it. I've only been here a few months. It be-longed to my uncle and aunt. They were killed by a drunk driver. Last July, they were on their way to the airport, and they were killed by a drunk driver."

"Any children?"

"Me? No."

"Your uncle and aunt."

"No." In Felicity's opinion, Uncle Bob had been too tightfisted to produce offspring he'd have had to support, but she didn't say so. According to Felicity's mother, he'd been stingy with Thelma, and it was certainly true that he and Thelma had given miserly Christmas and birthday pres-ents: cheesy sweatshirts, ten-dollar checks.

"The outer door. When you left the house, was it locked or unlocked?"

"Unlocked. If I lock it, packages get left outside. So I leave it unlocked for UPS and the post office and so on. The inner door was locked. So were all the other doors and win-dows. I'm careful about that. But the alarm system was off."

"So, what did you do when you got home? Walk me through it. Start with leaving the bookstore."

"I got in my car and drove home."

"Did you give anyone a ride? Stop anywhere?"

"No. I just drove home and put my car in the garage. I didn't get out of the car first. I used the garage door opener. Then I went to the front door."

"The front."

"I always use the front door unless I have packages to carry in."

"Did you notice anyone around? Any cars? Anyone out for a walk? Anything?"

"No. I mean, there wasn't anyone, and I didn't see any cars anywhere near here. I would've noticed."

"Any strangers around earlier today? Or this week? Anything unusual?"

"No. There's hardly ever anyone around here except lawn services. Oil trucks. People repairing things. Some of the people who live here have second or third homes and practically don't live here, and the others work all the time. You hardly ever see anyone."

"Sounds lonely," he said.

"I'm a writer. I need time alone."

"You might want to get someone to stay with you tonight. These things sometimes have a bigger impact than you expect. Anyone you could go and stay with? Friends? Relatives?"

"I couldn't leave the cat here all alone."

"Oh, we'll take it off your hands."

"No! No, it needs to stay here. He does. He was left for *me*. I can't abandon him. He's had a terrible time. He needs to be with someone who understands cats. Please! He needs to stay with me. I'll be fine. I'll set the alarm."

To Felicity's surprise, Dave Valentine didn't fight for possession of the cat. He did, however, return to the matter of her staying alone. Pressed, she admitted that she did have a friend she could call. When Valentine had taken down her phone number, the names of her late uncle and aunt, and a few other pieces of information, and when he had warned her that the police would be in her vestibule and yard for some time yet, he insisted that she call the friend she'd mentioned.

"A couple of other things," he said. "You're going to need to avoid talking about any of this. Don't discuss the details with your neighbors. Or the media. You need to avoid any contact with the media. If they call you, just tell them you've been asked not to talk about it."

Felicity felt the blood rush up her throat to her face, as if Dave Valentine had read her thoughts and decided to ruin her grand plans.

Before she had the chance to say anything, he thanked her for talking with him and handed her his card. "I'll be in touch," he added. "And if you think of anything else, call me. Anything. If it's something small, some little detail, call me anyway. And get that friend of yours over here."

With some relief, Felicity decided not to trail after the detective to observe the real investigation of an authentic crime scene. Instead, as soon as she'd ushered him out the back door, she called Ronald. She had no intention of asking Ronald to spend the night, but Ronald would certainly know what to do about the cat.

NINE

In the British mysteries that Felicity read at bed-time, the characters who nurtured and soothed the unfortu-nate finders of dead bodies fell into two categories, the first being loud, jolly women with large families and the second, blatant eccentrics. The eccentrics sometimes turned out to be murderers, as did the apparently traumatized body finders. In Felicity's experience, the fat, jolly women never killed anyone, probably because they were too busy taking care of their large families to have time to perpetrate so demanding a crime as murder.

Although Ronald clearly belonged in the category of ec-centrics, Felicity had little doubt of his innocence in the slaying of the gray man. The vestibule had been empty when Felicity left for Newbright Books. Even if Ronald had already stashed the corpse in the trunk of his car, there hadn't been time for him to leave his shop, drive to Newton Park, deposit the body in the vestibule, and drive back. Or had there? Could he have done it while Felicity was on her way to the signing? While she was in the shop? In any case, in Felicity's view, Ronald lacked sufficient interest in his fellow human beings to go to the bother of killing one. Also, he doted on cats and would have been far more likely to claim and keep the beautiful gray animal than to abandon it anywhere, never mind to incarcerate it in Felicity's vestibule with the remains of its presumed owner.

Felicity's reflections on Ronald's eccentricity made her think of Dave Valentine's question about strangers she might have noticed in her neighborhood. In the eyes of the police, Ronald would be a suspicious-looking character. His ancient gray Volvo sedan would be out of place in Newton Park, as would Ronald himself, with his straggly ponytail, his handmade leather sandals worn over loudly patterned fleece socks, and, most of all, his odd demeanor. Even when engaged in some wholesome and blameless activity such as restocking the shelves in his store or eating one of his natural-foods lunches, he somehow managed to look as if he were lurking. Somewhat belatedly, Felicity put on her trench coat and went out the back door to try to intercept Ronald before he aroused the attention of the police. By the time she reached the street, however, Ronald was speaking to Dave Valentine.

". . . a friend of Felicity's," Ronald was saying as if passing along a state secret to an enemy agent. "She called me."

Rather than undertake the impossible task of explaining Ronald, Felicity greeted him in a fashion meant to confirm his statements. "Ronald, you're here! Thank God!"

"Thank me," he said with a glance upward at the fog obscuring the view of the heavens.

In an effort to smooth over her friend's dedication to voicing his atheism, she said, "Ronald has a dry sense of humor." She made quick introductions: "Ronald Gershwin. Dave Valentine." The detective was looking at the cat carrier and the bags suspended from Ronald's hands. A devoted environmentalist, Ronald never allowed shops to place his purchases in paper or plastic bags, but provided string bags of the type popular in Europe before the introduction of the plastic bags to which Ronald objected and unpopular in the United States except among socially out-of-it intellectuals who hadn't been abroad for decades. Felicity considered telling the detective that Ronald had gone to Harvard and thus couldn't be expected to behave like a normal human being.

"Ronald, you've brought cat food. Thank you." The weird fishnet bags had the advantage of making their contents plainly visible. "And cat litter."

"I knew you'd never think of it."

"Of course I would." The fictional Morris and Tabitha managed their bodily functions in complete privacy, which is to say, never on the pages of Felicity's books. The litter needs of a real cat hadn't occurred to her. "But for obvious reasons, I haven't exactly had a chance to run errands. We'd better go inside. The poor cat may be in desperate need."

Satisfied to have ended Ronald's contact with police on the ordinary, practical note of feline excretion, Felicity hustled Ronald indoors to the kitchen, where he unpacked cat supplies and spread them on the table. Without consulting Ronald, Felicity opened a bottle of a wine called Mad Fish. Although Bob Robertson had been a drinker of single malt scotch and the occasional beer, the basement of the house had a small, cool room that served as a wine cellar. Felicity, who knew nothing about wine, had originally selected Mad Fish when she'd invited Ronald for a housewarming dinner. Her choice had been based less on his liking for red wine than on her sense that Ronald might accurately be described as something of a mad fish himself. The wine had been a success, and she'd taken to serving it whenever he visited. By the time she had uncorked the bottle and poured two glasses of wine, Ronald had placed a disposable cardboard cat box on the floor, added litter, and set out two dishes of cat food. One dish contained dry food; the other, wet pink glop that smelled remarkably like the salmon odor left by Felicity's own dinner.

"Ronald, I'm not having a litter box in the kitchen," Felicity said. "It's unsanitary. Besides, you haven't seen this cat. He's huge. He's twice the size of that little box."

"Once he knows there's litter here, you can move the box. He won't like it near his food, anyway."

"As if my opinion didn't matter! Ronald, what a horrible ingrate I am. I'm sorry. I'm in shock. Thank you for coming over. Sit down." She took a seat at the table. Ronald sat opposite her. Although he was examining a variety of cat toys he'd left there instead of paying attention to her distress, she said, "Ronald, someone did this to me! Why would anyone do that? Who hates me so much?"

"Your mother."

"My mother is little and old, and she hardly ever leaves the house. She couldn't have killed that man. And she couldn't have moved his body."

"Maybe your sister helped her."

"Neither one of them would've touched the cat. And

they're not the perfect relatives, but they're not murderers."

"They resent your inheritance."

"They were horrible to Bob and Thelma. I was nice. There's no more to it." Raising her glass, she paused for a moment. Ronald avoided the usual toasts to health and friends in favor of book titles. Felicity had picked up the custom. *"Living Well Is the Best Revenge,"* she said.

Ronald took a sip of wine. *"Mommy Dearest.* Do you have any idea where he is?"

"My mother is admittedly toxic, but she *is* female."

"The cat. Have you looked for him?"

"First of all, I have to remind you that I am the one who rescued the cat, so please stop making that face, as if I disliked cats. He was in the vestibule with the man. I told you this on the phone. Whoever left the body in my vestibule deliberately left the cat there, too. And when I made the mistake of getting my neighbors, the Wangs, Mr. Wang was horrible to the cat, so I picked him up, the cat, obviously, and carried him around to the back door and brought him inside. But then he took off. I put out tuna, and I called him, but I haven't seen him since I found him under a bed upstairs. Isn't that where cats always go?"

Ronald drank some wine and then evidently reached a decision about the cat toys he'd been examining. After picking up a long rod with feathers and jingle bells fastened to one end, he rose and said, "Let's go see."

The grand scale of Uncle Bob and Aunt Thelma's house made the search for the cat a challenging task. Felicity was sure that the animal hadn't gone down the stairs that led to the back door and to what Felicity persisted in thinking of as the basement even though the space contained a family room, a big exercise room, the little wine cellar, and other finished rooms. The upper floors, however, offered countless hiding places. Although Felicity used only the master bedroom suite, which had a dressing room and a luxurious bathroom, she kept the doors to the other five bedrooms open, mainly to remind herself that she wasn't living in a hotel. And, as Ronald pointed out, the cat wasn't necessarily still in the same place.

"Cats hide under beds!" Felicity insisted when Ronald got down on his belly to peer under the living room furniture.

"Cats hide," Ronald said. "That much is true. He isn't here."

"Well, I'm going upstairs where he was before. You can waste your time here if you want, but I'm telling you, Ronald, that's exactly what you're doing."

Felicity headed upstairs, and Ronald indulged her by following. In each of the five unoccupied bedrooms, he silently lowered himself to the floor and, raising the bed skirts in which Thelma had dressed the beds, searched in vain for the cat. It was only when Ronald had stuck his head under Felicity's king-size bed that he tapped a finger against his lips and mimed the instruction to her to close all the doors in the room. He raised the blue-and-white bed skirt, eased the feather-and-bell toy under the bed, and moved it slowly back and forth, in and out. Just as Felicity was on the verge of ordering him to crawl under the damn bed and grab the cat, a large paw shot out. And shot in again. It took Ronald a full five minutes of coaxing and luring to persuade the cat to emerge. Once Ronald was sitting on the floor holding it firmly his arms, Felicity's impatience and irritation turned to satisfaction: Exactly as she had told Ronald, the cat had been under a bed, and not just any bed, either, but *her* bed. She felt proud and flattered that it had moved to her room.

She also felt resentful that it was Ronald who was holding the cat.

"This is a magnificent cat," Ronald said. "I wonder what she is. We'll have to look her up. Russian Blue?"

"Oh, I think she's a beautiful gray alley cat," said Felicity with an effort to place no emphasis on the *she*.

"She is a she." Ronald now had the cat on her back and was stroking her chest. "Mature but still young. Clean teeth. No fleas. On the heavy side but not obese. She's in good condition. Did you notice her eyes?"

"Of course! They look like pieces of amber. How could I not notice them? They're incredible."

"The pupils are dilated."

"Oh, I think that's how they're supposed to be."

"Dilated? I wonder if she's been drugged. She's awfully calm. Mellow."

"Drugged by the murderer! He drugged the cat and slaughtered the man. Maybe he drugged the man, too. Before he killed him. And left them both for me."

"The whole business might have nothing to do with you, Felicity. You haven't been here long. Maybe it has to do with your uncle and aunt."

"Nonsense. Why would anyone leave a body and a cat for them?"

"Why would anyone leave them for you?"

"Because of my books!"

Ronald smiled and shook his head. "Authors," he said. "Well, I'd better be going. Could you get the carrier? It's in the kitchen."

"What for?"

"To carry the cat."

"Where?"

"Home."

"Oh, no! Ronald, that cat is staying with me. He . . . she is evidence in a murder. She was left for me. She is staying here. We're going to get her settled in one of my guest rooms with her litter box and lots of food, and she's going to learn that she is perfectly safe now." Reaching down, she tentatively stroked the top of the cat's head. The cat silently watched her.

Acting on her plan, Felicity left Ronald and the cat in her room and transferred the litter box, cat food, and water bowl to the largest of the unoccupied bedrooms, which were not, properly speaking, guest rooms, since Felicity hated having houseguests and never invited anyone to stay with her. Aspiring mystery writers on do-it-yourself book tours were always eager to avoid the cost of hotels by staying with fellow mystery writers, many of whom were happy to accommodate the out-of-towners, who, in turn, were happy to reciprocate when their hosts traveled. Felicity had always managed to weasel out of offering hospitality to these visitors and had no desire to camp out in other people's houses in strange cities. The cat, however, wouldn't expect her to cook breakfast or recommend it to her literary agent and could be counted on never to expect her to sleep on a foldout couch or on some makeshift bed in a messy sewing room or office.

When Ronald had carried the cat to its new room, he and Felicity returned to the kitchen, where Ronald finished his glass of wine and, as an obvious afterthought, presented Felicity with a small supply of Valium, a gift that she assured herself was the American equivalent of those British cups of sugary tea.

Before leaving, he also reminded her to activate her alarm

system. "And if your password is *Morris, Tabitha, Prissy,* or *LaChatte,*" he said, "change it."

She'd intended to replace Uncle Bob's password with *Morris*.

"Ronald, I know better than that."

She walked Ronald to his car, in part to assure the police that she had survived her encounter with this suspicious-looking character—not that the police seemed to care—and in part to see whether they were leaving soon. The investigators of a murder couldn't exactly be called guests. Even so, it seemed to Felicity that they were overstaying their welcome. When she invited people to dinner, she expected them to finish dessert, converse a bit over coffee, and go home so that she could go to sleep. Like after-dinner lingerers, the police, she feared, might continue to hang around well past her bedtime. How many photographs were really necessary? How long could it possibly take to gather trace evidence and to dust for fingerprints in one small vestibule? As it turned out, the police were, in fact, about to depart for the evening but would return in the morning to search the neighborhood by daylight. To Felicity's disappointment, Dave Valentine had left without saying good-bye to her, cautioning her to lock up carefully, or otherwise expressing any concern for her or her safety. Having studied hundreds, perhaps thousands, of accounts of police procedure in English villages, she knew better than to expect a policeman to be stationed protectively in her kitchen all night; such special treatment was inevitably reserved for the aristocracy and for friends and relatives of the chief constable. Consequently, she was surprised to learn that a cruiser would remain in Newton Park. She didn't actually feel threatened: If the murderer had wanted to kill her, she'd be dead by now, wouldn't she? Still, she appreciated what she took to be the show of attention.

Comforted by a sense of being looked after, she returned to her house, went to bed, fell asleep after only two pages of the new P. D. James, and dreamed neither of London and Dalgleish nor of vestibules and gray men but of the Highland Games and Dave Valentine, who wore his kilt and tossed the caber.

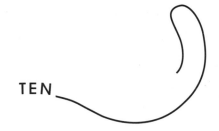

TEN

One male had come and gone. Another had arrived and, with him, the odor of food, both wet and dry. Still, Edith remained under the bed. Better safe than satiated. When the feathers and bell appeared, Edith was hip to the ploy, but prey drive triumphed, and Edith was nabbed. Now, under this new bed, she licks her paws as if she were smoothing ruffled feathers, as, in a sense, she is.

ELEVEN

Felicity allowed nothing to come between her and her commitment to regular grooming. At nine o'clock on Tuesday morning, she kept her appointment with Naomi, to whom she related the entire story of the small gray man and the large gray cat, including her tumble down the front steps; her rage at the perfidy of Mr. Wang; her rescue of the cat; her medicinal consumption of Uncle Bob's single malt scotch; her embarrassment at the reek of fish; and her memory of the caber tossing at the Highland Games and of the kilted Dave Valentine's oaklike legs. "Scots are famous for having knobby knees," she told Naomi, "but his aren't. They're all muscle."

In telling the story to Naomi, Felicity was aware of whipping off a rough draft that would be revised and edited before the police gave her permission to present it to newspaper, television, and radio reporters, her fellow mystery writers, and others in a position to distribute it to the mass market. Dave Valentine's knees would suffer deletion, and the nameless little man would move from the background to the foreground. It now seemed to Felicity that in responding to Valentine's questions, she had senselessly limited herself to a dreary recitation of facts and had underemphasized her observations of the body. In mystery writing, it was an old saw that no one cared about the corpse. The same couldn't be true of the police, could it? If so, why had there been no urgent message on her answering machine this morning, no plea for details she might have forgotten the previous evening, no request for her thoughts about means, motive, and opportunity? When she'd left for the salon, the police had been searching her yard and the surrounding area, but Valentine hadn't been there, and those present had merely nodded to her. Novels, she reflected, were far more satisfying than was real life, especially the novels she wrote herself. If she were working from one of her own outlines, for example, she'd know why Mrs. Valentine had abandoned Prissy and the irresistible Morris and Tabitha.

"Felicity," Naomi demanded, "are you with us this morning? Your eyes are glassing over." Painting a foil-encased strand of Felicity's hair with chemicals, she added, "You haven't gone and caught something from that stray cat, have you?"

Although a concern for hygiene was, Felicity thought, an admirable trait in a hairdresser, it seemed to her that Naomi was nearly obsessed with germs. The overwhelmingly white salon could safely have served as an operating room. Naomi's sanitary bent seemed to account for her hair, which was no more than two inches long and so devoid of color that Felicity suspected her of treating it with chlorine bleach. Fortunately, Naomi was only twenty-five and had excellent skin, so she carried off the startling effect. Felicity had never seen Naomi turn a client into a grotesque version of herself. Felicity considered her a gifted colorist and a clean one, too, of course. Naomi went through pair after pair of disposable latex gloves and always used freshly disinfected combs.

"This is no stray cat," Felicity said indignantly. "She is very well cared for. And what could I possibly catch from her?"

"Something she got from the dead body! You said yourself she was right there with it. It gives me the willies to think about! You ought to be careful. That cat could be carrying some kind of awful disease. Was the body decomposing?"

Felicity's corpses were fresh or embalmed. She'd lately come to favor skeletons. Halloween, skeletons, candy: Bones had a happy association with food. As the author of works of light entertainment, Felicity believed in honoring the needs of her readers, some of whom devoured Prissy LaChatte over dinner or snacks. Decomposition was disgusting and therefore did not occur.

"No," Felicity said. "He had died recently. And there is nothing wrong with the cat. On the contrary, she is obviously healthy."

"She could be incubating something."

"You know," said a woman seated in the next chair, "it's not a bad idea to take the cat to a vet."

Felicity's eyes had been fixed on her own fascinating image in the mirror before her. With most of her hair wrapped in pieces of foil and standing out from her head, she looked to herself like a freakish lion. She reluctantly turned her eyes toward the woman who'd spoken, a client who was having what was known as a "one process." Her long hair was thickly coated with black and foul-smelling stuff.

"If you don't know where the cat came from," the woman continued, "you might want to check for parasites. And have a vet give the cat a general going-over. What kind of cat is it?"

"Big," said Felicity. "A big gray cat."

"Longhaired?"

"No. Uh, normal."

"A blue shorthair. You know, you might have a Russian Blue."

Ashamed of the paucity of her knowledge of real cats, Felicity shrugged her shoulders. If the cat turned out to belong to some breed, she could always say that the information was vital to the murder investigation and that the police had ordered her to keep it to herself. She was now spared the need to respond. The colorist darkening the woman's hair handed her a kitchen timer, and the woman left for another part of the salon.

For the remainder of her hair appointment, Felicity avoided any detailed discussion of the cat and silently vowed to remedy her ignorance. She had intended to go directly home, but when Naomi finished blow-drying her hair, she drove to an ATM and then to a large chain bookstore. Out of loyalty to Ronald, she ordinarily bought books exclusively at Newbright, but now felt the need for privacy, as if she were shopping for sex manuals or treatises on hemorrhoids. The chain bookstore was in a mall and had all the newness and brightness that Newbright lacked, as well as six or eight times the floor space of Ronald's shop, and a coffee bar, too. Surveying the employees and customers, Felicity saw no familiar faces. After only a short search, she found the pet books, of which there were many more than she had expected. Suppressing the urge to hunt down the manager to suggest the wisdom of shelving some of her cat mysteries with the nonfiction cat books, she indiscriminately gathered a tall stack of works on cats and cat care, hurried to a register, paid using the anonymous cash from the ATM, and escaped with only a hint of disappointment that no one had asked, "Aren't you Felicity Pride?"

Driving home, she reminded herself that anonymity had, after all, been her goal, a goal achieved in part because her publisher always put her photograph inside the back flap of her books instead of placing it prominently on the back of the dust jacket. Newly possessed of the splendidly photogenic cat, Felicity would have to get an author-with-feline-muse photo that would simply demand to occupy the entire back cover of the next Prissy LaChatte. The mythical nature of her very own Morris's existence had its conveniences, but, by virtue of nonexistence, Morris had been unable to pose before the photographer's lens. And the real cat was far less trouble than she had imagined. In her haste to keep her appointment with Naomi, she had rushed out of the house without even bothering to open the door of the room it occupied. Furthermore, once she, Felicity Pride, had truly become an expert on all things feline, the gray cat really might enable her to solve the murder. Effortless promotion would follow. Felicity Pride and her crime-solving companion would be written up in the Boston papers, the stories would be picked by the wire services, and the term *mass market* as applied to paperback editions of the Prissy LaChatte series would become accurately descriptive of the hundreds of thousands of copies loaded into mammoth vans and transported to bookstores and mall department stores throughout the United States. Not to mention supermarkets! Throughout the country, supermarkets, the true mass outlet, would dump their copies of Isabelle Hotchkiss's silly mysteries and replace them with Felicity Pride's light entertainments.

Preoccupied though she was with visions of fame, Felicity managed to drive Aunt Thelma's Honda through the narrow streets of genteel Norwood Hill and into Newton Park, where there was no sign of the police and, as usual, no sign of anyone else, either. Especially notable for their absence were vans emblazoned with the names and logos of local television stations. But maybe the police and the media politely called first instead of just dropping in? Damn the taboo on interviews!

Felicity entered the house through the back door. When Prissy LaChatte got home, Morris and Tabitha leaped from the windowsill where they had been watching for their beloved owner, to whom they sometimes had important crime-busting messages to communicate. Having yowled in joy and transmitted their messages, they meowed for food and dove into the bowls that Prissy filled. Locked in an unused bedroom, the blue-gray cat could not emulate the delightful behavior of Prissy's cats. Instead of letting the cat loose or even saying hello to her, Felicity checked her answering machine, found no messages, made herself a tuna sandwich, poured herself a glass of milk, and settled down at the kitchen table with her lunch and her new cat books.

She began by looking up the Russian Blue. The photo illustrating the breed showed a cat not entirely unlike the big gray cat, but according to the text, Russian Blues had large, pointy ears and bright green eyes. Damn! But there were more alley cats than purebreds, weren't there? Therefore, the majority of her readers probably owned . . . What *was* the correct, inoffensive term? Another book supplied three possibilities: *domestic, mixed-breed,* and *nonpedigreed.* Considering herself to be a quick study, Felicity switched to a book about cat care that emphasized the need for physical, mental, and social stimulation. Illustrations showed carpeted cat trees, repulsively realistic plush mice, and feather-and-bell teasers like the one Ronald had used. Having mastered the topic of stimulation, Felicity picked up another book and had only begun to read about the sanitary needs of cats when she remembered her complaint to Ronald about the inadequate size of the disposable litter box he'd brought.

Abandoning her course of study, she ran upstairs and into the cat's room, where she found that the small box had indeed been used. Yuck! Morris and Tabitha never made such a stench! The cat herself was huddled under the bed, where, far from communicating the solution to the murder of her defunct human companion, she was communicating nothing except her wish to be left alone. Well, physical, mental, and social stimulation would shape her up! Then, too, there was the urgent need for a large litter box and a fresh supply of litter.

An hour later, Felicity was back home after a trip to a large pet-supply store. In uncharacteristic fashion, she had spent more money than she'd have believed possible on the props required to present herself to her public as the very model of the modern cat owner: a gigantic gold litter box with a hood, a bag of litter, a molded plastic cat carrier with a quilted pad, a velvety cat bed, premium dry and canned food, two brushes, feline cologne, nail scissors, and a dozen toys that ranged from colorful bits of artificial prey to a battery-operated device that whirled feathery lures enticingly through the air. She comforted herself with the reflection that these ghastly expenses were tax deductible.

Although the representatives of the media were still infuriatingly absent, she was gratified to find three messages on her answering machine, one from Dave Valentine and two from members of the local mystery writers' community, Sonya Bogosian and Janice Mattingly. Valentine's message was nothing more than a request to return his call. Sonya Bogosian was the president of the New England branch of Witness for the Publication, an organization of mystery writers and fans that met at Newbright Books. Felicity served on the board. Sonya's message was not, however, about board business. Ronald, she said, had told her about Felicity's misadventure, and she wanted to touch base before the Witness meeting tonight. Until recently, Janice Mattingly had been a "wannabe," an unpublished writer with hopes, but her first mystery had been accepted. She edited the local Witness newsletter, saw to the food and drink offered at meetings, and otherwise made herself useful. She, too, said that Ronald had told her what had happened. She hoped that Felicity's creativity and concentration weren't affected by the terrible experience. Would Felicity please call her? Felicity intended to return Sonya's call but not Janice's. Eager to hear that the baffled police were finally seeking her advice, she called Dave Valentine back immediately.

"Miss Pride," he said, "thank you for getting back to me. I just wanted to let you know that we're all done. You can use your front door again."

Struggling to keep the disappointment out of her voice, Felicity said, "Who was the man? Who killed him? Why was he left here?" *And how soon am I going to be able to milk this murder for its full promotional value?*

"We don't know just yet."

Felicity cursed herself for having failed to check the pockets of the gray suit. "You don't even know his name?" Should Prissy LaChatte ever find a corpse at *her* door, she'd be braver than her creator had been.

"Not yet."

"He didn't have a wallet? Did his shirt have a laundry mark?" A tailor-made suit with a name stitched in was too much to hope for, wasn't it? Did American tailors even do that?

"So far, we don't know anything."

"The people who were here this morning, searching the yards. Did they find any . . . evidence?" *Clues* were strictly for Nancy Drew and Miss Marple, weren't they? Even Prissy LaChatte avoided them in favor of evidence.

Without giving a direct answer, Valentine said, "The body was probably transported there in a vehicle."

"And the cat?"

"The cat, too. Probably."

"Was he murdered in my vestibule?"

"Sorry if that's been worrying you. No. No, he wasn't."

"That's not what's worrying me! What's worrying me is that a murder victim was left at my front door! What's worrying me is *me!* So, where do we go from here?"

Felicity's literary experience led her to feel certain that Valentine would insist that the murder was a police matter in which amateurs should remain uninvolved. Ignoring the *we,* he said, "Miss Pride, in real life, most homicides have simple solutions."

"Then why aren't they all solved?"

"Sorry, Miss Pride, but I've got run. Like I said, it's okay to use your front door now."

Infuriated, Felicity managed a loud but anticlimactic response: "I will! I definitely will!"

The ban on discussing the murder had convinced Felicity that as publicists, the police were useless. It now seemed to her that they were equally useless as homicide investigators.

TWELVE

Brigitte eyes the food dish, which is empty, as is the water bowl she customarily shares with Edith. Having repeatedly checked the bathroom and kitchen faucets, she knows that they are not dripping.

How long can a cat safely go without water? The question never occurs to Brigitte, who nonetheless jumps to the kitchen counter, scampers to the sink, and trains her amber eyes on the faucet. Just in case.

THIRTEEN

"I'm so surprised you're here," said Janice Mattingly, who had finished unpacking the plastic glasses, the
bottles of wine and soft drinks, and the cheese, crackers, and
fruit offered to members of Witness in the social hour before
the meeting began. Her eyes were not on Felicity but on a
mummified foot that formed part of the display set out by
the evening's speaker, a forensic expert whose presentation
Felicity had intended to skip. Her fellow Witnesses evidently
failed to share her distaste; perhaps thirty were milling
around, each wearing a name tag. Happily, the gruesome
objects and photographs were on one table at the back of
Newbright Books, the refreshments on another. It occurred
to Felicity that the fruit, especially the chunks of melon,
might easily have gone on either table without seeming out

of place. The watermelon had turned a sick red, as had the strawberries, and the honeydew looked slimy. "Me," Janice continued, "I'd be so shaken up!"

Janice was twenty years younger than Felicity and cursed with a day job. As Felicity had once done, she taught school. A hatred of classrooms was something the two had in common. Felicity had taught kindergarten in Wellesley, whereas Janice taught seventh graders in Brighton. Janice had shoulder-length brown hair and bangs, and although chalk was no longer ubiquitous in classrooms, her skin was white and powdery. In Felicity's judgment, her lipstick was too red and her eyebrows were overplucked. She favored handwoven garments and the color red.

"I *am* upset!" Felicity said.

"You probably won't be able to write for weeks. Maybe months. Or years!"

When the City of Somerville had torn up the street in front of Felicity's apartment building, the jackhammer hadn't stopped her from writing. She had worked despite the ends of love affairs, the pain of a broken wrist, and the discombobulation of the move from Somerville to Newton Park. The alternative was a return to classroom teaching. She had written two pages this same afternoon. "Well, if that happens, I'll file a civil suit against the murderer and retire on my settlement," she said.

"Can you do that?"

Felicity was about to say that one could indeed file such a suit when she noticed the object Janice had just picked up. "Janice, put that thing *down!*" The thing was the mummified foot, which Janice was absentmindedly fondling. Sounding like Naomi, she said, "You could catch something from it!"

"It's dry. Actually, it looks like it's been varnished. Bacteria grow in warm, moist environments."

"Janice," said Sonya Bogosian, "you aren't supposed to touch the exhibits. And that thing is disgusting. I don't know why you'd want to touch it, anyway. Hi, Felicity. How's your murder coming along?" Felicity had returned Sonya's call, but had had to settle for leaving voice mail. *Bogosian* was Sonya's married name. Her coloring was Scandinavian. Her long, naturally blonde hair was secured in a bun at the base of her neck, and, as usual, she wore so many layers of loose, flowing garments that her appearance suggested a well-scrubbed bag lady. "You know, if you don't mind my asking, I have a little professional curiosity about something. The blood. Would you say it looked like ketchup? Or more like red paint?"

"Sonya, it's going to depend on whether it's congealed," said Hadley O'Connor, who'd joined the little group. Hadley was Felicity's junior by ten years and almost ridiculously handsome, with wavy brown hair, bright blue eyes, and hard muscle. Five years ago, when he'd moved to Boston and begun attending Witness meetings, Felicity had had a brief fling with him that she'd ended as soon as she'd belatedly sampled one of his books. She occasionally read private investigator novels, especially hard-boiled mysteries so undercooked as to be barely coddled, and had wishfully supposed that Hadley's novels would suit her palate. Ten pages of gore and sadism had disillusioned her. She had, however, remained on cordial terms with Hadley. In fact, she went out of her way to be pleasant to him, mainly because the contents of his mind frightened her senseless.

"There wasn't any blood." Felicity made the admission with a sense of shame and inferiority, as if she'd had the bad luck to get a third-rate corpse. A first-rate one would have been mutilated, maybe even decapitated. Decapitation was hot these days, wasn't it? Second-rate would've been gory: brain matter and blood. The little gray man had been third-rate: He'd been just plain dead. Still, the duct tape counted for something, didn't it? "His mouth was sealed with duct tape," she hastened to add, lest anyone think that her very own corpse had simply had a heart attack after being frightened to death, a method favored by Isabelle Hotchkiss. "But the police have asked me not to share the details with anyone." Except hair stylists, who were clergy of sorts. Thank heaven for freedom of religion!

Her eyes eager, Janice asked, "What did he die of then? Asphyxiation?"

"No one knows yet," Felicity said smugly. "When the results are available, I'll be among the first to know. Obviously. I mean, this was not some random crime, although how it connects to me is, if you'll pardon the expression, a complete mystery." To Hadley, she said, "There was a cat left with the body. In my vestibule. I think I'm allowed to tell you that."

"Dead?" he inquired hopefully.

"Alive! She's with me now. Well, not here and now, but at my house. She was horribly traumatized, but she's beginning to recover. And she's just as sweet as she is beautiful. Ask Ronald! He met her last night. He came rushing over as soon as I called him."

"The poor cat!" Janice exclaimed. "I don't know what Dorothy-L would do if something like that happened to her." At Janice's first mention of her cat, Sonya and Hadley turned to the refreshment table. Janice was well known to be tediously devoted to the cat, who was named after Dorothy-L, an Internet list for mystery fans, which was, in turn, named in honor of Dorothy L. Sayers. "Her health is fragile enough as it is. I thought her thyroid was okay with the medication, but now I'm starting to think that maybe she needs the radioactive iodide treatment after all, even though it would be awful for her in the short term. They have to be isolated, and then even when they come home, you can't touch them because, of course, they're radioactive. I really don't—"

In desperation, Felicity said, "Any news about your book?" *Tailspin* was a cat mystery that Felicity had weaseled out of blurbing by pleading a deadline. ("I don't have time to read my own manuscript, never mind someone else's!")

"Sonya did a wonderful blurb for me," Janice said. "Really cute."

"I'm sure," said Felicity.

"Look," said Janice, "maybe this isn't the right time to raise it, but would you mind if I wrote about your murder in the newsletter? I'm always short of material. I'm supposed to be the editor, but people are lazy about sending me material, and I end up writing most of it myself, and it's hard to know what to say."

With great self-control, Felicity replied casually, "Well, if it would help you out, I guess I wouldn't mind, but I have to wait until the murder is solved. I am forbidden to give interviews."

The membership was now settling in chairs and on the floor in preparation for the business meeting, which would be followed by the forensic expert's presentation.

"I'll call you," Janice said. "For an interview."

The first of many! Felicity thought gleefully. "Fine," she said. "With luck, I'll be allowed to share the details in a day or two."

In spite of the welcome omen that her publicity plans were shaping up, Felicity felt suddenly tired and, in any case, had no desire to hear about mummified feet. Excusing herself, she headed for the front of the shop, where she passed the display of Isabelle Hotchkiss's new book. Instead of feeling the combination of jealousy, envy, and resentment that ordinarily assailed her when she came upon evidence of her rival's success, she felt an almost grandiose optimism to which she gave voice once she reached the privacy of Aunt Thelma's Honda. "Kitty Katlikoff, you better watch out! Better say bye-bye to your saccharine, sickening Lambie Pie and Olaf! Because here comes Prissy LaChatte." She paused and added vehemently, "And Morris and Tabitha, who are going to scratch your rotten eyes out!"

FOURTEEN

After taking her first mouthful of coffee—but before putting on her reading glasses—Felicity perused the morning paper. From her optometrically challenged viewpoint, the lead article on the front page began thus:

MYSTERY WRITER'S CAT SOLVES HOMICIDE
Felicity Pride, author of the Prissy LaChatte series of feline mysteries, returned home on Monday evening to a scene out of one of her own books.

Feeling somewhat dissatisfied, Felicity fortified herself with a slug of coffee and tried again:

FAMOUS MYSTERY NOVELIST'S CAT
SOLVES NEWTON MURDER

Felicity Pride, celebrated author of the bestselling Prissy
LaChatte series of feline mystery novels, returned home on
Monday evening from a well-attended signing of her latest
blockbuster, *Felines in Felony,* to discover a scene straight out
of one of her own spine-tingling tales. Or should that be
tails?

Once having donned her glasses, Felicity paged through
the paper until she finally came upon a short paragraph in a
column about local crime:

Police report that an elderly man whose body was found on
the front porch of a Brighton home on Monday evening
was the victim of foul play. Authorities are pursuing their
investigation.

Brighton home indeed! *Front porch!* No Felicity, no mystery novels, no Prissy, and no cat! Still, the murder had been
reported in the paper, no matter how inadequately, and instead of passively accepting her ignominious and anonymous relegation to two sentences deep in the interior of the
paper, Felicity decided to act. After all, her first three mysteries hadn't been hardcovers, had they? No, they had been
paperback originals reviewed in the newsletters of three
mystery bookstores and nowhere else. But those three paperbacks had been a start. So, too, was this stinking mini-
paragraph. Well, if the cat was indeed going to solve the
Newton homicide, best to begin with the cat and with her
own role as cat-worshiping cat novelist. To begin with,
she'd take the cat to a vet.

The late Morris had required nothing in the way of veterinary care and had thus left Felicity entirely ignorant about veterinarians and local veterinary clinics. Clearly, Felicity Pride's cat must see a posh veterinarian. But how was she to go about identifying one? By address, she presumed. Consulting the yellow pages of the West Suburban directory, Felicity studied the listings and, on the basis of its Newton location and the possibly feline connotation of its name, picked out Furbish Veterinary Associates. Having called the veterinary practice, stated her name, and requested an appointment for a cat, she was only somewhat surprised to be told that Dr. Furbish could see the cat at eleven o'clock this same morning. As Felicity was enjoying what she interpreted as evidence that her name had weight in the world of cats, she was taken aback by the request for the cat's name.

Stalling, Felicity said, "Her name."

"Yes. The cat's name."

It had never before occurred to Felicity that the cat possessed such a thing as a name. Furthermore, having named hundreds of characters in her many books, she hadn't even toyed with the possibility of giving the cat a temporary name that would do until the real one was discovered.

"The cat's name," she said, "is a mystery! The cat came to me under strange and baffling circumstances, and her true identity is, for the moment, entirely unknown. Let's think of her as X, shall we? The unknown quantity."

Felicity's self-congratulation for this inspired solution was short-lived. Before hanging up, the veterinary assistant informed Felicity that all animals needed to be restrained while in the waiting room. For a few seconds, Felicity could make nothing of the requirement. Restrained from doing what? Scratching people? It emerged that the cat would have to be in a carrier or on a leash.

The plethora of cat supplies Felicity had bought did not include a leash, but did include a large carrier complete with a quilted pad. Missing from the armamentarium, however, was any sort of clever device that would automatically entrap a cat and deposit it in the carrier; it would, alas, be necessary to perform the operation by hand—thus risking a scratched or bitten hand.

It was nine o'clock. To delay the cat-capturing expedition, which would take her into the wilds of one of her own guest rooms, Felicity took a shower, fixed her hair, and, in preparation for her first public appearance with her new PR agent, put on gray woolen pants and a patterned sweater with patches of amber. After locating a pair of leather gloves that would offer some protection against scratches, she postponed the daunting task that lay ahead by placing a phone call to her mother, who would inevitably hear about the gray man and, just as inevitably, find a way to blame or ridicule Felicity for the episode. If Felicity broke the news herself, at least her mother wouldn't be able to complain that she'd had to wait until someone else told her.

Although Felicity's mother, Mary Pride, lived a mere twenty-minute drive from Newton Park, Felicity visited her as seldom as possible. Whenever Felicity felt guilty about the infrequency of her visits, she reminded herself of other destinations that were also within twenty minutes of Newton Park: waste recycling depots, funeral homes, and slummy neighborhoods infamous for drive-by shootings perpetrated by drug-crazed maniacs on innocent bystanders such as herself.

Her mother answered the phone with a thick-voiced,

"Hello? Hang on while I turn down the television." Minutes later, she said, "Who is it?"

"Mother, it's Felicity."

"Who?"

"Felicity!"

"Who?"

"Your daughter. Your older daughter. Felicity. Remember me?"

"Oh, you. I thought it was Angie. She calls me all the time. Last night she called when I was in the middle of one those nature shows I love. About leopards." Mary pronounced *leopards* and, indeed, everything else, with the Boston accent that Felicity still labored to remove from her own speech. *Leopards!* And not *leh-puhds!* Truly, the accent was her mother tongue.

Mary's fondness for programs about wild animals had originally mystified Felicity. Her mother had never owned a pet of any kind and had refused to allow her children, Felicity and Angie, to have even so undemanding a pet as a solitary goldfish. It had finally occurred to Felicity that the attraction of the nature programs was their savagery: Program after program showed wild animals engaged in slaughtering one another.

"Mother, I called because something terrible happened. Monday night, I did a signing, and—"

"A what?"

"A signing. I was signing my new book at Ronald Gershwin's store. Newbright Books. You've been there."

"You know what he always puts me in mind of? 'Wee, sleekit, cowran tim'rous beastie.' "

"I can't imagine why."

"That's Robert Burns."

"I know it's Robert Burns. It's from 'To a Mouse.' "

"We're descended from Gilbert Burns, you know. Robert's brother. *Robert* Burns had no legitimate descendants."

It seemed to Felicity that every Scottish family in America claimed descent from Gilbert Burns. If all the claims were true, Gilbert Burns would have needed to father hundreds of children, so it was impossible that they'd all been legitimate. But Felicity limited herself to saying, "That's debatable." She took a deep breath. How had she once again let herself get sucked into the Burns Diversion? "Mother, when I got home on Monday night, there was a dead body in my vestibule." Knowing it was a mistake, she added, "And a cat."

"Cats! Do you remember that cat Thelma had when you were a little girl? It was an ugly thing, but you were crazy about it. You used to go running after it, but the cat had your number all right! It was always coming up to me and rubbing against me. Cats are attracted to me, you know. Dogs are, too. And I hate the damn things."

"Did you hear what I said? About the body? It was the body of some elderly man."

"I have very acute hearing. Well, don't worry, I won't say a thing."

"I have no idea who the man was or why the body was left here. There's no question of your saying or not saying anything."

"When they ask me, I'll say I don't know a thing about it. And Angie won't say a word, either. Blood's thicker than water, I always say, Felicity. Angie and I won't breathe a word."

After ending the conversation, Felicity could almost hear the braying her mother had emitted when Aunt Thelma's cat had run from Felicity almost fifty years earlier: *Cat's got your number! Cat's got your number!* And here was Felicity with yet another cat that evidently had her number as well. In catching the gray cat, she must remember not to chase it. In reality, Aunt Thelma's cat had run because it had been chased. It hadn't had Felicity's "number," whatever that was. It had simply run from an eager child who hadn't known how to behave around cats.

FIFTEEN

Felicity entered the cat's room on what she might have described in her books as "little cat feet." There was, however, nothing foggy about her mental state. On the contrary, she felt sharply determined to prove that *this* cat didn't hate her. Equally sharp was her awareness that her will left everything to Ronald Gershwin and, consequently, nothing to her mother or sister, both of whom she meant to outlive, anyway.

"If you chase cats," she said softly, "they run away. Cat, I am not going to chase you. Do you hear me? And do you see what I'm doing? I am ignoring you!"

The cat was hiding under the bed and thus easy to ignore. The level of dry food in one of the new bowls had dropped, and the bowl of canned food was empty except for a disgusting residue of dried brown crud. Peering under the hood of the gigantic gold litter box, Felicity saw that the litter had been used. Feeling confident that the cat was still alive, she sorted through the pile of supplies she'd bought, arranged the quilted pad in the cat carrier, and armed herself with a feather-and-bell toy identical to the one that Ronald had successfully used to lure the cat. After raising the bed skirt, she inserted the toy, but instead of twitching it slowly and enticingly, she shook it vigorously back and forth, and then repeatedly yanked it out from under the bed and shoved it back under again. Dropping the toy, she got down on her knees, peered under the bed, and saw that the cat was huddled directly beneath the center of the headboard and was thus out of reach. Bearing in mind that it was vital not to chase the cat, she resolved, on the Mohammed-and-mountain principle, to move the bed. This bed, unlike the king-size platform bed in the master bedroom, was full-size. The headboard ran down to the floor, but the foot of the bed stood on wooden legs. The bed should be light enough for her to move, especially since she could get a good grip on the oak headboard. Grip she did. And managed to drag the bed a good eighteen inches from the wall. Startled at what must have seemed like an earthquake, the cat ran out, dashed across the room, and jumped onto a dresser. Assuring herself that she wasn't *chasing* the cat, Felicity took long, smooth steps, encircled the cat with her arms, and, hugging tightly, transferred the hefty animal to the dark interior of the cat carrier. After a few minutes of puzzled fiddling with the latch, she finally managed to fasten the carrier shut.

It was in returning the bed to its normal position that Felicity discovered the fireproof box, which had lain between the headboard and wall, but, having been dislodged, prevented her from pushing the bed all the way back in place. What immediately struck Felicity about the box was, in addition to its peculiar location, its obvious age. Almost everything else in the house was new. Uncle Bob and Aunt Thelma had kept most of their possessions in the oceanfront estate in Ogunquit that had gone to one of Thelma's sisters. The box was old. Somewhat larger than a shoe box, it was made of tan-coated metal, like a cheap filing cabinet, and showed several scratches and small dents. Picking up the box, Felicity was reminded of the cat: Both felt much heavier than they looked, as if they were packed with lead. Felicity's speculation about the contents of the box, however, had nothing to do with lead weights or, indeed, any other metal, including gold bars that Uncle Bob might have cached for use in a national emergency or natural disaster. Rather, she was terrified that the box contained a heretofore undiscovered will leaving everything to Aunt Thelma's sisters or, worse, to her own mother and sister. The box was locked.

Happily for Felicity, there was no mystery about the location of the key, which she correctly guessed to be the small one she'd noticed in the same large kitchen drawer that contained a three-ring notebook of manuals and warranties for the refrigerator, range, washer, dryer, and other new appliances. After dashing down to retrieve the key and sprinting back up to the cat's room, she placed the box on the bed and opened it. The heavy contents were neither legal documents nor gold bars. The box contained a large amount of cash and a small, shabby notebook in which were recorded what were evidently deposits made at intervals of a week or two weeks: columns of dates and amounts ("May 15, 1968 40") with, here and there, a cumulative total preceded by a dollar sign. The dates began thirty years earlier. The amounts varied, but had increased in size over the years from twenty or thirty dollars to eighty, a hundred, or two hundred dollars. The grand total in the notebook was $120,555. With only a half hour to get the cat to the vet, she nonetheless took the time to count the cash, most of which was in one-hundred-dollar bills. Her total agreed with the one in the notebook.

She hurriedly replaced the contents in the box, locked it, and put it where she'd found it, between the headboard and the wall. Ill-gotten gains? In what nefarious enterprise had Uncle Bob been engaged? There was no such thing as a Scottish Mafia. Or was there? Although the bills looked used, they might, for all Felicity knew, be counterfeit. When she got back from seeing Dr. Furbish, she'd take a closer look.

Transporting the cat proved to be a weightier task than Felicity had somehow imagined. The carrier had a handle on top, but was as heavy as a big suitcase. Felicity lugged it downstairs and out to the garage, and, after some hesitation, put it on the front passenger seat of the Honda and fastened it with a seat belt. Preoccupied with the matter of Uncle Bob's hidden money, as well as ignorant about cats, she failed to appreciate the silence of the drive to the veterinary clinic; it hadn't occurred to her that the cat might howl.

Furbish Veterinary Associates occupied a small brick building with parking spaces in front, one of which was empty. Detained by her unexpected discovery, Felicity arrived in the waiting room at the precise time of her appointment and was directed to a small examining room before she had a chance to do more than glance at the room and its human, feline, and canine occupants. To Felicity's surprise, Dr. Hilary Furbish was female, a woman of about

Felicity's age who wore green scrubs and had short, straight hair going gray, no makeup, and unvarnished nails. Felicity decided that if Dr. Furbish became the cat's regular vet, a quiet word or two about Naomi might be appropriate. Naomi and Dr. Furbish would like each other's cleanliness.

Evidently more concerned with the cat than with her own appearance, Dr. Furbish, after introducing herself, lifted the heavy carrier with no sign of effort, settled it on a metal examining table, and looked in. "What a beautiful cat!" she exclaimed.

"Thank you." Fearful of making a fool of herself, Felicity was determined to say as little as possible about the cat. Did Dr. Furbish or her staff recognize Felicity's name? Did they know who she was?

"I take it that she's new."

"She was left at my doorstep," Felicity said. "On Monday evening. I thought she ought to have a checkup."

Dr. Furbish opened the carrier door, reached in with both hands, removed the cat, and placed her on the table. "You're a big girl, aren't you?" She stroked the head of the unprotesting cat. "Amazing eyes. Magnificent." Casually touching the cat and speaking gently, she conducted a thorough examination. The cat cooperated when Dr. Furbish applied a stethoscope, looked in her ears, checked her teeth, and used a thermometer to take the cat's temperature. "Spayed female," she told Felicity. "Healthy. Young. Three or four." She then moved a small scale to the table, lifted the cat onto it, and said, "Thirteen pounds. Let's consider this her maximum acceptable weight. She's not obese, but I don't want to see her any heavier." She then raised the cat's head and pointed to a small area on the throat. "That's been shaved recently. Within a day or two."

"What on earth for?" Felicity asked. She immediately regretted the question. For all she knew, shaving a spot on the throat was an essential part of routine cat care.

"It's a venipuncture mark. A blood test maybe." Without asking Felicity's permission, she retrieved a small electronic gadget from a shelf and slowly passed it over the base of the cat's neck. Studying it she said, "Okay." Then she reached for a pad of paper and a pen, and wrote down a string of numerals. "Microchip number. With luck, in no time we'll know whose cat she is. She's a beauty. And so mellow. Someone will be relieved to have her back home."

SIXTEEN

"She isn't one of ours," said the young woman behind the high counter. "We keep the numbers for all the animals we microchip on our computer, and her number isn't here. Dr. Furbish would've recognized her, anyway. If you want to have a seat, we'll call the company, and they'll look up the number."

And what if I don't want to have a seat? thought Felicity. *What if I want to take my cat and go home and reexamine Uncle Bob's money?* Reluctantly seating herself on one of the wooden benches that lined two walls of the waiting room, she concentrated on behaving herself. Only a few minutes ago, when Dr. Furbish had been examining the cat, Felicity had enjoyed the rare sense of being able to relax while kind, competent adults managed practical matters better than she could have done herself. Then Dr. Furbish had said, "I'm sorry, but we can't release the cat to you until the registered owner has been contacted."

The cat was now somewhere behind the scenes at the clinic while Felicity was stuck here in the waiting room. Registered owner, hah! Murder victim! And Dr. Furbish rather than Felicity would get all the credit for discovering the identity of the little gray man, who had definitely been left in Felicity's vestibule for Felicity. Particularly galling was the reflection that the cat, just like Morris and Tabitha, had possessed information about the murder that she had "communicated," albeit not in the mysterious fashion favored by Prissy LaChatte's cats but via a microchip and a scanner. So what! The cat was Felicity's, the information belonged to her, and she deserved the credit; Dr. Furbish and her staff deserved none.

The young woman behind the counter put down the phone and said, "The number's busy. I'll try again in a minute."

Eager though Felicity was to return home to the fireproof box and its puzzling contents, she was unwilling to do anything to suggest that she had abandoned the cat. Still, she was tempted to tell the young woman that she'd be back soon and to zip home to pursue her investigation.

The clinic door opened and in stepped a well-dressed woman with a well-groomed golden retriever. The woman greeted an elderly couple seated far from Felicity on the other wooden bench. She'd barely noticed them. There was a small green cat carrier at their feet, but they'd been speaking neither to each other nor to the cat that was presumably in the carrier. After checking in at the counter, the woman with the golden retriever took a seat near the couple. Her dog sat on the linoleum next to her without so much as sniffing the cat carrier. Neither the people nor their animals were of interest to Felicity, who continued to focus her thoughts on tax-free cash until a phrase drew her attention.

". . . tract mansions!" the elderly woman exclaimed. "That's what they're called."

"McMansions," the elderly man said. "Like McDonald's. I think that's quite clever. And very appropriate. Do you know that those people pretend that their development is in Newton? Someone was telling us about some scheme of theirs to have their mail delivered with Newton addresses."

Felicity knew all about the so-called scheme. To her disappointment and that of her neighbors, it had failed, as had the effort to have trash collected by Newton trucks.

"They're more than welcome to their pretensions," said the woman with the golden retriever. "All I object to is the traffic. And the way they drive! Our streets aren't meant for all those cars, and those people treat them like speedways. One of these days, someone's going to be run over and killed. I don't know why they can't use their own entrance."

"Because it's in Brighton!" the elderly woman crowed.

All three Norwood Hill residents had a laugh at what Felicity felt to be her expense. To her relief, the young woman behind the counter had the phone at her ear and was reading off a number. Felicity gave her a questioning look, and she nodded. After hanging up, she said, "The chip number's on file. They'll call the owner, and then the owner will call us."

"Do you have any idea how long this is going to take?" Felicity asked.

"It depends on whether they can reach the owner."

Felicity cursed herself for having failed to bring her

notebook computer along. A veterinary clinic would have been the ideal setting in which to work on the latest adventure of Prissy and the cats. Since the little gray man was dead, he wasn't going to answer the call from the microchip company, so she'd probably have to sit here for hours with nothing to do. In case she ever wanted to have Prissy take Morris and Tabitha to a vet, she studied the waiting room and made mental note of details. A board with removable letters gave the names of the clinic's veterinarians, veterinary technicians, and veterinary assistants. What was the difference between technicians and assistants? If she got it wrong, an irate reader would let her know. The elderly couple and their cat carrier vanished into an examining room. Two new clients arrived with dogs. The phone rang several times, and a young man who'd replaced the young woman behind the counter dispensed advice about bringing animals to the clinic. When the phone rang again, Felicity assumed that the caller was once again a pet owner. This time, however, Felicity overheard the young man say "microchip." She rose and stepped to the counter.

"My cat," she mouthed to him as he took notes.

"So you're the breeder," he was saying. "California?" After a pause, he said, "If you wouldn't mind. Yes, she's right here." To Felicity he said, "This is the breeder. She'd like to talk to you." He handed the phone to Felicity.

"Hi. My name is Felicity Pride. I'm the one who found the cat. Or rather, she was left in my vestibule."

"*The* Felicity Pride? The author?"

"Yes. I'm a mystery writer."

"I know! I just love Morris and Tabitha. And *you're* the one who found Edith?"

"Edith," Felicity said flatly. Edith? What a bland, disappointing name! How was she supposed to do effective publicity with a cat named—damn it all!—Edith! "Yes. I didn't exactly find her. I think that she was left for me. On Monday night."

"Well, where on earth is Quin? He must be frantic. He's devoted to his Chartreux." It took Felicity a second to connect the spoken word with the name she'd seen in one of her new books. The woman said "Char-troo," whereas Felicity had assumed that *Chartreux* should be pronounced with an effort at a French accent. The accompanying picture had shown a big gray cat with greenish-hazel eyes. Why had she of all people trusted a *book* to be accurate! Especially a book about cats! "He must be worried sick," the woman continued. "Why didn't he call me? Why didn't he call the microchip company? He has Edith's microchip number. He should have reported her missing. And what about Brigitte?"

"Who?"

"Quin's other Chartreux. She's a fluffy. Edith has her premiership, but you can't show fluffies. Well, some people are starting to, but not as Chartreux."

Nervous about exposing her ignorance to a member of her adoring public, Felicity limited herself to making a small sound that she hoped would indicate comprehension.

"Edith Piaf and Brigitte Bardot." To Felicity's relief, she anglicized the pronunciations. It was more than enough effort to remember to pronounce *r*'s in English words without having to twist her tongue around an unpronounceable foreign language just to say the names of cats. And *Chartreux*! Or "Char-troo." In either language, that rotten *r* was lurking in wait for persons slaving to throw off the chains of a Boston accent. "Those aren't their registered names, but Quin is a professor of Romance languages, and he wanted French names."

"Quin is . . .?" The young man behind the counter handed Felicity a slip of paper. "Oh, I have it here. Quinlan Coates." Now that her attention had been drawn to the veterinary assistant or technician, whichever he was, Felicity saw that he was impatient and belatedly realized that she was monopolizing the phone line. "Look, I think we need to talk more. If it's okay with you, I'll take, uh, Edith home with me, and I'll call you from there."

"It's more than okay. Obviously, Edith couldn't be in better hands. And I'm sure you're as worried about Brigitte as I am. Really, your love for cats just shines through in your books. Look, take Edith home with you, and I'll call Quin right now, and we'll get this whole thing straightened out. You didn't give Edith any vaccinations, did you? Because she's up to date . . ."

After listening to a brief lecture on the risks of immunization, Felicity obtained the name of the breeder, which was Ursula Novack, and her phone number and e-mail address, and once Ursula had given permission to the clinic to release Edith to Felicity, Felicity was finally allowed to take the cat and go home. Driving Aunt Thelma's car back to Aunt Thelma and Uncle Bob's house, she alternately fumed about Edith's plain, flat, unliterary, and throughly unmysterious name and, as was habitual with her, plotted the next steps in a murder investigation. Usually, it was Prissy LaChatte who took those steps. This time, it would be Felicity Pride, assisted, of course, by her prescient, communicative, and lovable feline companion, Edith. Edith! By her prescient, communicative, and lovable feline companion. Period.

SEVENTEEN

In Felicity's years as a kindergarten teacher, she had been forced to write lesson plans. She'd hated the task, and ever since liberating herself from her day job, had luxuriated in the freedom of having no fixed schedule, not even a self-imposed one. Felicity attended meetings and made and kept appointments, but she shunned daily to-do lists, weekly calendars showing tasks to be accomplished, and other activities that would have felt like personal lesson plans doomed to transform her life into one more classroom. A prolific writer, she had no need to impose deadlines on herself and had never missed a contractual deadline for the delivery of a manuscript. Consequently, her recent experience in planning events consisted mainly of outlining her Prissy LaChatte books and of scrambling to think of ways to promote sales.

Now, returning home from the veterinary clinic, she prioritized her tasks in the way most familiar to her, namely, by asking herself what Prissy LaChatte would do first. Call Ursula Novack? Return a call to Detective Valentine, who had left a message on her machine? Examine the fireproof box of cash? Certainly not. Prissy would first take care of the cats. Then, based on the clues she'd found, she'd get one step ahead of the police by discovering the identity of the murder victim. In other words, she must feed Edith—and, incidentally, herself—and then rush to the rescue of poor Brigitte.

In reality, her first step was to release Edith from the cat carrier, which would be needed for Brigitte. Instead of returning Edith to the confines of the upstairs bedroom, Felicity left the carrier on the kitchen floor. Having watched the skilled Dr. Furbish, she was prepared to reach in and gently remove the big cat. As it turned out, once Felicity had managed to undo the latch and open the little metal door, Edith emerged on her own and, to Felicity's surprise, didn't bolt out of the room, but hopped onto the kitchen table and sat there looking like a sphinx come to life. Prissy's cats stayed off dining surfaces. Edith's large, placid presence on the table didn't bother Felicity, who had, in any case, no inclination to respond to the cat's apparent effort at friendliness by scolding or punishing her. With the inscrutable Edith still planted on the table, Felicity quickly made a salmon salad from the previous night's dinner and carried her own plate and a saucer of salmon salad to the table. Perhaps Felicity moved faster than Edith liked. Or maybe Edith had had all the human contact she could tolerate for the moment. For whatever reason, she took a muscular leap off the table and vanished in the direction of the front hall.

With hurt feelings, Felicity ate her lunch, cleared the table, rinsed her own plate and put it in the dishwasher, and put Edith's saucer on the floor.

She began her detective work by dialing the phone number for Quinlan Coates that she'd copied from the veterinary assistant's slip of paper, which also showed an address on Commonwealth Avenue in Brighton. No one answered. Her next step was to use the Web. In modern mystery novels, the amateur sleuth was often a computer illiterate who needed the help of a young relative, a teenage employee, or some other techno wizard to retrieve even the simplest information from cyberspace. Felicity had nothing but scorn for the device of the youthful assistant. The female amateur detective should be self-reliant! Had Nancy Drew gone around whining for help with machinery? On the contrary, in the Nancy Drew books of Felicity's childhood, Nancy had capably driven her roadster without complaining that she had trouble shifting gears and without turning over the wheel to Beth or George. Capably steering with mouse and keyboard, Felicity soon had directions to Quin Coates's address and a map of its location, which was only about a mile from Newton Park and almost no distance from Boston College. Within seconds, her favorite search engine, Google, confirmed her hunch that Quinlan Coates was indeed a professor of Romance languages at that same institution.

She also found his office phone number, dialed it, and reached a woman who informed her in a heavy Boston accent that Professor Coates was on sabbatical. "He comes in every couplah days. You wanna leave a message? Or you want his voice mail?" *Mail* was "may-ull."

Felicity declined the offers. Arming herself with her cell phone, Detective Valentine's number, and the cat carrier, she set off to rescue Brigitte, whose name was damned well going to be pronounced "Bree-zheet" and not "Brih-jut." The cats' names could've been much worse than they were, she reflected. Neither *Edith* nor *Brigitte* constituted a pronunciation pitfall for persons laboring to rid themselves of Boston accents. The worst words weren't actually the obvious ones like *car* and *Harvard* that simply required speakers aspiring to standard English to remember to pronounce the letter *r*. No, the tricky words were those that demanded a decision about whether an *r* was or was not present. Sneaky words like *elegy* and *sherbet* put Felicity at such extreme risk of pronouncing the hateful letter *r* when it was supposed to be absent that she avoided the words altogether. Iris Murdoch's husband's memoir was just that and never *Elegy—Elergy?—for Iris*. She ordered ice cream and never that other stuff that was always *sherbet* and never *sherbert*. Wasn't it?

Even via the circuitous route down Norwood Hill, the drive to Quinlan Coates's address on Commonwealth Avenue was so short that Felicity's musings on the serendipity of the cats' names occupied her until she pulled into a parking (not "pahking") place. The Web had prepared her for the building's proximity to Boston College but not for what she perceived as its intimidating grandeur. It was an old-fashioned, monumental apartment building constructed of gray stone, with a wide flight of stone steps leading up to an imposing wooden door. The oversized cat carrier that she'd brought with her banged against her legs and made her feel ridiculous. The outer door was unlocked. She had trouble simultaneously holding it open and maneuvering the carrier inside. Once inside the foyer, she regained her self-confidence. Despite high ceilings and wood paneling, the interior of the building was shabby. Discarded junk mail and freebie local newspapers lay on the stone floor beneath the mailboxes, and the glass door that led to the main hallway was dirty. More to the point, it was locked. The numerous doorbells were marked with apartment numbers. Next to the numbers, residents' names appeared on business cards, scraps of paper, and, in few cases, tattered strips of masking tape. Quinlan Coates's name was on one of the business cards, albeit a yellowed one. Felicity rang Coates's bell, but the ancient-looking speaker near the bells remained silent, and no one buzzed her in.

What would Prissy do? Rather, what would Prissy's creator cause Prissy to do? Felicity searched the cards, scraps of paper, and bits of masking tape in search of a building manager or caretaker. In her mysteries and in other people's, the apartment building the amateur detective wanted to enter invariably had some sort of concierge, doorman, or manager who could be conned into believing a trumped-up story about a distant cousin making an unexpected visit or a paralegal desperately eager to deliver crucial documents that couldn't safely be left in a mailbox. As Felicity was grumbling to herself about the absence of anyone to whom she could tell her perfectly genuine story about the need to rescue an abandoned cat, the outer door opened and in walked a man of about her own age. He had curly black hair and dark eyes, and wore a dark suit. In his hand was a ring of keys.

"Pardon me," she said. "Do you happen to know Quinlan Coates?"

"He's on sabbatical. He might be away."

"Yes, I know he's on sabbatical. You haven't seen him lately?"

"His car's out back. But he could be traveling. I haven't seen him for a couple of days."

"Actually," Felicity said, "I have reason to believe that something may have happened to him. He seems to have abandoned his cats!"

"I doubt that," the man said. "He boards them when he goes away. That's probably where they are. At Angell Memorial."

"Well, at the risk of sounding melodramatic, I have to tell you that I came into possession of one of his cats under extremely sinister circumstances. And the other cat may very well be in his apartment. You don't happen to know anyone who has a key, do you?" To emphasize the nature and urgency of her mission, she lifted the carrier by its handle.

"I have one. Quin's apartment is right above mine, and the plumbing's old. I have a key to let the plumber in if something leaks when Quin's away. He wasn't too crazy about the idea, but then he had to pay for my ceiling, and he wasn't too crazy about that, either. He's an old tightwad, but I hope he's all right." The dark man inserted his key in the door, held it for Felicity, and took the cat carrier. "Let me take that thing for you. If anything's happened, he'll want the cats to be all right. It's on the second floor."

Felicity followed him up a flight of carpeted stairs. The carpeting was dark brown, the walls a muddy beige, and the atmosphere oppressive. At a door with "24" printed on adhesive tape, he stopped, searched through his key ring, and finally found the right key and let Felicity in. "I have to warn you, you're going to want to open a window. Quin won't hire anyone to clean, and he doesn't get around to taking out his trash all that often. I've got to go. You can let yourself out."

After thanking the neighbor, Felicity moved the carrier into the apartment, closed the door, and, in spite of the thick, rancid odor, smiled broadly. She stood in a large living room with a high ceiling, dark wood doors and trim, and walls that had once been white. The furniture had probably been sold as Scandinavian and had certainly been bought a long time ago. A sectional sofa and two soft chairs had also been white or possibly the color called "oatmeal." The arms of one chair had turned brown, and the patterned rug in front of it bore black stains. The tops of the side tables were invisible under piles of scholarly books and journals, but the legs were teak or maybe teak-stained pine. Dust and cat hair were especially prominent on the standing lamps and table lamps, which, like the other furnishings, were domestic Scandinavian in style. Their condition was battered. Strands of gray fluff clung to stained lampshades.

On the only clear surface in sight, the top of the coffee table, sat a single hardcover book, which proved to be an anthology of short stories presented in English and in French, English on the left-hand pages, French on the right. The editor of the collection was Quinlan Coates. Although the term "crime writing" always struck Felicity as an absurdity when applied to cozy mysteries, especially her own, she had attended enough presentations by forensic experts and law-enforcement personnel to know that the first rule for behavior at crime scenes was: Don't touch anything! It was also the second rule, the third rule . . .

But was the apartment really a crime scene? And she'd already touched the door and a light switch. What's more, having picked up the book and leafed through it, she'd already contaminated it and was therefore free to examine it yet more, as she promptly did by flipping to the back flap of the dust jacket, which showed a photograph of Quinlan Coates, Ph.D., Professor of Romance languages at Boston

College, who was unmistakably the small gray man. The weirdly long and thick eyebrows were the clincher; they were as prominent in the photograph as they'd been on the deceased Coates's face. Why on earth hadn't he had them trimmed? One of Naomi's assistants did a splendid job on Felicity's eyebrows, and there was no reason Quinlan Coates couldn't have had comparable care taken of his, not that he should have had his brows waxed and plucked until they arched, but why had he chosen to go through life looking bizarre?

But Quinlan Coates's eyebrows were a trivial concern except to the extent that they established the identity of the murder victim. Felicity retrieved her phone from her purse, found Detective Valentine's number, and dialed. She'd been tempted to conduct a thorough search of the apartment before calling the police but had felt that it would be just her luck if Detective Valentine and his associates, all on their own, were to put a name to the body as she was looking over Coates's possessions. Besides, the police wouldn't arrive instantly. She'd have time to find Brigitte and investigate the place, too.

Luck was on her side. Unable to speak directly to Valentine, she left a message that consisted only of Quinlan Coates's name and address. Then, remembering not to touch anything, she began to search for Brigitte—and, incidentally, for anything else of interest she might spot. Through a large archway was a dining room with a mahogany table and chairs, and a matching sideboard, all at least eighty years old. Displayed in a built-in cupboard with glass doors were sets of venerable china and glassware. The contents of the room proclaimed inheritance from a grandmother. Few men would have wanted these possessions, which Felicity guessed

to be a woman's family treasures, probably those of an unknown Mrs. Quinlan Coates, of whom she'd seen no other
sign. The dusty table bore the marks of plates and glasses.
Through another and smaller archway was the kitchen,
which was obviously a major source of the foul odor that permeated the apartment. The sink was full of dirty dishes, but
the stench probably emanated from every surface. The walls
and counters were coated in grease, and the old linoleum
floor was so filthy that Felicity's shoes almost stuck to it. Two
stainless steel bowls on the floor were empty.

Returning to the living room, Felicity tried to open a
closed door, but found it locked. She decided to pursue her
investigation and her search for Brigitte in the three rooms
with doors that stood ajar. One proved to be a bathroom so
disgusting that she did no more than peep in; the caulking
around the tub was black with mold, and the white fixtures
and tiles were stained yellow. The second room was the only
clean area she'd found so far. Its furniture and most of the
items in it were for cats. It contained two plush cat beds, a
carpeted cat tree that rose to the ceiling, two large litter
boxes in need of scooping, and dozens of small cat toys. Also
in the cat room was a canister vacuum cleaner that had obviously been used here and nowhere else. A bookcase held a
large collection of cat mysteries, including what seemed to
be the complete collection of Isabelle Hotchkiss's Kitty
Katlikoff series, many of Lilian Jackson Braun's *The Cat
Who . . .* books, and works by Rita Mae Brown, Shirley
Rousseau Murphy, Carole Nelson Douglas, Marian Babson,
and, of course, Felicity Pride herself. It did not escape Felicity's notice that Quinlan Coates had owned all of Isabelle
Hotchkiss's mysteries and only a few of her own. Furthermore, although she was anything but embarrassed about

writing light entertainment, she was struck by the contrast between the feline subgenre fiction in the cat room and the academic tomes and journals in the living room. It crossed her mind, too, that most of her readers were women. The explanation for all the cat mysteries was, she thought, identical to the explanation for the cleanliness of the room and the cat beds, cat tree, and toys: Quinlan Coates had been a man who really loved cats.

The next room she entered was obviously Coates's bedroom. Although the shades were down, Felicity avoided touching a light switch. In the gloom, she saw a floor deep in discarded clothing and a rumpled bed topped with a heavy duvet. As her eyes adjusted to the dark, she saw a length of fur in the center of the comforter. For a moment, she was unable to tell head from tail, but she then realized that the creature was on its back, its head twisted to one side, its tail stretched out full length. It reminded her of an exceptionally long and narrow gray bird with thick and ruffled feathers, a bird lying inexplicably dead. She had found Brigitte.

EIGHTEEN

When the apparently dead thing stretched, Felicity was able to discern four legs and, soon thereafter, a head and a tail. With presence of mind worthy of Prissy LaChatte, instead of lingering uselessly in the dim, musty bedroom and instead of making a quick grab at Brigitte, she tiptoed to the living room, opened the bothersome door of the cat carrier, and, using one hand to keep the metal door quiet, transported the carrier to the bedroom and put it on the carpeted floor. Faced with the task of moving the small cat from the smelly bed to the carrier, she hesitated almost as if she were hearing echoes of her mother's raucous laughter and the inevitable taunt about Aunt Thelma's cat: *Cat's got your number, Felicity! Cat's got your number!*

Whether Brigitte had her number or not, the cat had to

be shifted from the bed to the carrier. Was there a correct method for picking up cats? Should Felicity scoop the animal up in her arms? Grasp it in some manner known to the cat savvy and kept secret from people like her? Oh, my, yes, kept hidden from people whose numbers cats inevitably had, people whose essential character cats sensed and from whom cats therefore fled. Cats did sense things, didn't they? Self-doubt, for example. Consequently, it was vital to act with a show of self-confidence that even a cat's extraordinary powers of perception couldn't spot as fakery.

Taking a deep breath, Felicity bent from the waist, wrapped both arms around Brigitte, and pulled the cat to her bosom. Edith's body had the density and solidity of steel, and her coat was like wool. Brigitte, in contrast, was almost weightless and remarkably silky. Felicity did not, however, pause to stroke Brigitte and, in the darkness of the smelly bedroom, did not even get a good look at her. Rather, in one swift motion, she transferred the cat from her arms to the carrier. Only when she was fastening the latch did she realize that Brigitte hadn't clawed, squirmed, or yowled. On the contrary, she'd shown no sign of wanting to run away.

Far from boosting Felicity's confidence in her ability to handle cats, the observation made her wonder whether Brigitte was ill, perhaps seriously dehydrated or weak from starvation. She did not, however, linger in Quinlan Coates's apartment to offer the cat food and water, but immediately left. On her way out, she was pleased to see nothing of the police, who, she assumed, would detain her for questioning without hailing her as the brilliant amateur sleuth who'd solved the mystery of the murder victim's identity. Thank heaven that she hadn't reached Detective Valentine himself but had been able to buy herself time by leaving him a message.

As always, Felicity drove home through Newton. When she reached Norwood Hill, the unhappy memory came to her of the unkind remarks she'd overheard in the waiting room of Furbish Veterinary Associates. Dr. Furbish's snobbish clients, she now decided, had been jealous of the luxury enjoyed by the residents of Newton Park. Some of the old houses she passed had slate roofs that probably leaked. The wood of some houses was so old that it wouldn't hold paint, and many of the kitchens must date to the twenties and thirties. Imagine the bathrooms! Furthermore, every house was defaced by ugly power lines and cables that stretched from utility poles inadequately camouflaged by overgrown trees. Newton Park, in contrast, had underground utilities. New roofs. New kitchens. New bathrooms. New everything! No wonder the snobs were jealous!

Arriving home, Felicity lugged the big, awkward carrier inside via the back door. She wasn't exactly avoiding the vestibule, she told herself; she was simply taking the expedient route. After a moment of debate, she decided not to haul the carrier up to the bedroom, but to look through the grill of its door and examine its occupant, Brigitte, here in the bright light of the kitchen. After all, once Brigitte was loose, she'd disappear under a bed, where she might remain indefinitely. If the preliminary examination warranted an immediate trip to the vet, there'd be no need to hunt her down and repeat the ordeal of getting her into the carrier; the carrier, with the cat inside, could go promptly back out to the Honda. With these thoughts in mind, Felicity put the carrier on the kitchen table and looked in. Far from languishing, Brigitte was pressing her slate-gray nose against the mesh door, thus displaying eyes of an amber even richer and deeper than Edith's. Expecting Brigitte to bolt, Felicity unlatched the door. Before she had time to open it, Brigitte pushed against it, boldly sauntered onto the table, and dropped lightly to the floor. Felicity could now see that the blue-gray of her long, fluffy coat was identical to the blue-gray of Edith's. Brigitte, however, was a dainty little creature who moved lightly and gracefully. As if blessed with the dowser's gift for sensing sources of water, she leaped to the counter next to the sink, planted herself there, and trained those extraordinary eyes on Felicity.

"Wait!" Felicity whispered. "Don't run away!"

The plea was entirely unnecessary. Moving swiftly, Felicity filled one of Aunt Thelma's new cereal bowls with water and placed it on the floor. Brigitte flew off the counter and, as she drank, Felicity opened a can of cat food, spooned it into a bowl, and deposited it next to the water. Abandoning all appearance of delicacy, Brigitte attacked the food as if hammering it with her little head. Convinced that her touch would frighten off the cat, Felicity controlled the impulse to run her fingertips along the silky fur on Brigitte's back. Instead, she made do with watching quietly as Brigitte emptied the bowl. Having done so, Brigitte still failed to run away. Unintimidated by her new surroundings, she dashed across the kitchen and, as if on invisible wings, rose to a counter and then to the top of the refrigerator, where she perched and peered around, like a bird that had alighted on a treetop.

The phone rang. Expecting a call from Detective Valentine, Felicity was startled to hear the voice of Ursula Novack, who moved rapidly through preliminaries to ask about Brigitte.

"She's right here," Felicity said. "She was hungry and thirsty, but she's fine now."

"There's nothing shy about her!" Ursula said. "She couldn't be any more different from Edith. That's why Edith was Quin's to begin with. She *hated* cat shows."

Shy? The concept of a shy cat was new to Felicity. "Edith is traumatized," she said. She went on to relate the story of finding Edith with the body of her owner, Quinlan Coates. "The police haven't identified him," she finished. "I've left them a message with his name and address."

"Just like in one of your books!" exclaimed Ursula, whom Felicity was starting to like a great deal.

"It is like that, isn't it?" Felicity asked, as if the similarity had previously eluded her. "And I must say that I did feel a little like a detective when I went to rescue Brigitte. A neighbor let me in. In one of my books, he might turn out to be the murderer."

"Maybe he is!"

"He didn't do anything suspicious. But maybe. Ursula, was Quinlan Coates a friend of yours?"

"No, not really. We stayed in touch about Brigitte and Edith. He was very good about that, letting me know that they were doing well. But I never met him. When he decided he wanted a Chartreux, he got in touch with a friend of mine in Connecticut who has one of my cats, and she sent him to me. That's when he got Edith. I was showing her, and she did very well. I granded her, but she hated shows, and I wanted a good pet home for her. And then when I had a litter with a fluffy, I thought he might be interested, and that's how he got Brigitte. He really loved his cats. I think he was lonely. He was a widower. Why in God's name would anyone murder him? And leave him at your doorstep?"

Granded? Felicity made a mental note to look up the word, which must be a piece of cat show jargon. "I have no idea," she said. "I never met him, either. I'd never even heard of him. The only connection is cats. I write about them, and he owned them. But beyond that? Millions of people own cats. I have no connection with most of those people."

"Well, it must be someone who reads your books. But that doesn't narrow the field down a lot, does it? Your books are so popular."

Do go on, Felicity wanted to say.

But before she could say anything, Ursula resumed. "I see your books all over. Even at airports. Speaking of which, you can ship Edith and Brigitte back to me. Quin has a son, but I have the feeling they're not on good terms, and Quin always said that his son didn't like cats, so Edith and Brigitte better come home here. I always take responsibility for the cats I breed. A direct flight would be best. There are plenty from Boston to San Francisco. That's the nearest airport to me. I don't know if you've ever shipped a cat before, but it's pretty simple. Edith and Brigitte have flown before. That's how they got to Quin. I'm never comfortable when my cats are flying, but I've never had a problem."

Brigitte, maybe. But Edith? Edith, who was so timid, so *shy,* that her response to finding herself with the freedom of a big, luxurious house was to huddle under a bed? Lock her in a cage and condemn her to hours in the roaring, terrifying belly of an airliner? No!

"Edith can't possibly fly. She is—"

"Oh, that's just Edith. Has she come out from under the bed yet?"

"Yes, but she does spend a lot of time there."

"Edith always has to do everything on her own time schedule."

"She's beautiful. So is Brigitte. Their eyes are . . . Look, Ursula, is there some reason they can't stay with me?" Forgetting for once that she was *the* Felicity Pride, she rushed to establish her reliability: "I have a big house, plenty of room, no other cats, no dogs. Dr. Furbish seems very good. I'd take them to her all the time. I've bought the best food I could find, dry and canned, and toys and cat beds. They'd be inside cats. There's no one here but me, so they wouldn't get out accidentally." Recollecting her place in the world, she added, "They'd have their pictures on the covers of my books!" She paused. "Only if they wanted to. If Edith was too shy, she wouldn't have to have her picture taken. I'd be more than happy to buy the cats. I can pay you."

"You really don't need to present your credentials. I know who you are! And you don't owe me anything. But if you change your mind, I'm here. Edith and Brigitte are always welcome. Just stay in touch with me, would you?"

"Of course."

"And let me know what turns up about Quin."

"I'll call you soon."

"You'll want the cats' registration papers. We'll get them transferred to you, unless you change your mind. And if you have any questions, I'm here, not that you of all people . . ."

"You never know," said Felicity, who already had a question that Ursula would be unable to answer. It was this: *What am I doing adopting two cats?* A second followed: *Have I gone totally out of my mind?*

As if in answer, the phone rang. The caller was a reporter from one of the two major Boston newspapers. Had he reached the author of the cat mysteries? He had. And had

Ms. Pride found a cat and a dead body on her porch? No, she had not. Both had been in her vestibule. Would she be agreeable to an interview sometime in the next few days? She would not. The police had ordered her not to speak to the media.

Not until the murder was solved.

NINETEEN

Felicity's considerable experience as a con-
sumer and producer of mystery fiction had given her a great
fondness for emotional magnetism between female amateur
sleuths and male homicide detectives. When the attraction
became outright romance, the relationship often fell victim
to author-imposed impediments cruelly placed between the
would-be lovers to prolong tension from book to book, thus
smoothing a series potentially chopped up by discrete murders. In some cases, the author found it useful to unite the
duo in a consummated affair or in marriage, thus allowing
the amateur gumshoe ready access to information otherwise known only to the police; it was far easier to write
a little pillow talk than it was to invent complex sub-
terfuges whereby the amateur protagonist discovered the

results of a postmortem, learned which suspects had or lacked alibis, or became privy to the secret of exactly what bewildering object the murderer had left as a signature at the scene of the crime. Ah, love! What a splendid literary convenience!

Thus at six-thirty that evening, after Felicity had re-counted the $120,555 in the fireproof box and added 1,353 words to her new Prissy LaChatte book, she was delighted to find Detective Dave Valentine at her back door. Having left her phone off the hook and her cell phone off, she was, not however, surprised. He'd have to reach her somehow, wouldn't he?

"Come in," she said. "You got my message?"

"Your phone's out of order," he said. "And you must've had your cell phone turned off. But I take it that you got there first."

In more ways than one, Felicity wanted to say. "I didn't touch anything except the book on the coffee table. I had to get Quinlan Coates's other cat. The one that was left here is Edith. They're Chartreux cats. I took Edith to the vet this morning, and it turns out that she has a microchip. The number on the microchip was registered to the breeder, who's in California, and she had his name and address. She made me promise to get his other cat right away. That's Brigitte. They're Edith Piaf and Brigitte Bardot. He was a professor of Romance languages."

Possibly in response to the sound of her name, Brigitte flounced into the kitchen. Picking up speed, she leaped onto the counter by the sink and began to sniff the salmon fillet that Felicity had been seasoning.

"You see? She was starving." As Prissy would have done, instead of asking whether Dave Valentine would like to share the meal, she told him to have a seat and set about fixing food for two. "It's not for her. Cats need cat food. It's Scottish salmon." She turned the heat on under one of Aunt Thelma's expensive new skillets.

"Smoked?"

"No. Farm raised. I tried it out of loyalty, but it really is good." She paused in the hope that he'd mention the Highland Games or, indeed, anything else about Scotland. "Besides, it was on sale."

He laughed. "How much more Scottish could it get?"

"I have to confess something," Felicity said coyly. "I saw you at the Highland Games."

"Making a fool of myself."

"Not at all!"

"In a skirt. And I'm only three-quarters Scottish."

"Me, too. But I've been to Scotland. Have you?"

"Never."

"It's beautiful. Everything is wonderful except the food. The food is horrible. Microwaved potatoes. Salmon is the only thing Scottish cooking doesn't ruin." With that, Felicity poured a little olive oil into the skillet, waited a moment, and put in the salmon fillets. Then she set the table with Aunt Thelma's new place mats, napkins, plates, and stainless steel flatware.

When she set a place for Detective Valentine, he didn't object, but he did abandon the topic of their shared heritage. "I need to ask you a few questions."

When Prissy conversed with policemen, they often warned her off her investigation or sought her brilliant insights. They didn't just interrogate her. Felicity reminded herself that fiction was to real life as Scotland was to everywhere else: better.

As Felicity tossed salad, he said, "Quinlan Coates was a professor at B.C." The abbreviation for Boston College pleased Felicity, to whom it suggested collaboration in the investigation. "His speciality was French. Does anything about that connect with you? Did you go to B.C.?"

"No. It's only about a mile from here. I drive by it all the time. Nothing else."

"Do you speak French?"

"A few words."

"You don't own a dog, do you?"

"A dog? No."

"Have you had any visitors who brought their dogs with them?"

"What is this about? No."

"Your relatives who left you this house, the Robertsons. Did they have a dog? Or a cat?"

"No. A long time ago, when I was a child, Aunt Thelma had a cat. As far as I know, that was the last pet they had. They had a house in Ogunquit and a condo in Florida. It wouldn't have been very convenient for them to have had pets." Felicity served the salmon, the tossed salad, and a loaf of French bread. "You obviously found dog hair," she said. "What kind of dog did it come from?" She picked up her fork.

Dave Valentine, too, reached for his fork. "This is the best meal I've had in front of me in a year. Probably more."

Although the detective didn't hammer his head at his food as Brigitte had done, Felicity was happy to see that he ate with gusto. Was his wife a terrible cook? Just what you'd expect from someone who *used to* read Felicity Pride! Or maybe she was just Scottish. Or, with luck, *had been*.

"Quinlan Coates was a widower," he said. "His wife died ten years ago. Her name was Dora. Does that ring any bells?"

"Dora Coates. No. It doesn't sound familiar."

"There's a son, William. Bill."

"William Coates. Bill Coates. Billy Goats! The poor thing!"

Valentine smiled. "I hadn't noticed that." He paused to eat. "Everything is delicious. Thank you."

"You're welcome."

"If you don't mind, let's go over this business about the cat and the microchip. Just tell me about it."

Felicity was happy that he hadn't said "in your own words." Whenever she heard the phase, she wondered whose words she was expected to use. Shakespeare's? Still, she had to choose between her own nonfiction words, so to speak, and her storytelling words. After her regrets about the unimaginative first interview she'd had with Valentine, she longed to embellish the account of taking Edith to Dr. Furbish, speaking to Ursula Novack, discovering the victim's identity, and pulling off the daring rescue of darling Brigitte. With a sense of disappointment in herself, she settled for giving a simple account that did, however, emphasize her effort to reach him and her concern for Brigitte.

When she'd finished, she returned her attention to her food and then added, "While I was looking for Brigitte, I noticed that there were a lot of cat mysteries, including mine."

"A few of yours. Others, too. What do you make of that?"

"Not much. Lots of people read mysteries."

"The other books are all about the French or in French, or biographies, academic journals, that kind of thing."

"Professor Coates was entitled to a little relief, wasn't he? And he loved his cats."

"The choice is kind of, uh, feminine."

"Men read mysteries, too!"

"Cat mysteries?"

"Some men do."

Perhaps because he was finishing a meal she'd cooked, Valentine didn't argue the point, but switched to asking her to think about anyone who might have a grudge against her. "About anything," he said. "Something that might seem like nothing to you."

The two people who came immediately to mind were her mother and sister, whose resentment, far from seeming negligible, felt monumental. "I can't think of anyone," she said.

"I want you to dig deeper. Go through your appointment book and see if it brings back anything. Letters you've sent. Or received. You use e-mail?"

"Of course." Did he think of her as belonging to the generation that feared the Internet? "I use it all the time. Nonstop."

"Good. I want you to go over any e-mail you've saved. Sent and received. Look for anything at all that might have made someone want to retaliate. Anything that might've hit someone else the wrong way."

After again thanking Felicity for dinner, Detective Valentine rose to leave. Although she had read hundreds of times that police detectives weren't allowed to drink on duty, she couldn't resist reminding him that they were both Scots. "I don't suppose you'd like a wee deoch an doris, would you?"

But after smiling and refusing, he said, "Another time."

Felicity waited until he was out of earshot before bursting into song. She did not sing the Harry Lauder song about a wee drink at parting. Rather, at the top of her three-quarters-Scottish lungs, she bellowed the chorus of "Scotland the Brave."

TWENTY

One thing Felicity never ate for breakfast was oatmeal. She had acquired the prejudice against it from her
mother, who had been raised on "mush," as the Scots called it,
and who especially loathed the innocent combination of oatmeal and raisins known as "mush torra laddy." On the morning of Thursday, November 6, Felicity ate scrambled eggs
and went so far as to offer some to Brigitte, who sniffed with
interest, but then resumed her favorite activity, which was
zipping around the house, upstairs and downstairs, and leaping in and out of bathtubs. Although the ravenous Brigitte
had devoured canned cat food when Felicity had first brought
her home, she had refused it since then, and although she eagerly sniffed at Felicity's own food, she limited her actual in-
take to dry cat food.

Over eggs and coffee, Felicity read the morning paper, which included a short article about the murder:

MURDER VICTIM IDENTIFIED

The homicide victim whose body was found on Monday evening at the door of a Brighton home has been identified as Quinlan Coates, 63, of Brighton. Coates, a professor of Romance languages at Boston College, died of a blunt trauma to the head. The victim's remains were left in a housing development at the entrance to a unit occupied by Felicity Pride, 53. Authorities are pursuing their investigations.

Felicity was incensed. Exactly how did her age pertain to the murder! And a "housing development"! A "unit"! A "unit" in Brighton! She'd have preferred *minimansion*. Furthermore, in the normal course of things, the appropriate response to receiving a personal insult in the newspaper was to write an outraged letter to the editor. But what could she write? That she was fifty-three, but didn't look it? That she did not, as the paper had suggested, dwell in public housing, but lived in a house the size of a small cruise ship? That within feline mystery circles she was a bona fide celebrity and, as such, expected to be treated with respect? Impossible. All of it. Impossible.

The best response was obviously to solve the murder— and to claim credit for having done so. Toward that end, when Felicity had finished grooming herself and dressing for the day, she settled herself in Uncle Bob's Harvardian den and began to comply with Detective Valentine's instructions to go through her correspondence in search of a clue to the murderer's motive in having left Coates's body for her. His cat, too, of course. In Felicity's opinion, therein lay her advantage over the police: Whereas they dismissed the importance of Edith's presence, she did not. Therefore, the more feline the clue, the better! She began with a folder of letters from readers. She kept only a little of what other authors called "fan mail." Felicity received some correspondence that merited the term, but she preferred to think of thank-you notes as just that. In most cases, she read the thanks, sent a brief reply, and tossed out the note. She kept letters that pointed out errors. If a reader found a typographical error, she photocopied the offending page of the book, marked the correction, and sent the page to her editor. Her file contained a few such letters from readers, but who would dump a corpse in an author's vestibule because *cats* had been misprinted as *cast*? She kept letters in which readers advised her about the proper care and feeding of Morris and Tabitha. Because of such advice, Prissy hadn't given the cats milk for many years, fed them human food only as a rare treat, and took care not to let them play with long cords that might cause strangulation. No motive there. A few readers had expressed strong opinions about series characters. Some readers wanted Prissy to marry the chief of police; others cautioned against the alliance. There were several letters from correspondents who urged Prissy to adopt a third cat from a shelter. Nowhere did Felicity find anything even remotely suggestive of a wish to harm her.

As Felicity was returning the file to a drawer, she was distracted by the sound of voices. In her apartment in Somerville, she'd have ignored this evidence of human presence. In Newton Park, the employees of lawn services sometimes talked or even shouted to one another, but the lawns had already received their final mowings of the season, and all the leaves had been removed. One of the voices was deep, male, and angry. Making her way to the dining room, she peered out and saw Mr. Trotsky standing in the road in front of his house. About a yard away from him, also on the pavement, was a woman with a golden retriever, indeed, the same woman Felicity had seen in the waiting room of Furbish Veterinary Associates. To Felicity's horror, Mr. Trotsky was hollering at her. The subject of his anger was evidently the dog, at which he kept jabbing a finger. If it had been possible for Felicity to open a window and eavesdrop, she might have done so. She was, however, fearful of getting caught. The Norwood Hill view of the residents of Newton Park was bad enough, and now Trotsky was making it worse! What was he doing home, anyway? Felicity grabbed a coat from her front hall closet. In her haste, she considered going out through the vestibule, but retained a superstitious desire to avoid it. If the snob with the dog assumed that anyone emerging from the back door must be a servant, too bad.

Striding down the paved path from the back door to the road, Felicity heard Mr. Trotsky yell, "And they are killing my grass, these dogs! Look at that! Dead! And do you know how much I pay for this lawn?"

"What's killing your grass," the woman said calmly, "isn't dog urine. It's drought. If you'd water the grass here by the street, it would be fine." Her pronunciation of the word *water* irked Felicity, who never disgraced herself by saying "wat-uh," but who could never get that first vowel quite right. This condescending Norwood Hill dog walker pronounced the miserable syllable with the effortless perfection of someone who hadn't merely overcome her Boston accent, but had never had one to begin with. She probably didn't have to think twice before uttering *cork* or *caulk*.

"This neighborhood is private property," Mr. Trotsky

informed her. He swept an arm around. "All private property."

"If I'm trespassing," countered the woman, "perhaps you should call the police. The Boston police will undoubtedly come running when they hear that my dog put her paw on your lawn."

"Pardon me," Felicity said, "but—"

Mr. Trotsky ignored her. "No dogs! No pets! No trespassers!"

"You know something?" asked the woman. "People who don't know how to live in good neighborhoods shouldn't move to them. Or anywhere near them. Until these houses went up, Norwood Hill was the quietest, safest place you can imagine, and now we have cars speeding down our narrow streets and ruining everything. As a matter of fact, a complaint has been lodged with your condominium association."

Before her Russian neighbor could respond, Felicity said, "I'm so sorry there's trouble here. There's no reason at all to object to having people walk through here. Most of us—"

"No pets!" shouted Mr. Trotsky. "A cat! I saw a cat in your window!" He turned his back on her and stomped to his house.

"Charming neighbor you have," said the woman.

"He really is the exception," said Felicity.

"I'd hope so. At least you're not all Russian. There's that to be thankful for. How they get their money out of Russia is a mystery to me. And how they made it to begin with!"

"This neighborhood is actually quite diverse," Felicity said. "And I suspect that back in Russia, people found him pretty rude, too. If your dog wants to walk on a lawn, let him walk on mine. It won't bother me."

"Her. *Her*. She's female!" With that, the woman clucked to the dog and walked briskly away.

Felicity went back inside and resumed her examination of her correspondence. It seemed to her that some of the reviews she'd received would have provided grounds for justifiable homicide, but the blurbs she'd written for the covers of other people's mysteries, feline and otherwise, had been laudatory. She had, of course, declined to blurb some books, and she'd begged off reading some manuscripts, but it seemed to her that her refusals had been kind and tactful. For instance, to Janice Mattingly, she'd written, "How sorry I am not to have the treat of reading your manuscript right now! As it is, I am up against a looming deadline and barely have time to read my own book. I look forward to enjoying *Tailspin* when it comes out and certainly wish you the very best of luck with it." She'd previously weaseled out of recommending Janice to her agent, too, but to the best of her recollection, she'd been equally inoffensive on that occasion.

As she was turning to old e-mail in search of slights and grudges, the phone interrupted her.

"So," said her sister, "you find a corpse at your door, and you don't even bother to tell me?" Angie's Boston accent was intact: *corpse* was "cawpse," *door* was "dough-uh."

"I'm sorry. I told Mother." Felicity had long ago discarded *Ma*. "I assumed she'd tell you. But I should've called. It's been very stressful."

"Poor you. At least you don't have to go to work every day."

"Angie, I work at home, but I *do* work. And I'm the first person to say that I don't miss teaching. I'm sorry you're still stuck in the classroom."

"Well, thank God for cell phones. They're the only thing that keeps me sane."

Angie taught in a middle school in an impoverished city

that had once been a mill town. Whenever Felicity read or heard about laudable efforts to recruit bright, well-educated college graduates to teach economically disadvantaged students in public schools, she thought of her sister, who was exactly the kind of teacher in immediate need of replacement.

"I was a rotten teacher myself," Felicity said.

"I am not a rotten teacher! Why would you say such a thing when you know that I'm stuck here with these obnoxious kids who don't give a damn about anything, least of all school. Wasn't it enough that you had to go and suck up to Bob and Thelma without rubbing it in?"

"Speaking of Bob and Thelma—" Felicity began.

"Don't! Just don't! The less I have to hear about them, the better! I gotta go." And she hung up.

On the theory that toxins might as well be consumed all at once instead of little by little, Felicity immediately called her mother, who had bored her with family stories for five decades and should therefore be easy to pump for information about Uncle Bob. He wouldn't have told his sister about financial shenanigans that would account for the cash, but Mary might know something without understanding its significance.

Mary answered the phone with a thick, "Hello?"

"Mother, it's Felicity."

"Who?"

"Felicity!"

"Let me turn down the television." After the inevitable and, in Felicity's opinion, unnecessarily prolonged delay, Mary returned to the phone. "Who did you say you were?"

"Felicity!" The impulse to shout was uncontrollable and had become more so after Felicity, in desperation, had dragged

her mother to an audiologist. The result of the exam had been unequivocal: Mary Pride had exceptionally acute hearing. After arranging to visit her mother that same afternoon, Felicity slammed down the phone. How could she have imagined that her mother bore her a strong enough grudge to retaliate by leaving a murder victim at her front door? Far from bearing her a grudge, her mother couldn't even remember who she was.

TWENTY-ONE

Newton Park Estates could properly be called a housing development: A developer had bought a tract of land and built houses on it. Because the collection of multimillion-dollar houses was organized as a condominium, each dwelling was a unit. If Felicity had felt secure about the position in the world to which her recent inheritance had elevated her, she would have recognized the absurdity of referring to her opulent abode as a unit in a housing development; in reading the morning paper, she would have responded with amusement rather than outrage. Her hypersensitivity to the perceived slight stemmed largely from the irrational feeling that the innocent, if misleading, little newspaper article had mistaken her living situation for her mother's. Mary Robertson Pride occupied a one-bedroom unit in a new and attractive complex intended to provide senior citizens with affordable apartments. The Robertson clan unanimously agreed that Mary lived in a garden apartment in a small retirement community. No one, not even Felicity, ever said that Mary Robertson lived in public housing.

The complex certainly bore no resemblance to the notoriously rundown and crime-ridden projects of the inner city. On the contrary, its two-story buildings were covered in cedar shingles, their trim was freshly painted in cranberry, the foundation shrubs were neatly pruned, and mulched paths ran from building to building and down to a small pond. Inside, the hallways and apartments were bright, and a social center offered many activities in which Mary refused to participate on the grounds that she was a better Scrabble player and bridge player than anyone else there, and she had no interest in yoga, nature walks, or, indeed, any other form of physical exercise. Still, it was because of the retirement community's overall excellence that Bob Robertson had used his considerable clout to move his sister to the top of the long waiting list for available units. He had also been responsible for the negligence with which Mary's application had been examined. In particular, no one had raised the question of whether she was, in fact, a widow, and no one had asked whether her financial circumstances were, in fact, severely reduced.

When Felicity parked Aunt Thelma's unpretentious Honda CR-V in front of her mother's building that afternoon, she uttered a short prayer: "Dear God, thank you for allowing the illegitimate nature of my mother's occupancy to remain undetected. Gratefully yours, Felicity Pride."

If a thorough and conscientious administrator ever

examined the details of residents' applications, would Mary be booted out? Sent a hefty rent bill for past years? Perhaps even charged with fraud? Probably not. Although Uncle Bob had been a man of influence, there was no reason to suppose that his sister was the only resident who'd slipped in under false pretenses. For all Felicity knew, not a single occupant of the attractive units was actually entitled to subsidized housing; the entire place was probably populated by the relatives of persons of financial or political power. And the units *were* attractive. The entrance hall of her mother's building was spotless. A low table held a mixed bouquet of flowers in a glass vase. Tacked to a cork bulletin board above the table were notices of events: Children from a local school would give a concert on Thursday afternoon, a shuttle bus would transport people to a Boston theater on Saturday for the matinee performance of a musical comedy, and lessons in watercolor painting would begin on Monday at ten A.M.

Felicity rapped her knuckles on the first door on the left. "Mother?" She could hear the television. After a long wait, she rapped again and called loudly, "Mother! It's Felicity!"

Eventually, there was a sound of shuffling, and Mary said, "Who is it?"

"Felicity!"

"Who?"

"Felicity!"

The door opened. Mary wore a cotton duster, a flower-patterned garment halfway between a bathrobe and a dress. She made as if to hug and kiss Felicity, but succeeded only in scratching Felicity's face with the brush rollers that covered her head. "Come in! Don't stand out there. You're letting in a draft. Those shoes are new. I always think that a woman with big feet should look for something with a short vamp."

"They're boots," Felicity said. "It's cold out."

Mary settled herself in a padded lounger that faced the television. "I wouldn't know," Mary said. "I can't get out very much."

Won't, thought Felicity as she turned off the TV.

"Sit down and tell me all about your murder," her mother said. "It puts me in mind of my grandmother. She loved a murder. She spoke broad Scots, you know, and when the paper came, she always opened it and said, 'Any guid meerders today?'"

"This wasn't a particularly good murder. It wasn't exactly pleasant to find—"

"Do you remember that woman who shot her husband and threw him over the bridge? You and Angie and I followed that in the papers. It went on for weeks. She and her boyfriend killed the husband. What was her name? Nancy? And the boyfriend was ten years younger than she was. She shot her husband in the head, but he didn't die right away, so she called the boyfriend to finish him off and help her get rid of the body."

"Could I have a cup of coffee?" Felicity asked. "Do you want one?"

"Help yourself. Nothing for me. I had a nice poached egg for lunch. You know, Felicity, there's something I've been meaning to ask you. This review you sent me? Of your book?"

"Yes?"

"There's something I don't understand."

"Yes?"

"It says here you're funny."

"What do reviewers know?" Felicity moved to the small kitchen, which was separated from the living room by a divider. She put the kettle on and got out instant coffee, sugar, milk, and a cup and saucer. Her mother disapproved of mugs. As she fixed coffee for herself, her mother reminisced about other murders that the family had enjoyed following in the papers throughout Felicity's childhood: husbands who had hired thugs to brain wayward wives with baseball bats, doctors and nurses who had habitually done in patients, mothers who had drowned their children in bathtubs.

Returning to the living room and taking a seat, Felicity said, "I've wondered whether the body was left at my house by mistake. It's occurred to me that maybe someone didn't know about Bob and Thelma and thought that Uncle Bob still lived there."

"Why would someone dump a body at Bob's doorstep?"

"Why would someone dump a body at mine?"

"You'll know more about that than I will. I've never believed in interfering in my children's lives."

"I don't know a thing about it. That's why I'm wondering about Uncle Bob."

Mary put her hands on the arms of the recliner and leaned forward. "My brother was a fine man until Thelma got her clutches in him. She could see he was going places, and she set her cap for him. She was always greedy, Thelma was. A sly one, that's what she was. Did I ever tell you what she did when my mother died?"

Ten thousand times. But having diverted her mother from sensational murder cases to Bob and Thelma, she said, "What was that?"

"She stole my mother's jewelry right off her body! After the funeral, right after, she went to the undertaker and got him to give it to her. My mother's opal ring and her gold chain. Of course, I don't believe in an open casket myself, but I had no say in it, and look how it ended up!"

"A new argument for closed caskets. Worried about the family kleptomaniac? Shut that lid!"

"What was that, Felicity?"

"Nothing. Look, Mother, this business of the murder and Uncle Bob. I know you thought a lot of him before Thelma came along, but was there anything not quite on the up and up in his past? Anything that would lead anyone to . . . I don't know. Anything I might not know about?"

Mary closed her mouth and locked her jaw. "I don't know what you're talking about."

"A family secret."

"In our family?"

"In our family. About Uncle Bob."

"You know, Felicity, the Depression was a terrible time for men. It's hard for a man to worry about not having a job."

And easy for a woman. "So, Uncle Bob worried?"

"There's no real harm in rum-running. A lot of people did it."

"He was a bootlegger? Uncle Bob?"

"Not a bootlegger, really. No. He just had friends at Seabrook Beach. It wasn't *bootlegging.* It was just rum-running. He wasn't much more than a boy, anyway. That's how he got started in the liquor business."

"Mother, rum-running *is* bootlegging."

"It was a long time ago. And he gave it up, after all."

"Of course he gave it up! Prohibition ended!"

Mary laughed hoarsely. "It wasn't very profitable afterwards, was it? Hah! It wasn't very profitable after that!"

TWENTY-TWO

Felicity arrived home to find a message on her answering machine from a neighbor named Loretta who more or less ran the condo association. Loretta was a single mother with two young children fathered by two different men, neither of whom Loretta had married. As far as Felicity could tell, Loretta had somehow managed to grow up in the United States and reach the age of thirty or thereabouts without encountering the notion that society expected women to marry before having babies and frowned on those who violated the expectation. Loretta didn't seem to defy the rules, nor did she seem to have liberated herself from them; she seemed not to realize that they existed.

What puzzled Felicity and the other residents of Newton Park was not, however, Loretta's startling openness about having given out-of-wedlock birth to two children with two different fathers. Rather, the mystery about Loretta was the source of her apparently boundless wealth. Frugality was anything but the norm in Newton Park, but even by the extravagant standards of the neighborhood, Loretta threw away money with abandon. Although her house had been brand new when she'd bought it, she'd immediately redone the entire kitchen. Dissatisfied with the result, she'd then had the second new kitchen torn out and a third one installed. When she'd decided that the medium beige of her house was a bit more yellow than she liked, she'd had it repainted in a shade indistinguishable from the original. She clearly had a job: She left the house early every morning and returned home in the evening, and her children were known to attend an expensive day care center. She was rumored to do something with computers, but it was hard to imagine what she could possibly do to earn what she spent.

In any case, she generously hosted meetings of the condo association and dealt with neighborhood matters. According to her message, the Norwood Hill Neighborhood Association had sent a letter complaining about traffic, and Mr. Trotsky had lodged a formal objection to the presence of a cat in Felicity's house. "Don't worry about the cat!" Loretta said in her little-girl voice. "No one else minds! Just come to the meeting!"

Felicity had just finished listening to Loretta's message when she got a call from Ursula Novack, Edith and Brigitte's breeder. "I mainly wanted to hear how the girls are doing," she said.

"Fine. Splendidly, in fact," said Felicity, who hadn't seen either cat since returning home from her mother's.

"Excellent. Any news about Quin?"

"Nothing. Not that I've heard."

"Too bad. Oh, there's something I forgot to tell you. Two things. First of all, Quin used Angell, so all the vet records are there. You know Angell?"

Boston's Angell Memorial Animal Hospital was so famous that even Felicity had heard of it. "Of course."

"And the other thing is that Edith is a blood donor there. You don't have to keep that up if you don't want to, but it's a good thing to do. There's always a great need for blood, and Edith is *so* suitable."

It had never before occurred to Felicity that cats had blood, never mind donated it or needed transfusions. "Suitable," she repeated.

"Because of her size. They have to be over ten pounds. Brigitte is too small. Also, Edith is so mellow. And she's young and healthy. You'd just have to drop her off there and pick her up every so often, and you get free exams and shots. But it's up to you."

"I'll think about it," Felicity promised.

True to her word, as she sautéed chicken breasts and steamed fresh asparagus for her dinner, she mulled over the possible consequences to a cat that received Edith's blood. Would the animal vanish under a bed and remain there forever? But Edith was shy, she reminded herself. Cats could be shy. Edith was. As if to prove that she was anything but shy, Brigitte ran into the kitchen, jumped up onto the counter, and strolled along it. Instead of shooing her off, Felicity dared to run her hand all the way from Brigitte's head to the base of her tail. In response, the silky little cat rubbed her head against Felicity's hand. In gratitude, Felicity cut off a small piece of chicken breast, minced it, placed it in a saucer, and offered it to Brigitte, but after a sniff of curiosity,

Brigitte darted to the bowl of dry cat food and ate hungrily. Instead of reading or listening to the radio over dinner, Felicity watched the cat, who brazenly jumped onto the table, but didn't try to eat off Felicity's plate. Felicity pondered the possibility of speaking to Brigitte but decided that in real life, conversing with cats was a sign of serious eccentricity if not outright madness. Still, despite the lack of conversation, Brigitte hung around, and although Felicity did not admit it to herself, she enjoyed the companionship.

Indeed, many a sensible person would have preferred the company of the cat to the company afforded by the residents of Newton Park present at the condo association meeting. The first time Felicity had attended one of the meetings, she had made the mistake of assuming that it would be a social occasion or one that would combine the business of condo affairs with the pleasures of socializing. Expecting to meet her new neighbors over coffee and dessert, Felicity had turned up at Loretta's with a contribution: a box of pastries from Rosie's Bakery. Neither food nor drink had been offered at the meeting, and Felicity had tried to pretend that the pastries were a hostess gift for Loretta. Tonight, she walked empty-handed to Loretta's, which was at the far end of Newton Park, near the Brighton entrance. Six or eight large cars were parked in the street. Had the murder made her neighbors afraid to go out at night? It was only seven o'clock. Felicity hadn't considered driving.

Although Thanksgiving was three weeks away, next to the front door of Loretta's house sat a large basket in the form of a cornucopia. Artfully arranged as if spilling from the cornucopia were gourds, Indian corn, pots of purple mums, and other inedible objects symbolic of a bounteous harvest. Felicity rang the bell. Before the door opened, she heard the clicking of several locks.

"Felicia, isn't it?" Loretta greeted her. "Come in. Half the people aren't here yet." Loretta had masses of dark curls and wore heavy eye makeup.

"Felicity, actually."

"Felicity. Sorry. Felicity. I'll remember next time. This shouldn't take more than twenty minutes."

How had Loretta managed to call her a few hours ago and forget her name in the intervening time? "It's very nice of you to have the meeting here, Lucille," she said.

"Who's Lucille?"

"Loretta. Sorry."

"I have to tell you," Loretta said, "that we've been driven crazy by the police. Everyone's been questioned, and our yards have been searched. But we're not going to waste time going over that. We just have to settle the business about your cat and decide what to do about this nasty letter."

Felicity followed Loretta into the living room, which had off-white walls, off-white carpeting, and off-white furniture that provided ample seating. Ten or twelve people were gathered there. There was no food or drink in sight. The fireplace contained an oversized vase heavily decorated with gilded cherubim.

"Hi. Sorry if I'm late," said Felicity, who was exactly on time.

Loretta left to answer the doorbell.

Zora Wang smiled at Felicity and said, "Any more murder?"

"What?"

Zora laughed and repeated her question. "Any more murder? Joke! Any more murder?"

"No, no more murders," said Felicity.

Loretta returned with Mr. and Mrs. Trotsky, Brooke and her husband, and a man named Omar. "Let's get started," she said. "This should take no time. Everyone should have a copy of the letter from the Norwood Hill Neighborhood Association. They're on the table. Take one if you don't have one already."

Felicity took a copy of the letter and seated herself next to Zora Wang, who had at least tried to act friendly. "Tom isn't coming?"

"Work. Work all the time," Zora said.

"Could we pay attention to business?" Mr. Trotsky said. "We have a no-pet clause. Cats are pets. No cats allowed."

"That clause is there in case anyone gets a dog that becomes a nuisance," Brooke informed him. "So we could do something if a dog barked all the time. Or ran loose and bothered us." Brooke looked even more silvery and showy than usual. Her platinum hair and fingernails matched.

"No pets is no pets," Trotsky responded.

Careful to avoid revealing the presence of two cats and not just one in her house, Felicity said, "The way to make sure that cats live long, healthy lives is to keep them indoors. I would never let a cat roam the neighborhood. I cannot see how an indoor cat could be a problem."

"Enough said," Loretta decreed. "All in favor of allowing Felicia to keep her cat, raise your hands."

"Felicity," said Brooke. "Not Felicia. You apparently don't know that Felicity Pride is a well-known author."

"Oh, what do you write?" asked a woman Felicity didn't know.

"Mysteries," said Felicity.

Brooke elaborated. "Mysteries about cats."

"Oh, I've read those!" a woman exclaimed. *"Purrfectly Sleuthful* was my favorite. I just love Olaf and Lambie Pie! But I didn't know you wrote under a pen name. I thought Isabelle Hotchkiss was your real name."

Loretta cut short the discussion. "Could we vote, please? Raise your hand if you want her to be able to keep the cat."

All hands except Mr. Trotsky's popped up. Mrs. Trotsky lifted hers only briefly before her husband grabbed her wrist and lowered her arm. "My wife doesn't speak English," he explained.

Mrs. Trotsky was a short, stout woman with unnaturally red-black hair. She wore a deep purple suit that somehow looked foreign as opposed to imported. "Speak English!" she cried. "Yes, cat!"

"Well, it doesn't matter one way or the other," Loretta said. "The vote is overwhelmingly for the cat. Now, the letter. If you haven't already read it, please do so now."

Felicity had read the offending letter and now simply glanced at it. It was on Norwood Hill Neighborhood Association letterhead. A logo depicted a tree that Felicity considered in need of pruning. The text read:

Until the erection of the Newton Park Estates development, the narrow streets of Norwood Hill carried almost no traffic. The recent influx of vehicles traveling at high speeds disturbs the tranquility of Norwood Hill and poses a threat to public safety. Thus the Norwood Hill Neighborhood Association respectfully requests that residents of the development, which is in Brighton, enter and exit through Brighton.

"It's no accident," said Harry, Brooke's husband, "that they've chosen this particular time to fire off this condescending missive. What's not said here is that they see urban crime at their doorstep. Not without reason, of course."

Felicity felt everyone's eyes on her. "That letter requires no response," she said. "If they have a traffic problem on their streets, they should call the police. Do we look like traffic cops?" A few people tittered. Encouraged, Felicity added, "And I am as concerned about the horrible event that took place here as everyone else is. More so. But it does seem clear that the man, Quinlan Coates, was killed somewhere else. There is no reason to suppose that we're seeing the start of some sort of crime wave."

Trotsky angrily shook his copy of the letter. "We are going to take this insult lying down?"

"In my opinion," Brooke said, "Felicity is right. Our best course is to be perfect ladies and gentlemen. In other words, we should do nothing."

"Place the burden on the opposition," a man agreed. "I'm for that."

"All in favor of no reply," said Loretta, "raise your hands! Done! Same as the last vote. Mr. and Mrs. Trotsky, you're seeing American democracy in action here. You win some, you lose some. That's the American way. Well, we wrapped this up fast, didn't we!"

Everyone stood up. Loretta moved swiftly to the front hall and opened the door. "So nice to see you!" she said. "Until next time!"

Hustled out, one couple headed for the next house. All the others except Brooke and Harry got into the cars parked on the street.

"Chickens," said Brooke. "We're not afraid to walk, are

we? Sorry about that mix-up with Isabelle Hotchkiss. Your books are much better than hers."

"Thank you," Felicity said. "Loretta certainly knows how to run a meeting, doesn't she?"

Harry said, "She kept that Trotsky under control. I have to give her that."

"Actually," Felicity said, "you were right that something triggered that condescending letter, but it wasn't having the police here. It had nothing to do with the murder. It had to do with Mr. Trotsky. He had a nasty encounter with some woman who was walking her dog. He accused her dog of killing his grass. She acted quite entitled and supercilious, and he got nasty. I tried to smooth things over, but I didn't have any luck."

"As if the relationship between the neighborhoods weren't bad enough to begin with," Brooke said, "without him making things worse." Like the Norwood Hill woman with the golden retriever, Brooke sounded as if she'd never had a Boston accent to lose, but Felicity didn't resent the apparent effortlessness of Brooke's correct vowel sounds. Brooke preferred Morris and Tabitha to Olaf and Lambie Pie, and she was as close as Felicity came to having a Newton Park ally.

"He creates a terrible image of our neighborhood," Felicity agreed. "Among other things, the woman thinks that Russians are gangsters."

"Gangsters?" Harry said. "Trotsky's a legitimate businessman. A publisher. He's an oaf, but he isn't a gangster."

"How do you know that?" his wife asked. "Russians are notorious for pirating American software."

"They pirate American books, too," Felicity said.

TWENTY-THREE

Brigitte sits on top of the refrigerator. Her tail twitches, and her amber eyes scan the kitchen. She drops weightlessly to the floor, rockets to the front hallway, skids across the slate floor, zooms to the living room, slides across a low table, and bolts back to the hallway, up the steep stairs, and into the room where Edith remains huddled under the bed. Boring, boring, boring Edith! What that cat needs is a good bite on the head! Brigitte dives straight through the bed skirt, pounces on Edith, delivers a hard nip to Edith's neck, and flees before Edith can retaliate.

In the upstairs hall, Brigitte follows her nose to a room heavy with the scent of cosmetics. The bed in here is larger than the one under which that fat, silly Edith is hiding. Brigitte soars upward, lands, and settles herself on a pillow. Although she goes instantly to sleep, the tip of her tail resumes its twitch. She dreams of prey.

TWENTY-FOUR

When Felicity returned home from the condo association meeting, she saw no sign of the cats and made a mental note to herself about Morris and Tabitha, who, she now realized, had spent far too much time awake in her previous books. Real cats were dedicated sleepers. Furthermore, as amateur sleuths, they were duds. Morris and Tabitha would simply have to stay as prescient and communicative as they'd always been. After all, one of fiction's most important functions was to misrepresent reality.

Loretta had kept the meeting short. It was now only quarter of eight, and Felicity wished that she'd delayed her dinner and could call Ronald to suggest that they meet at a restaurant. Better yet, she wished that Detective Dave Valentine would appear at her door to announce that the murder had been solved and that she was consequently free to talk about it to the press. And free to accept an invitation to go out with him? She reluctantly settled for calling Ronald, who answered his phone but said that he couldn't talk because he was listening to Glenn Gould, with whom he was, in Felicity's view, obsessed. Felicity had no ear for music and couldn't tell one Goldberg Variation from the other, and although she'd enjoyed *Thirty-two Short Films About Glenn Gould* when Ronald had dragged her to a theater to see it, she'd been bored the first time they'd watched the video together and, after the third time, had refused to see it again. She did, however, manage to divert Ronald from his music long enough to make him promise to go out for dinner with her the next evening. At the end of the short call, having failed to ask her how she was, he neglected to utter any of the usual formulaic phrases about how glad he'd be to see her or how much he was looking forward to dinner, but simply hung up.

Felicity longed to call Detective Dave Valentine but could think of no pretext. She'd tell Valentine about the animosity between the Norwood Hill and Newton Park neighborhoods, but the antagonism hardly suggested a motive for Coates's murder. Even Felicity found it unimaginable that some disgruntled resident of Norwood Hill had slain a professor of Romance languages simply to cause trouble in Newton Park by leaving his body in a vestibule. Could Quinlan Coates have planned to buy a house in Newton Park? No realtors' signs hung in the neighborhood, and nothing in Coates's apartment had hinted at any intention of moving. What connection could there be between Coates and Newton Park? Had he fathered one of Loretta's children? Had a book he'd published been pirated by the horrible

Mr. Trotsky? Had he allowed Edith or Brigitte to put a paw on Trotsky's grass?

In lieu of phoning the detective, she went to her computer in the hope that someone had e-mailed her, but nothing of interest had arrived. She again searched the Web for information about Quinlan Coates but found nothing she didn't already know. On impulse, she entered Dave Valentine's name and, to her delight, retrieved a photograph of him in his kilt at the Highland Games. To her even greater delight, she discovered something for which the thousands of mysteries she'd read had failed to prepare her, namely, that unlike the wives of the attractive male detectives, both amateur and professional, who populated mystery fiction, the woman hadn't left or divorced Valentine, thus making him bitter, regretful, self-recriminatory, or mistrustful. No, novels to the contrary, Mrs. Valentine had died!

The wives of fictional detectives did die once in a while, Felicity reminded herself, but the cause of death was usually cancer, wasn't it? And in those cases, instead of developing the detective's character by having him respond with bitterness, regret, self-recrimination, or mistrust, the author revealed the protagonist's devotion during his wife's illness, his subsequent grief, and thus his capacity for deep, complex emotion. Mrs. Valentine, however, hadn't died of cancer, been killed by terrorists, been run over by a drunk driver, committed suicide, or perished in some other fashion that might be expected to add sharpness and profundity to an author's depiction of her husband. Rather, according to the obituary that had appeared in a Boston newspaper two years earlier, she had died of endocarditis, an infection of the heart that she had contracted during a routine dental appointment. As a literary device, the cause of death had nothing to recommend it, and, indeed, so far as Felicity could remember, nowhere in mystery fiction had a detective's wife ever died from having her teeth cleaned. Still, Dave Valentine had probably mourned her despite the unliterary nature of her demise, and to her credit, Mrs. Valentine had an excellent excuse, indeed, the only acceptable excuse, for having abandoned her reading of Felicity's books.

After turning off the computer and shutting off lights, Felicity made her way upstairs. Entering her room, she found Brigitte asleep on her pillow. The little cat was not sprawled awkwardly on her back at she'd been when Felicity had discovered her at Quinlan Coates's apartment. Rather, she was curled up in what Felicity saw as normal cat fashion, her head tucked in, her tail curved around her body. Inexperienced cat owner that she was, Felicity never considered reclaiming her own pillow and her own side of the bed by picking up Brigitte and moving her; although she now knew that cats slept a lot, she had no understanding of the depth of feline sleep, nor did she appreciate the capacity of awakened cats to return instantly to oblivion. Consequently, motivated mainly by the fear that Brigitte, like Aunt Thelma's cat, would get her number and run away, she performed her bedtime preparations in near silence. Entering the bathroom that adjoined the bedroom, she left the light off until she'd gently pulled the door shut, and, after finishing her ablutions, turned off the light before opening the door. On tiptoe, she moved her book from the nightstand on Brigitte's side of the bed, carried it to the other side, and returned for a flashlight that she kept in the nightstand drawer. Easing herself between the sheets, she curled up on her side and read by flashlight until she joined Brigitte in sleep.

In the morning, Brigitte was no longer on the pillow but had moved to the top of a high dresser, which she had draped herself upon in a manner that looked precarious; she seemed to be a sort of feline scarf carelessly tossed on the dresser and in danger of slipping off. She remained there while Felicity put on her robe and slippers, and when Felicity descended to the kitchen, Brigitte followed her. To Felicity's surprise, in the middle of the kitchen floor was a little pile of gray fur that was far too long and silky to have come from Edith. When cats groomed themselves, were they in the habit of pulling out dead hair, gathering it together, and leaving it for their owners to clean up? After starting the coffeemaker, Felicity topped off the bowl of dry cat food and opened a can of vile-smelling but supposedly gourmet cat food. As usual, Brigitte danced around, sniffed the stuff with great interest, and then turned to the dry kibble and ate lustily. Not long thereafter, while Felicity was examining her morning paper over her eggs and coffee, Edith appeared at the door to the kitchen and simply stood squarely there on all four paws with a bewildered expression on her face, as if she couldn't understand why she wasn't still under the bed. Then she uttered a single brief, soft, high-pitched meow that sounded as if had come from the mouth of a tiny kitten. With some notion that animals disliked being stared at, Felicity kept one eye on the paper and the other on Edith, who suddenly ran across the floor, came to a halt by the dish of canned food, huddled down, and began to eat. Whereas Brigitte moved lightly and gracefully, Edith, with her short legs and big, bulky body, looked to Felicity as if she hadn't been designed for running and didn't trust herself to perform the act competently.

To avoid making Edith self-conscious, Felicity concentrated on the newspaper, in which she found an obituary for Quinlan Coates. The accompanying photo was not the one on the jacket of the book in his apartment, but seemed to have been taken decades earlier. Coates's hair and his distinctive eyebrows were dark rather than gray, and the face belonged to a man in his late thirties or early forties. The obituary was almost exclusively about his professional achievements: his publications, visiting professorships, and honors. His beloved wife, Dora, had died ten years earlier. He was survived by a son, William G. Coates, of Brookline. A funeral mass would be celebrated at the Church of Saint Ignatius of Loyola at Boston College the next morning. There was no mention of his cats.

It was the thought of representing Edith and Brigitte that gave Felicity the idea of attending the funeral mass. Once having thought about going, she firmly resolved to do so. In mystery novels, homicide investigators invariably showed up at victims' funerals, usually in the hope that the murderers would do the same. Would Detective Dave Valentine be there? Detective Dave Valentine, the widower! Would the murderer be there? In any case, if Coates's funeral had been set for tomorrow, the postmortem must be complete. Why had she been foolish enough to arrange to have dinner tonight with Ronald, when she could have invited Dave Valentine to share a meal? And to share the autopsy results, too. Even if Valentine failed to attend the funeral, it wouldn't be a complete waste of her time to go. To the best of her recollection, she'd never written a Roman Catholic funeral mass. She hoped that the church had stained glass windows, dark recesses, and an odor of incense strong enough to overpower anyone except Prissy LaChatte.

After her morning shower, Felicity kept her promise to

Ursula Novack to inquire about the blood donor program in which Edith was enrolled. A quick Web search informed Felicity that Boston's famous Angell Memorial Animal Hospital had changed its named to the Angell Animal Medical Center. She also found its phone number and learned that it was on South Huntington Avenue in Jamaica Plain and was thus a short distance away. The drive from Newton Park to Angell would take perhaps twenty minutes. Having ascertained that Edith's participation wouldn't cut deeply into her writing time, she dialed the number and was eventually connected to someone in the blood donor program.

"I am the new owner of a cat that participates in your program," Felicity said. "And I've been advised to call you for information."

"Which of our cats is this?" asked a young-sounding woman.

"Her name is Edith."

"Oh, Edith! Edith is a lovely cat. And she's an ideal donor. I hope she'll still be participating."

"I need to know what's involved."

"Well, not a great deal, and there are a lot of benefits. You just bring her here in the morning and pick her up in the late afternoon. You'll need to get her here between seven and eight, and she'll be ready to go home at about four. Let me send you some material."

When Felicity asked to have Edith and Brigitte listed as her cats, and gave her name and address, the woman did not exclaim, "*The* Felicity Pride?" She did, however, again promise to mail the information and went on to say, "But you won't need to do anything right now. Edith was just here on Monday, so she can't donate again for at least six weeks."

"Monday?"

"I think it was Monday. Let me look. Yes. The third. That was Monday."

"Good lord!"

"Is something wrong?"

"No. Never mind. Just send me the information."

"If you have any questions about it, give me a call."

"Oh, I will. I definitely will," said Felicity, who doubted that she'd have questions about the blood donor program, but was certain that she and the police would have a great many questions about Edith's visit to Angell on Monday. For example, at what time did Quinlan Coates pick up Edith? At what time did he leave Angell? Was he alone? If not, who was with him? But the important point was that she, Felicity Pride, with the assistance, more or less, of her cat, Edith, had discovered where Quinlan Coates had been only a few hours before he'd met his unnatural death. At about four o'clock in the afternoon, he'd been at the Angell Animal Medical Center on South Huntington Avenue in Jamaica Plain. No wonder the detective had asked whether there had been dogs in her house and whether Bob and Thelma had owned a cat. Coates had been at Angell, where animal fur must have attached itself to his clothing. About four hours later, his dead body had been in her vestibule. Oh, hurrah! Hurrah for Edith! Just like Morris and Tabitha, she had "communicated" information vital to the solution to the murder! Felicity hastily called Detective Dave Valentine. She no longer needed a pretext. Now, thanks to Edith, she had a real reason to call.

TWENTY-FIVE

Felicity reached Dave Valentine. As soon as she heard his voice, she announced that she had important new information and needed to see him as soon as possible. If a mystery writer wasn't entitled to be mysterious, who was? To her delight, he said that he'd be right over. After hanging up, she realized that her news might not be news to the police; maybe every investigator from the attorney general on down already knew that Quinlan Coates had been alive in the late afternoon, when he'd gone to Angell to get Edith. Felicity's self-doubt worsened when she checked her kitchen and found nothing wonderful to serve Dave Valentine with the coffee she was already brewing. In particular, her cupboards and refrigerator lacked such components of a Scottish breakfast as mush, canned beans, and kippers. She cheered up after remembering that in Scotland itself, she had once been served Nescafé cappuccino; to prepare an authentically Scottish breakfast, she should substitute instant coffee for her good French roast. If Valentine had any sense, he'd be happy with the bagels she removed from the freezer.

The cats posed a problem. The bold Brigitte would put in an appearance, but it was desirable to have Edith the Heroine in view when her key role was revealed. Desperate to set the scene properly, Felicity went upstairs to the guest room where she'd dumped her purchases from the pet supply store and chose a toy that consisted of a yarn ball and jingle bell on a string fastened to a stick. Neither cat was in sight. She shook the toy vigorously. Brigitte immediately responded to the jingling by rushing into the room and batting at the toy. Shortly thereafter, the stolid Edith warily emerged from under the bed and joined Brigitte in aiming a paw at the yarn ball. Gradually moving to the hall and down the steep stairs, Felicity shook the toy, paused, and resumed her progress until she had finally lured both cats into the kitchen, where she hastened to open a can of food for Edith. It occurred to Felicity that a market existed for odorless canned cat food or possibly for a deodorizing powder to be shaken on the existing products. As it was, she had to settle for hoping that Edith would eat fast. While Edith savored her stinky second breakfast, Felicity shut all the doors to the kitchen to prevent the shy cat from escaping. Then, just in case the fresh coffee had lost its freshness, she acted with un-Scottish wastefulness by dumping it into the sink and making a new pot.

Valentine had said he'd be right over. Where was he? As the coffee brewed, Felicity went to the powder room, brushed her hair, and reapplied lipstick. When the doorbell rang, she was pleased that Dave Valentine—or, as Felicity thought of him, Dave Valentine the Widower—had had the sensitivity to go to the back door instead of to the scene-of-the-crime door, so to speak. When she opened the door, he wished her good morning and accepted her offer of coffee. He was wearing khaki pants and a navy blue fleece pullover. How much friendlier than a suit! With the big, strapping Scot sitting there at Aunt Thelma's kitchen table, Felicity felt a wave of guilt for having looked him up on the Web and found his picture.

"Well," she said, "maybe it's not news to you at all, but I know where Quinlan Coates was late on Monday afternoon." Without asking, she sliced a bagel and popped it into the toaster, which was a four-slice chrome appliance and, like all the other appliances in the house, brand new.

"His movements on Monday would be news," Valentine said. "We have his appointment book, from his apartment, but the entries are in some kind of personal shorthand. Not really shorthand, but notations, abbreviations that meant something to him. What's there for Monday looks like the letters *a, b, d.*"

"Angell. Blood. Donor. Edith, the cat who was left here, is a blood donor at Angell Memorial. Angell Animal Medical Center. It's changed its name."

Where *was* Edith? She was somewhere in this kitchen. How irritating of her to disappear! As Felicity was scanning the room, Brigitte suddenly leaped onto the counter by the toaster and began to lick cream cheese from a tub that Felicity had opened and left there. Felicity threw out the cream cheese and substituted butter and jam from the refrigerator.

"Edith is around somewhere. She was very traumatized

by her horrible experience, but she's beginning to recover. Anyway, the cats' breeder, a woman named Ursula Novack, who lives in California, told me that Edith was a blood donor, and when I called Angell, the woman at the blood bank told me that Edith had given blood on Monday. So, Quinlan Coates must've driven her there in the morning and picked her up in the afternoon."

"I didn't know cats gave blood."

Instead of admitting that she hadn't known it, either, Felicity said, "They do. There's a great need for blood. And Edith is the perfect donor. She's big and young and healthy. Brigitte is too small. Anyway, the woman there said that the cats are usually ready to go home at about four o'clock. So, sometime in the afternoon, probably the late afternoon, he must've been at Angell. Which is not all that far from here." She put the bagel on a plate, buttered it, and served it to Dave Valentine with blueberry jam that she'd spooned into a little bowl. After supplying him with a knife, she poured herself a cup of coffee and joined him at the table. "It's maybe twenty minutes."

"More at that time of day," he said. "But that's interesting. Helpful. Did the woman there have any more to say?"

"No, I don't think so."

He bit into the bagel and chewed. Felicity wished that she'd given him something quicker to swallow. "We'll go and talk to them," he finally said. "Good coffee. Thank you. Good bagel. And thank you for calling right away. We'll get going on it this morning."

"His car was at his apartment building," Felicity said. "The neighbor who let me in told me that. Maybe he was with someone else, in someone else's car, when he went to get Edith. Or maybe someone else got her, of course."

Dave Valentine's eyes, Felicity noticed, were an exceptionally clear blue. In police procedurals, the detectives his age tended to look tired, but Valentine didn't. On the contrary, he looked as if he'd had ten hours of sleep.

"We'll find out," he said.

"Quinlan Coates's obituary is in today's paper." She paused. "So the body must have been released."

"That's something I wanted to ask you about." His eyes met hers. "Besides writing mysteries, you read them. You'd have to, wouldn't you?"

"Not necessarily. But I do. It's not an obligation."

"Sorry if . . . Look, see if this sounds familiar from a book. The victim sustains a blow to the head. Then his nose and mouth are sealed with tape."

"Duct tape."

"Any tape. Any strong tape. And then his head is covered with a plastic bag. Is there a book where that happens?"

"Not that I can think of. Not offhand. The three methods separately, I'm sure. But all three? It's possible, but nothing comes to mind. So that's how Quinlan Coates died?"

So, here was Felicity seated at her kitchen table with a handsome, burly police detective who was tapping her knowledge of mystery fiction and confiding the results of a postmortem. He was eating food she'd prepared, and the two were sipping coffee. Beautiful cats added a touch of domesticity. Specifically, Brigitte was now draped across the top of the refrigerator, and Edith was crouching beneath the kitchen chair at the built-in desk near the telephone. Ah, bliss!

"The actual cause of death wasn't head trauma," Valentine said. "The papers got it wrong. It was suffocation." To

Felicity's disappointment, he added, "It'll probably all be in tomorrow's papers." He drank some coffee and asked, "Have you had a chance to go through your old mail? E-mail?"

"Yes. But I didn't find anything, really. I've refused to blurb some books, to write things to be quoted on the cover, but I've always been tactful about saying no. I usually say I don't have time, and in most cases, that's been true. I've declined some invitations to be on panels at libraries, do signings at bookstores and events, and so on, but I've never said anything to offend anyone, I think. And every published writer gets requests to read people's manuscripts, and sometimes new writers want me to recommend them to my agent, that kind of thing. I just can't read *everyone's* manuscript. I don't have time. And I'm a writer, not a book doctor or an unpaid editor. But the letters and e-mail I've sent have been apologetic. Gentle. Polite." She shrugged her shoulders. "If anyone has a grudge against me, it's an unjustified grudge."

"Most grudges are. Do you ever write book reviews?"

"No."

"Anything else?"

"Well, not about books, but there is something. There's a lot of conflict between this neighborhood and the adjoining one in Newton. Norwood Hill. The Norwood Hill Neighborhood Association sent a letter to our condo association to complain about traffic. The Norwood Hill people want us to enter and exit through Brighton. There's resentment on both sides."

"Does that have anything to do with you? With you personally?"

"No. The only personal animosity, I think, is with the guy who lives next door, Mr. Trotsky. He just cannot get along with anyone. I overheard him being very nasty to some woman from Norwood Hill who was walking her dog here. And last night, there was a condo association meeting about the letter. Also about me, in a way. Our condo agreement has a no-pet clause, and Mr. Trotsky complained that I had a cat, but he was outvoted. Anyway, there are probably a lot of people who can't stand him."

A little smile crossed Dave Valentine's face.

Felicity gave him a knowing look. "Including whoever interviewed him about the murder. That must've been a challenge. He's a difficult person. Crabby. His wife seems nice enough, but she doesn't speak English. But there's one other thing about Mr. Trotsky, and this is pure speculation. About five years ago, a Russian publisher wanted to buy the rights to some of my books. The contracts arrived, they were signed and so on, and then my agent and I were told that the deal had fallen through. The Russians were in bad shape. They didn't have any money. End of story until just recently, when someone turned up at a signing I did with a book of mine in Russian. It was a hardcover edition of my first two books. So, the deal fell through in the sense that I was never paid an advance and haven't been paid any royalties, but the Russians went right ahead and translated and published my books. It's called pirating. Well, someone at the condo association meeting last night told me that the Trotskys are publishers. So, I couldn't help wondering. . . ."

"If that's the case, it sounds like you'd have something against them and not vice versa."

"That's true. I just thought I'd mention it."

Valentine looked inexplicably uneasy. "There's one other thing." He reached into one of the pockets of his pullover, extracted a folded sheet of paper, unfolded it, and smoothed it out on the table. "I want you to take a good look at this sketch and see if it's anyone you've ever seen." He slid the paper toward Felicity.

Even before she had picked it up, she knew that there was only one person she'd ever encountered who resembled the woman shown in the black-and-white drawing. "The obituary didn't mention a sister," she said. "Why on earth doesn't she do something about the eyebrows?"

Eager to please the detective, she silently studied the sketch, which hit her as a bit too sketchy even for a police sketch, as it obviously was. It showed the head and shoulders of a woman with shoulder-length brown hair, regular features, and thick, bushy eyebrows that were even more bizarre on a woman than they'd been on Quinlan Coates. The effect was ludicrous.

"Who is this person?" she asked.

"Have you ever seen her?" he asked flatly.

"No. Never."

"At a bookstore?" he prompted. "A meeting? A conference?"

"I don't go to many mystery conferences. They're expensive. Authors get a little break on registration fees, but we pay for airfare and hotel rooms and so forth. I can't afford to go to all that many of them. Until I inherited this house from my uncle, I lived in a little apartment in Somerville. Anyway, I've been to a few conferences, and there were lots of people at them, but I don't think I could have forgotten this woman. She's so weird! Who could forget her?"

"Just asking. Doing my job." He rose and again thanked her for the bagel and coffee.

"You'll remember about Angell. The blood bank."

"It's next on my agenda," he said. Looking embarrassed, he said, "One other thing. Men in your life."

"Right now, there aren't any," she said. "Except Ronald, who doesn't count. Ronald Gershwin. From the bookstore. But he's just a friend. He came over the night . . . You met him then. But as I said, there's no one else."

After Valentine left, Felicity out got her notebook computer and sat at the kitchen table, where she spent many hours in the world of Prissy LaChatte. Morris communicated an important piece of information to Prissy, who handed it along to the grateful chief of police. When he announced his intention of following up on the tip by interviewing a suspect, he invited Prissy to come along. Prissy happily accepted.

TWENTY-SIX

Whenever Ronald and Felicity wanted to eat out together, they confronted one of the many incompatibilities in their friendship. Ronald favored small ethnic restaurants that Felicity dismissed as "third-world holes in the wall." She claimed to be more than happy to eat anywhere else, but habitually rejected suggestions of establishments she considered to be either shamelessly expensive or suspiciously cheap. She also insisted that a restaurant be within a twenty-minute drive of her house and that it offer ample parking, by which she definitely did not mean valet parking, a service that she viewed as a form of legal extortion. She insisted that she loved food and enjoyed almost anything, with such minor exceptions as broccoli, cabbage, hot peppers, curry, fennel, shrimp with the shells left on, and all seeds and nuts, including oils and extracts, especially sesame oil and that detestable almond flavoring that ruined so many potentially delicious chocolate desserts. If pressed, she admitted to disliking bitter flavors. She was none too crazy about rice.

On Friday evening, Ronald and Felicity compromised by choosing a restaurant in Brookline that neither of them particularly liked, a seafood place with branches throughout the city. Although Newbright Books was open on Friday evenings, Ronald had left an employee in charge, but instead of driving the short distance from the store to his apartment in Lower Allston to change clothes, he arrived wearing the hopelessly stretched out green sweater and faded jeans that he'd had on all day. His hair looked clean and was neatly gathered in its ponytail, but Felicity was irked to notice that he had on Birkenstock sandals over woolen socks. Was it necessary for him to be so annoyingly counterculture?

"You look nice," he said as he greeted her in the crowded bar where would-be diners waited for tables. "Silk."

"Basic black. Thank you." Felicity had bought the dress on eBay ("new with tags") for a fifth of its retail price: NWT Eileen Fisher Silk Dress Sz S.

Unable to find seats at the bar, they settled for ordering drinks and standing near a wall. In what struck Felicity as a moment of unusual connectedness, Ronald chose the title of her new book as a toast: *"Felines in Felony!"*

For a moment, she felt embarrassed and wished that her books had serious, dignified titles like *War and Peace* or *Pride and Prejudice,* even though she knew nothing about any war except Caesar's campaign against the Gauls and could hardly use a title that contained her own last name. Besides, neither title would be suitable for a cat mystery, would it? On impulse, she said, *"Cats!"*

Ducking his head as if making an improper inquiry, Ronald asked in a near whisper, "How are they?"

"Edith is providing valuable assistance in solving the murder of Quinlan Coates," she announced. Then, in less dramatic fashion, she caught Ronald up on her discoveries. As she was finishing, the bleating of an electronic device in Ronald's hand signaled that their table was ready.

When they'd been escorted to a comfortable booth and presented with menus, Ronald turned his attention to making his dinner selections and, to Felicity's disgust, chose littleneck clams on the half shell and a curried shrimp dish with rice. Raw seafood could transmit hepatitis, and the shrimp probably had shells on their tails. When a waiter appeared, she ordered clam chowder and a lobster casserole, and then, hoping to set a good example for Ronald, asked him about himself and his cats, George and Ira, even though listening to people drone on about their pets was an onerous hazard of her occupation.

Ronald's initial response was ideal: "We're fine." He went on to say that George and Ira had inspired him to think about writing a mystery. "A cat mystery. I have a lot of notes for it. When I have something to show, I wonder if you'd be willing . . ."

"For you? Of course."

Without thanking her, he launched into confidences about the ghost writers who had actually written two current blockbusters. After that, he told her everything about an author who was suffering from chronic fatigue syndrome and panic attacks attributable to the capricious behavior of her notoriously volatile editor. Finally, when he said a few words about authors who'd be signing at Newbright, Felicity took the opportunity to encourage him to install an espresso bar and to think creatively about planning events at the store to enable him to compete successfully with chain stores and online booksellers.

"I'm not Starbucks," he said, "and I like the store the way it is."

"I do, too! Everyone does. Ronald, really, I'm not criticizing. I just worry, that's all."

"Don't. So, how's your murder? We got interrupted."

"Actually, the murder itself was very odd. Listen to this: Coates was hit on the head with a blunt instrument, and then his nose and mouth were sealed with duct tape, and then his head was encased in a plastic bag. The police asked me if all that sounded familiar from a mystery. I couldn't think of one. Can you?"

The appetizers arrived. Ronald chewed a raw clam and apparently mulled over the murder at the same time. After swallowing, he said, "No. You know what it sounds like to me? You know what it suggests?"

"No," said Felicity, who was averting her gaze from the raw clams and concentrating on her chowder.

"It suggests a murderer who doesn't know how to kill someone and can't tell if the victim is dead. A self-confident, capable murderer does what he's going to do. Let's say he smothers the victim. And when the victim's dead, he quits. But three methods? He tries one. He can't tell whether it worked. He uses another. And he's still not sure. And then he uses the third. So what we've got is a murderer who didn't know what he was doing."

Felicity felt chagrined. "I'll mention that to the police. I hadn't thought of it, and I don't think they have."

Ronald dipped a clam in a red sauce that was nauseatingly reminiscent of blood. "Have you been able to get any writing done with all this going on?"

"Less than usual. But speaking of my writing, Irene called me this afternoon. She had lunch with some other agents, and they discussed the whole business of Russians pirating American books."

"It happens all the time."

"Yes, it does. I just didn't know about it until it happened to me."

"You and a lot of other people. Isabelle Hotchkiss's were pirated. Her agent made a big stink. I read about it somewhere."

Felicity contained her competitive curiosity about whether her own books had been stolen before or after those of her rival. "And?"

"And nothing. Her agent got nowhere."

"None of them have. That's what Irene says, and she's a terrific agent. She's as furious as I am. We have the signed contracts. But what are we going to do? Get a Russian lawyer and take the whole thing to court in Russia? But there is one . . . let's call it a remote possibility."

The waiter appeared, cleared the table, and served the curried shrimp to Felicity and the lobster casserole to Ronald, who immediately spoke up. When the waiter had corrected the error and left, Felicity told Ronald about her suspicions of Mr. Trotsky. "How many Russian publishers can there be? How many who pirate American books?"

"Hundreds?" Ronald replied. "Living next door to you? I don't believe in coincidence."

"Maybe it isn't a coincidence."

With a sweet smile, Ronald said, "I don't believe in your

paranoia, either. But what just happened with the food made me wonder about a mistake. The houses in your neighborhood are all alike."

"No, they're not!"

"They are. Same size, same color, same basic design."

"Ronald, that is not true."

It was, in fact, more true than not.

"They all look the same to me. And the house numbers are hard to find."

"You're right about that." She peered at his shrimp, which were completely peeled. He probably hadn't contracted hepatitis from the clams, either.

"So, maybe the body got left for you by mistake. Switched. Like our dinners. It could've been meant for the Trotskys. Or someone else."

"Well, if Quinlan Coates had been a professor of Russian, that would be a connection. But I don't think Trotsky has any connection with Romance languages or Boston College. And he hates cats. He tried to get the condo association to enforce our no-pet clause. No one supported him. But it's easy to see how someone could have something against Trotsky. He really is unpleasant. Needlessly unpleasant. There's friction between our neighborhood and Norwood Hill, and he makes everything worse, but he's also nasty to the other people in Newton Park, and for no good reason. He was horrible to some woman from Norwood Hill who was just walking her dog by his house, and when I tried to pour oil on troubled waters, as it were, he went stalking off, and the woman said that he must be a gangster." *Stalking.* Had she said "stocking"?

"Maybe he is."

"He's a publisher. Maybe he pirates books, but there's

no reason to think he's a gangster, and I don't like it that the people on Norwood Hill have that image of us."

"How did he afford that house?"

"By being a publisher, I guess. How else? Just because you don't know where people got their money, it doesn't mean that they're crooks." As soon as Felicity spoke, she thought of Uncle Bob's fireproof box of money. That was a special situation, she told herself. It was one thing to have money in the bank and money to buy expensive houses, and quite another thing to keep a large amount of cash hidden behind a bed.

"Is something wrong with your lobster?" Ronald asked.

"It's dry and tough. Anyway, what offends me is the assumption based strictly on nationality that someone is a crook."

"Felicity, you're the one who suspects Mr. Trotsky because he's Russian."

"Ronald, whoever stole my books and published them in Russian is likely to *be* Russian. And it's possible to be a crook without being a gangster."

"The point is, Felicity, that you don't know."

"True enough. For all I know, people suspect me of being a criminal because I live in a big house."

"No, they don't. If they don't know about your uncle, they assume that you bought the house with your royalties."

Felicity, who was delighted to have people make exactly that assumption, said, "If that's what they think, they're fools."

"They're naïve, that's all. The wannabes who come to Witness meetings think they're going to be able to quit their day jobs when their first royalty statements arrive. Take Janice Mattingly."

"You take her. Ronald, why did she invite that forensics guy with his mummified foot? That thing is revolting. I wish someone else would take charge of lining up the speakers. I don't know what makes it her job."

"No one else wants to do it. Are you volunteering?"

"Of course not. I'm too busy."

"So is everyone else. That's why Janice does more than her fair share for Witness. Refreshments—"

"Which she does badly. It's the worst food I've eaten since school lunches."

"The newsletter."

"Which she is supposed to edit, not to write."

"How can she when no one sends her anything?"

"When Sonya did the newsletter, people sent her things. She plagued us. It worked. Besides, Janice likes doing the newsletter. She's going to interview me as soon as the police let me talk publicly about the murder."

"As you can hardly wait to do."

"Admittedly, Ronald. As I can hardly wait to do."

TWENTY-SEVEN

Quinlan Coates's funeral was a big disappointment. For one thing, instead of attending in solitary dignity, Felicity was dragged down, as she saw it, by Janice Mattingly and Sonya Bogosian, who had insisted on accompanying her. When Sonya called on Friday evening, she said that she and Janice were determined to offer moral support. Felicity was convinced then and remained convinced that Sonya and Janice were merely looking for a pretext to gather material for their books. The nerve! This was Felicity's very own murder, and Janice and Sonya had no business trying to exact shares to which they weren't entitled. Had the body been left at *their* front doors? Certainly not! If they wanted to attend the funerals of murder victims, let them find their own corpses and their own last rites!

Quinlan Coates belonged to Felicity, as did his funeral mass, and it was greedy and unprofessional of Janice and Sonya to hone in on, and thereby diminish, another mystery writer's research opportunity. Moral support, indeed! The hypocrites!

But there they were, seated on either side of Felicity in the Church of St. Ignatius of Loyola, which was so dishearteningly light, bright, and unmysterious that it could practically have been Presbyterian—and Scots Presbyterian at that. Furthermore, the wholesome young priest now delivering a eulogy about Quinlan Coates's professional accomplishments, his contributions to the Boston College community, and his extreme devotion to his late wife, bore no resemblance to the elderly, doddering figure Felicity had imagined, a satisfyingly sinister character who kept lapsing into Latin, thus rendering his insinuations about the deceased unintelligible except to Felicity and a handful of Jesuits with whom she would converse over the funeral meats.

The apparent failure of William Coates to provide funeral meats was another source of disappointment. In neither yesterday's paper nor today's had there been any mention of a postfuneral gathering, nor was such an event announced in the little memorial program Felicity had been handed when she had entered the church. As if deliberately to exacerbate her disgruntlement, Sonya and Janice had both inquired about Felicity's plans to go back to the house after the service. In informing them that she knew of no such gathering, Felicity had felt herself slip in their esteem, as if she had presented herself as more central to Coates's life and death than was actually the case, and had now been found out and deservingly shamed.

Leaning toward Felicity, Janice whispered, "There must be *something* afterwards. If the family isn't doing anything, the college must be. His department, maybe? *Someone?*"

"No," Felicity murmured. "No one is. You sound as if you expect me to."

"Certainly not," Janice whispered. "You've done more than enough already."

"What do you mean 'more than enough'?" Felicity eyed Janice with annoyance. In selecting the medium blue suit she wore, Felicity had taken care to avoid the black-from-head-to-toe apparel suitable for close relatives. Janice, a stranger, was in deep mourning. A wisp of black lace was pinned unflatteringly on top of her head, and she had on a black dress and black high-heeled shoes.

"Finding him. Taking his cat."

"Cats. Plural."

Sonya put a finger to her lips. Who was she to enforce the rules of propriety? In Felicity's view, Sonya's loose layers of pale blue cotton and, worse, her espadrilles were as inappropriate as Janice's formal black. In British cozy mysteries, churchwomen were always arranging flowers and polishing brasses, activities for which Sonya was suitably costumed. If Felicity had known no one in the church, she'd still have been embarrassed to be seen with Janice and Sonya, but, just as mystery novels had led her to hope, Detective Dave Valentine was in attendance. At Janice and Sonya's insistence, the three women were in the last row, so Felicity had a good view of Valentine, who was only three rows ahead, in a pew toward the right. Despite the distraction of her companions, she'd seen him enter, and she'd also studied everyone else in church, which was perhaps a third full. No one bore even the slightest resemblance to the weird woman in the police sketch. Felicity had, however, been able to identify William Coates—poor Billy Goats!— who had entered from the front of the church just before the mass had begun. The late Dora Coates had perhaps had very thin eyebrows or had carried the genes for them: A dilution of his father's genetic influence had left William with normal eyebrows and, indeed, with an altogether ordinary appearance. The priest had gone on and on about the depth of Quinlan Coates's grief for Dora. Maybe her husband had missed being married to someone with corrective eyebrow DNA. In any case, William was of medium height and had brown hair. The only distinctive thing about him was that he sat all alone at his father's funeral. The newspaper hadn't mentioned a wife, but didn't he have relatives or friends?

Felicity's observations were interrupted by the rising of the congregation. Unfamiliar with Roman Catholic practices, she was contenting herself with standing when others stood and sitting when they sat. Sonya was doing the same. Janice, however, had genuflected when the three women had entered the sanctuary, and, despite her propensity for whispering during the mass, kept kneeling and crossing herself with the other worshipers.

Leaning across Felicity, Sonya violated her own ban on talking to whisper, "Janice, I didn't know you were Catholic."

"I'm not. I just want to fit in."

Unable to contain herself, Felicity muttered, "When in Rome . . ."

Sonya smiled silently and dug Felicity in the ribs, but Janice made a sour face and focused her attention on the priest. For the remainder of the mass, the women said nothing aloud, but Felicity took the opportunity to address the Almighty.

"Dear God," she prayed, "Quinlan Coates's worth as human being falls in Your purview and not mine, but in case You've forgotten, as would be understandable at Your advanced age, he was wonderful to his cats, Edith and Brigitte, who, if they could, would implore You to show the same love and generosity to his immortal soul that he lavished on them. Sincerely yours, Felicity Pride." As an afterthought, she added, "Amen."

By the time she had finished composing and dispatching this piece of correspondence, Quinlan Coates's casket was being carried down the aisle. People rose and began to file out.

"Are we going to the cemetery?" Janice asked brightly.

"The interment is private," said Felicity, who had no idea whether or not it really was. "Excuse me. There's someone I need to speak to. I'll be right back."

By then, the women were outside the church, where clusters of people were lingering. The hearse and one black limousine were at the curb. Felicity rapidly made her way toward the limousine and thus toward William Coates, who was gazing at the gray November sky while moving his feet back and forth on the concrete as if trying to scrape something off the soles of his shoes.

Felicity introduced herself, but sensing that William Coates wouldn't return a handshake, did not offer one. "I'm very sorry about your father."

"I'm not," he said.

"Well, in case you're concerned about his cats, I wanted you to know that they're safe. I have them."

"Keep them. He treated every cat he ever owned a lot better than he treated me."

It occurred to Felicity that if Quinlan Coates had hated cats, he might have been the perfect match for her mother. Now was not, however, the time to organize a support group for adult children whose parents didn't like them. "I'm sorry to hear that," she said.

"Were you a friend of his?"

"I never met him."

"You didn't miss much. Well, thanks for coming."

"You're welcome," she said.

As she walked away from William Coates, she experienced a disconcerting sense of gratitude toward her mother, who had had the decency to insist on good manners. Preoccupied, she nearly bumped into Detective Dave Valentine, who wore a dark suit and looked well groomed in some male fashion that Felicity couldn't identify. Had he had a haircut?

Fresh from her encounter with William Coates, she exclaimed, "What a rude man!"

"I didn't expect to see you here," Valentine said.

"I felt as though I should come."

"It was nice of you. Look, this is an awkward time, but there's something I need to ask you about your uncle and aunt. The Robertsons."

"Yes?"

"You told me they were killed in a car accident."

"They were."

"By a drunk driver."

"Yes."

"There was a little something you didn't mention."

Felicity silently gazed into Valentine's eyes, which the cloudy sky had turned an especially attractive shade of blue.

"The little something," Valentine continued, "concerns the drunk driver."

"Yes."

"The driver in question was Robert Robertson."

"Yes," Felicity agreed, "the drunk driver was Uncle Bob himself."

TWENTY-EIGHT

The funeral left Felicity in a foul mood. As she changed out of her blue suit and into corduroy pants and an old sweater, she glared at her unmade bed and cursed herself for having skipped the housework to concentrate on her appearance. For all the good it had done to fuss with her hair, her makeup, and her outfit! Rather than inviting her out to dinner, or at least flirting with her, Dave Valentine had caught her in a stupid lie. Furthermore, he'd seen her with Janice and Sonya, and he'd probably overheard the silly whispering of women acting like schoolgirls. William Coates had been horrible, particularly because his antagonism toward his father had reminded her of hers toward her mother. As material for a writer, the church and the priest had been useless.

The funeral had been brief and nearby, and it was only quarter of twelve. Still, the bed should have been made by now, and the presence of both cats on the rumpled comforter was uncomfortably reminiscent of the dishevelment of Quinlan Coates's apartment. Was it slovenly to let cats sleep on the bed? Felicity felt incapable of shooing them off. When she removed the pillows and yanked the top sheet and blanket toward the headboard, Brigitte, as if recognizing the start of a delightful game, began tearing around the room, leaping off and on the bed, and diving under the sheet. The large and stolid Edith, however, remained where she was, in the exact center of the bed, and her weight made it almost impossible to straighten the covers. Felicity, who was too intimidated to remove Edith, settled for pulling hard on the covers with both hands. She then plumped and replaced the pillows, but when she neatly folded over the top of the comforter, Brigitte flung herself onto the bed, dove under the fold, and wiggled. Felicity finally gave up.

After vacuuming downstairs, Felicity ate a light lunch and, resisting the urge to take a nap, went to her computer and visited the Web site of a large online bookseller to see how *Felines in Felony* was doing. Mistake! The new Isabelle Hotchkiss, *Purrfectly Baffling,* was selling better than *Felines in Felony.* Furthermore, two disgruntled readers had given *Felines in Felony* low ratings and posted nasty reviews. According to one of the readers, the book was "too feline and insufficiently felonious," and according to the other, "the premise that Morris and Tabitha communicate with Prissy LaChatte in some unexplained fashion is utterly preposterous." In search of consolation, Felicity looked at the ratings and reader reviews of *Purrfectly Baffling,* but found no comfort. "Olaf and Lambie Pie are even more lovable in *Purrfectly Baffling* than in its charming predecessors," wrote one reader. "With twitching tail, I eagerly await the brilliant Isabelle Hotchkiss's next recounting of the spine-tingling adventures of Kitty Katlikoff." Was it possible that Mary Robertson had a computer hidden somewhere in her apartment and secretly visited this Web site to pan her daughter's books and praise those of her principal rival?

To remind herself of just how badly Isabelle Hotchkiss wrote, Felicity decided to read some of the sample pages of *Purrfectly Baffling* available at the click of a mouse. She soon came to a section in which Isabelle Hotchkiss's fictional cats were conversing with each other:

> "I am not sure I feel like telling the Furless Person everything I know," the hefty Olaf opined stodgily. "What has she done for us lately?"
> "Fed us!" exclaimed the soft, fluffy little Lambie Pie. "Oh, yum! Dry food! Yum, yum, yum!"

"'Hefty Olaf opined stodgily.'" Felicity spoke with the joy of one who has found precisely what she sought. "Pass me the antiemetic, please." Despite the claim to nausea, she devoured two full pages about Olaf and Lambie Pie. Although she believed in keeping an eye on the competition, she had read only a few of Isabelle Hotchkiss's books and none of her recent ones. In *Purrfectly Baffling,* the cats were as saccharine as ever, but something about them was elusively different from what she remembered. When she'd read the old Kitty Katlikoff books, she hadn't owned cats; the new element might be her own perception and not Hotchkiss's depiction. Had soft, fluffy little Lambie Pie always draped herself on the edges of furniture? For that matter, had little Lambie Pie been soft and fluffy? Had she been little? As to Olaf, had he been compact and stodgy? Then there were the food preferences. Had Olaf always preferred canned food? And when Kitty Katlikoff opened a can of food, had Lambie Pie always danced eagerly around, sniffed the wet food, and then eaten dry food?

Clicking her mouse and scrolling down the pages, Felicity happened on a scene in which Kitty Katlikoff was making her bed. Lambie Pie ran madly around, leaping under the covers and hiding in the folds of the bedspread, whereas big, placid Olaf planted himself in the center of the bed and refused to budge. The bed-making scene settled the matter: Isabelle Hotchkiss seemed to be describing the late Quinlan Coates's cats.

Had Hotchkiss and Coates known each other? But Edith and Brigitte were young, four and two years old, respectively, and the first Hotchkiss mystery had been published about a dozen years ago. Unless all cats acted alike? Or unless all Chartreux cats acted alike, and Isabelle Hotchkiss owned the breed? But Edith and Brigitte were both Chartreux, yet differed radically from each other in ways that mirrored the differences between Olaf and Lambie Pie. And neither of Ronald's cats, George and Ira, bore a strong resemblance to Olaf and Edith or to Lambie Pie and Brigitte. Both George and Ira were only moderately active. Felicity had never seen either cat drape himself on furniture. Mystified, Felicity decided on a visit to Newbright Books, where she could question Ronald about cat behavior and Isabelle Hotchkiss's identity while simultaneously preparing to investigate Olaf and Lambie Pie as they had been portrayed in Isabelle Hotchkiss's early mysteries.

Forty-five minutes later, soon after Felicity entered Ronald's store, she felt a wave of guilt. Tucked in the wallet in her shoulder bag was a one-hundred-dollar bill from Uncle Bob's fireproof box. Back at home, when she'd decided on the efficient course of acquiring Hotchkiss's books while interrogating Ronald about cats, she'd had to confront her reluctance to contribute to Hotchkiss's royalties. The public library would have some of the old Hotchkiss mysteries, but the new one, *Purrfectly Baffling,* would—damn it all!—have a long waiting list, and Felicity wanted to study its depictions of Olaf and Lambie Pie without having to read the whole book at her computer. With luck, Newbright Books would have some used Hotchkiss paperbacks, but to acquire *Purrfectly Baffling,* she'd have to buy a new hardcover. The bill from Uncle Bob's stash represented a compromise: Although Isabelle Hotchkiss would get paid for the book, Felicity herself wouldn't have earned the money that ended up in Hotchkiss's bank account. Entering the store, Felicity found Ronald conferring with a customer about the perfect present for the woman's elderly aunt who doted on her cats. He immediately introduced the customer to Felicity and, as if engaging in some secret and probably illegal transaction, advised the woman to have Felicity inscribe a copy of *Felines in Felony* to the cat-loving aunt. And in Felicity's wallet was the ill-gotten and possibly even counterfeit hundred-dollar bill that she'd intended to palm off on this dear friend, this sweetest of men, this promoter of her books!

After Felicity had inscribed her book to the aunt, she headed to the section of used books, where she found satisfyingly cheap paperback copies of the first Isabelle Hotchkiss, *Purrfectly Poisonous,* and three later books in the series, *Purrfectly Murderous, Purrfectly Deadly,* and *Purrfectly*

Sleuthful. With regret, she moved to the shelves of new paperback mysteries, where she picked up *Purrfectly Criminal.* Finally with an emotion close of pain, she added *Purrfectly Baffling* to the stack of books she carried.

"Her new hardcover?" Ronald inquired in an undertone. "And her new paperback? Felicity, how unlike you!"

Felicity was about to say that it was unlike Ronald to discourage a customer from buying books when she realized that it was actually something he habitually did: If he thought that a customer wouldn't enjoy a book, he said so. She settled for responding with a noncommittal nod before demanding, "Ronald, who *is* she?"

"What do you care?"

"I'm just curious."

"I have no idea. No one does. Presumably. Felicity, you know all this. Mystery writers used to write under pseudonyms all the time. Nicholas Blake was Cecil Day-Lewis. The poet laureate. Michael Innis was—"

"J. I. M. Stewart. Amanda Cross. Carolyn Heilbrun. I know! Carolyn Heilbrun wrote about it somewhere. Academic types were stigmatized if their colleagues knew that they wrote mysteries. Michael Innis was a don at Oxford. Except that everyone knew who he really was. And it was no secret that Carolyn Heilbrun was Amanda Cross. So why all the secrecy about Isabelle Hotchkiss?"

Ronald shrugged. "Have you looked up copyright information? It's on the Library of Congress Web site."

"I hadn't thought of that."

"It won't tell you anything."

"Then why would I look there?"

"Because you're stressed. It would give you something to do. I wish I could persuade you to listen to—"

"I don't want to listen to Glenn Gould!"

"Look, Felicity, why don't you take the rest of the weekend to relax. Play with your cats. Cats are great stress reducers. They're so mellow."

"Brigitte isn't. She's wild." Felicity lowered her voice. "Speaking of which, is it normal for cats to hang around in bathtubs?"

"Cats are individuals. They have eccentricities. Likes and dislikes. Just the way we do."

Felicity felt dissatisfied. Among other things, she suspected that Ronald knew more about Isabelle Hotchkiss than he was willing to say. Even so, she paid for the books with her debit card and left Uncle Bob's hundred-dollar bill in her wallet. Ronald didn't deserve to get stuck with it, but maybe she'd encounter someone who did.

TWENTY-NINE

With some justification, Felicity had a high opinion of her own ability to comprehend the written word and thus had no intention of reading Isabelle Hotchkiss's books sentence by sentence or paragraph by paragraph. Rather, she intended to go through the books with her goal in mind, that goal being to trace the development of Olaf and Lambie Pie. In the case of the first book in the Kitty Katlikoff series, Felicity, having actually read it some years ago, needed only to refresh her memory. Armed with a fresh cup of coffee, a yellow legal pad, a pen, and the six Kitty Katlikoff books she'd bought at Newbright, she settled into an armchair in Uncle Bob's study and opened *Purrfectly Poisonous,* which had introduced Kitty, Olaf, and Lambie Pie. The copyright page confirmed Felicity's recollection that the book had been published twelve years earlier. The first chapter was of no interest, concerning as it did the life circumstances of Kitty before her acquisition of Olaf and Lambie Pie, an event that occurred in the second chapter when the protagonist rescued the cats from a ramshackle house where they had been abandoned by a villain who, as Felicity remembered, turned out to have murdered his three wives. In *Purrfectly Poisonous,* Olaf and Lambie Pie were what Felicity had recently learned to call "domestic shorthairs." Olaf was black and white, and Lambie Pie was orange. When discovered in the ramshackle house, both were thin. In subsequent chapters, the cats gained weight, but Olaf did not become notably solid or compact. Furthermore, the gratitude of the cats to their savior was such that both animals displayed extreme friendliness to Kitty right from the start. In temperament and behavior, there was almost no difference between the cats. Their only striking behavior was their mastery of spoken English, a gift they used to inform Kitty about their previous owner's crimes.

In *Purrfectly Murderous* and *Purrfectly Deadly,* the third and fifth books in the series, respectively, Olaf and Lambie Pie were much as they had been when first introduced, except, of course, that they were now healthy and well cared for. They chatted as much as ever, usually on the subject of murder. The only major change in the description of the cats was Isabelle Hotchkiss's increasing reliance on adverbs: The cats didn't just speak, but exclaimed, interjected, cried, voiced, articulated, and uttered things jauntily, saucily, teasingly, and naughtily. In *Purrfectly Sleuthful,* published three years earlier, both Olaf and Lambie Pie enjoyed dry food and canned food. Olaf hadn't gained weight. To Felicity's professional disgust, the murderer did in her victims by injecting air bubbles into their bloodstreams, a method that Felicity scorned as nonfatal as well as passé. Isabelle Hotchkiss should have attended educational presentations for mystery writers and thus should have known that contemporary mysteries favored multiple gunshots to the head and chest, good old reliable strangulation, and other such simple, dependable forms of homicide.

In *Purrfectly Criminal,* published in hardcover a year earlier and presumably written in the year preceding its publication, Felicity finally found what she sought. Olaf was suddenly much bigger than Lambie Pie, whose fur was longer, softer, and fluffier than it had been before. Indeed, Lambie Pie went so far as to behave *fluffily.* Olaf was solid, stolid, and mellow. Lambie Pie was light and quick. The differences between the cats grew pronounced in the final book, *Purrfectly Baffling.* Olaf continued to be omnivorous, but Lambie Pie now turned up her darling little nose at canned food and chomped away at dry food. When taken to stay at a motel while Kitty followed up a clue, Olaf hid under a bed, whereas Lambie Pie ran wildly around the room.

Having no plans for the rest of the day, Felicity was tempted to call Dave Valentine, who, despite the unfortunate business of the drunk driver who'd killed Bob and Thelma, could be lured to dinner with the promise of a fascinating discovery about Quinlan Coates's cats, couldn't he? Prissy LaChatte's pet police chief would come running, but would Dave Valentine find the discovery as fascinating as he should? Would he consider it a discovery at all? More to the point, was it one? Calling William Coates was clearly impossible. His father had been buried today. What's more, the son had made it clear that he resented his father's affection for cats. Consequently, he couldn't be expected to respond in a helpful manner to questions about a connection between Isabelle Hotchkiss and Coates, Brigitte, and Edith, a connection that Felicity had to admit to herself was somewhat tenuous. When Quinlan Coates had acquired Brigitte and Edith, Isabelle Hotchkiss had transformed Kitty Katlikoff's cats, Olaf and Lambie Pie, in ways that made them resemble Coates's cats. How had Isabelle Hotchkiss known Edith and Brigitte? Who *was* Isabelle Hotchkiss? Felicity cursed herself for having neglected to open the copies of the Hotchkiss books that she'd seen in Coates's apartment. For all she knew, Hotchkiss had signed them using her real name. Could Hotchkiss be a friend of Coates's? A relative? The weird woman in the police sketch, perhaps?

Faced with such frustration, what would Prissy do? Well, she'd *do* something. As would Felicity. But only when she was dressed to meet her adoring public, a few members of which simply had to work at the newly renamed Angell Animal Medical Center, where Edith was a blood donor, and where both Edith and Brigitte were patients. According to Coates's neighbor, Coates had never used a cat-sitter, but had boarded his cats at Angell when he traveled. Therefore, the people at Angell knew Coates and knew his cats. If he'd ever been there with the real Isabelle Hotchkiss, someone might remember her. With luck, she'd been with him on Monday only a few hours before his murder.

Forty-five minutes later, Felicity drove Aunt Thelma's Honda CR-V past a long brick wall on South Huntington Avenue in Jamaica Plain and made a left turn into the grounds of Angell, which occupied a building far larger than she had expected. And what were all these cars doing here late on a Saturday afternoon? Felicity found a parking space in a lot to the side of the building and, avoiding the

MSPCA adoption center—the last thing she wanted was another pet—made her way to the main entrance, where she
had to wait while a man gently encouraged a limping dog to
pass through the doors. Once inside, Felicity was struck by
the resemblance of the animal hospital to what she thought
of as a "real hospital." No one was selling flowers or Mylar
balloons, of course; one wall was packed with bags and
cases of pet food; and on the long reception counter sat a
miniature doghouse with a slot on top and a sign asking for
donations to the shelter. Still, prominently posted in this
reception area was a list of medical and surgical departments
together with the names of veterinarians who specialized in
cardiology, oncology, and other familiar fields; and the human clients with their animals were reminiscent of able-
bodied spouses and caregivers with ailing human charges at
their sides. Some small animals were in carriers like the one
Felicity had bought, but most of these carriers were far less
spacious and splendid than hers. How many people who escorted cranky or demented relatives to hospitals would be
delighted to have the option of locking the difficult human
beings in secure cages for transport? As in the hospitals
Felicity had visited before, staff hurried around. Here, some
wore green scrubs or white lab coats, and others had on blue
shirts with the word *Angell* stitched on the left breast in
place of an alligator or a pony. The entire scene was far more
professional and complex than Felicity had imagined. Angell was not some slightly larger version of Dr. Furbish's
clinic; it was a big institution where she shouldn't have expected to be able to drop in for a chat about Quinlan Coates
and his cats.

   As Felicity was trying to decide whether to leave, a man
with a black dog addressed her. "You look lost."

"I am," she said. "Well, not really. I need to check on my cats' records. Their owner died, and I need to make sure that the records are in my name now."

The man pointed to the long reception counter. "Ask the people over there," the man said. "They'll check their computers. What kind of cats do you have?"

Was it *Chartreux* or *Chatreux*? "Gray," said Felicity. "Gray cats. One of them is a blood donor here."

"What a good thing to do! I'd sign Charlie up"—he nodded at the black dog—"but he has cancer. They're doing what they can for him. This is the best place there is."

"He looks happy."

"That's all you can ask for. Well, good luck."

When the man moved away, Felicity took his advice by joining one of the lines at the reception counter and was soon talking with the white-haired woman in front of her whose carrier turned out to contain a gigantic white rabbit that had just been treated for a foot injury. Then, as the woman was paying the bill for the rabbit, a little fawn-colored dog whose owner was filling out a form suddenly approached from Felicity's right and jumped up on her leg. The dog's owner, a pale, elderly woman, apologized. "Christine, that was very naughty!" she told the dog. "Tell the lady you're sorry!"

Before Christine the dog even had time to obey, the woman with the rabbit left, and Felicity found herself facing a hefty young woman in one of the blue Angell shirts, who asked, "How may I help you?"

"I need to check on my cats' records," Felicity said. "My cats used to belong to someone else, a man named Quinlan Coates. I want to make sure that the cats' records are in my name now."

"You could have called us," the woman said.

"I did. But what if I were an imposter? Just claiming to own the cats now? I assumed that you'd need to see some identification." Felicity fished in her shoulder bag, pulled out her driver's license, and put it on the counter, mainly in the hope that the woman would read and recognize her name.

"Are your cats currently hospitalized?" The woman ignored the license.

"No. They're at home. They're fine. They're healthy. One of them is a blood donor. That's the other thing I want to check on." In a place this big and complicated, no one would realize that she'd already spoken to someone about Edith's participation in the program, or so Felicity told herself.

"What did you want to know?"

"What's involved," Felicity said impatiently. "What do I need to do to have her give blood."

"If you'll give me your name and address, we'll mail you the information. Let me see if you're already in the computer. What's your name?"

Enunciating with great clarity and at unnecessarily high volume, Felicity said, "Felicity Pride." She added, "The cats are Edith and Brigitte. They were owned by Quinlan Coates."

The woman was tapping at her keyboard and looking at her monitor. "They're here," she said. "Under your name. Is that all?"

"When is Edith due to give blood again?"

"Six to eight weeks after the last time. Let's see. She was here on the third. So about five to seven weeks from now. No sooner than that. We'll mail you all the information."

"Did you know Quinlan Coates? Is there anyone here who knows Edith?"

"I'm sorry. I can't remember everyone."

A young man in green scrubs with slicked-back hair and a pierced ear was standing nearby behind the counter and suddenly spoke up. "Is that Edith who gives blood? The Chartreux?"

"Yes! I'm her new owner."

"Do you think you two could take this somewhere else," the woman said. "There's a line."

The man with the pierced ear gave a wry smile and gestured to Felicity to wait. In seconds, he appeared in the reception area and then led her through a half-door to a long corridor with a bench along one wall. He did not, however, take a seat. "I'm Eric," he said. "Edith is a great cat. She has real character."

"Thank you. I'm just getting to know her."

"She's beautiful. So is the other one. What's her name?"

"Brigitte. How do you know Brigitte?"

"She boards here. I work there sometimes. And at the blood bank. I move around." He waved his hand toward a large waiting room visible through an opening in the wall above the bench.

"You *do* know that their owner was murdered."

"The police have been here. I talked to some guy, but I couldn't tell him much. I'm the one who took Edith out to the owner, but I just gave Edith to him. That was all."

"What time was that?"

"I don't know. Five. Around five."

"Was anyone with him?"

"Not that I saw. I gave Edith to him right here. There could've been someone out in the reception area. Probably not, though. He must've waited here for a while before I had a chance to get Edith for him."

"Is five the normal time to get a cat? After she's given blood?"

"It's on the late side. The way it works is that we call when the animal's ready to go home. With cats, we sedate them, so we have to wait until they're awake and doing okay. And before you get the animal, you have to see the people out there where you were. So, that can take a while if we're busy. It's the same as if you were picking up an animal after a procedure. Except that you don't pay. In fact, you get free cat food if you want it."

"Did Quinlan Coates do that? Edith's owner."

"I don't know. The people at the front desk take care of that. Hey, I better go. It was nice meeting you. I hope Edith will be back."

"She probably will."

Before departing, Felicity stepped into the big waiting room, where owners sat with dogs on leashes and small animals in carriers. Then she returned to the corridor and examined a decorative metal tree espaliered on the wall opposite the bench. Each shiny leaf bore the name of a pet. Felicity found herself surprisingly moved by the memorial tree. At the same time, she wondered exactly how much it cost to buy a leaf. On her way out, she again noticed the miniature doghouse with its sign asking for donations to the MSPCA animal shelter. On impulse, she reached into her bag, found Uncle Bob's suspect hundred-dollar bill, and inserted it in the slot on the roof of the donation box. If there was, in fact, something wrong with Uncle Bob's cash, there'd presumably be a public fuss about someone's having donated hot or fake money to the MSPCA. And if not? She'd have supported a good cause.

THIRTY

The board of the New England Chapter of Witness consisted of Sonya Bogosian, Janice Mattingly, Hadley O'Connor, Jim Isaac, and Felicity. At the group's inception, it had been emphasized to the founders that to avoid tie votes, it was crucial to have an uneven number of board members. In fact, as the board was now constituted, votes were nearly always unanimous. Sonya, as president, chaired the board meetings and the general meetings, and Jim Isaac, as vice president, was prepared to fill in for her in her absence. Sonya, however, was always present. Felicity, in the position of clerk, dealt with correspondence by handing it over to Janice, whose official position was that of treasurer. Janice also took notes on meetings and, at each meeting, read the minutes of the last one. Hadley O'Connor attended board meetings. As the two best-known authors on the board, he and Felicity privately believed that their willingness to serve on the board was in itself a valuable contribution to the organization.

On Sunday, November 9, the board meeting was held at Janice's apartment, which was in a multifamily house on a narrow street in Lower Allston. The neighborhood was known for providing affordable housing to students and musicians. Although Felicity professed to find the area interesting, she actually considered it a slum. Her prejudice against anything even remotely like a tenement had been handed down to her by her maternal grandparents, both of whom had been born in Glasgow, a city with such a notable history of urban poverty and overcrowding that it now welcomed tourists to a museum called Tenement House. Still, in Felicity's family, as in all other Scottish-American families, the elders had always passed down the information that their own ancestors had been the kings of the Highlands, thus generating the universal question of Scottish-American children, namely, if they were the kings of the Highlands, why did they leave?

In any case, on Sunday afternoon when Felicity squeezed the Honda into a small parking space on the narrow street where Janice lived, she experienced an atavistic dread at finding herself about to enter what she must not refer to as a tenement. After all, Harvard was buying up property here, wasn't it? Albeit with the intention of tearing down the existing buildings, among them, Janice's perfectly nice dwelling in this ever-so-interesting and culturally diverse neighborhood. After taking no more than her usual care to make sure that the Honda's windows were firmly closed and its doors locked, she made her way up a short flight of wooden steps in need of paint and pressed the doorbell next to a tattered card that read "Janice Mattingly and Bruno Balboa." As Felicity knew, Bruno was a fiction who existed strictly for Janice's protection against evildoers who might harm her if they realized that she lived alone. It had never occurred to Felicity that Bruno inhabited the same universe as her very own late Morris, for whom she was still grieving. Indeed, Felicity half-believed in the existence of Bruno and would have been unsurprised if she'd been at Janice's and heard the door open and a deep male voice call out, "Janice, I'm home!"

On this Sunday afternoon, Bruno was, of course, out. When Janice answered the bell and led Felicity upstairs to her one-bedroom apartment, Sonya, Jim, and Hadley had already arrived, and Janice's cat, Dorothy-L, occupied a place on the couch. Dorothy-L was a thin and elderly calico with greasy-looking fur. Janice attributed the poor condition of the cat's coat to a thyroid disorder for which the cat took an evidently ineffective medication. Since Janice had a tedious habit of talking at great length about Dorothy-L's many ailments and of debating aloud about treatment options available at Angell, Felicity took care to say nothing about the cat. Instead, she greeted her fellow members of the board and apologized for being late.

"You're not late. We're early," said Jim Isaac, a Jewish-Chinese-African-American lawyer whose detective was a Jewish-Chinese-African-American lawyer.

"Help yourself to food," Janice said. "It's in the kitchen."

Mainly to give herself something to do during the meeting, Felicity accepted the offer of food. Entering the small kitchen, she found the table spread with cold cuts, ham, American cheese, pickles, iceberg lettuce, tomatoes, rolls, bread, and dishes of mayonnaise and mustard. The kitchen had cheap cabinets and appliances installed perhaps ten years earlier. In Felicity's view, the landlord should have left everything as it was in the hope of passing the place off as retro. Here and elsewhere, the walls and trim were thick with layers of old paint that a fresh coat of white had done nothing to disguise. Why did Janice insist on living in Boston, albeit in Lower Allston? Janice's rent was probably even higher than Felicity had paid in Somerville.

After making herself a half sandwich, she returned to the living room, which was lined with brick-and-board bookshelves that held hundreds of hardcover mysteries in protective plastic jackets. Janice was known to collect autographed first editions and always bought Felicity's new hardcovers at Newbright Books and had Felicity sign them, but Felicity had had no idea of the great size of Janice's collection.

Sonya called the meeting to order. "Janice, could we have the minutes of the last meeting? And keep it brief, please." Sonya took a bite of a thick sandwich.

"All of us were present," Janice said. "The minutes were read and accepted. Ditto the treasurer's report. We agreed to make December's meeting a holiday party with no speaker. Pending Ronald's approval."

"Thank you," said Sonya, her mouth still somewhat full. "Old business? None? New business?"

"Speakers," said Hadley O'Connor, who looked handsome enough to remind Felicity of why she had had a fling with him. She also remembered the intolerable violence of his books. She consoled herself with the reflection that he lacked the strength to toss the caber. "We're getting repetitious," Hadley said. He had made himself a sandwich even thicker than Sonya's. When he lifted it to his mouth, slices of meat, cheese, and tomato began to slide out, and he was forced to take a big bite to prevent the food from falling into his lap.

"Enough forensics," Felicity agreed.

"There's an anthropologist who'd talk about cannibalism," Janice said.

"On some South Sea island?" Jim asked. "Or homegrown, so to speak?"

"The Donner Party. That kind of thing." Janice, too, began to eat.

"That's not really very relevant, is it?" Sonya said. "Cannibalism would be fine, but it has to be *criminal* cannibalism. No one's going to want to hear about some pitiful group of starving people who ate each other just to survive. And if the, uh, victims were already dead, I mean, if they'd starved to death, well, that has nothing to offer us, does it? We are crime writers, after all."

"Then there's a forensic psychiatrist," Janice said.

"All they're interested in is serial killers," said Hadley, "and a lot of psychologizing about unhappy childhoods."

"Would it be possible," Felicity asked hesitantly, "to have something upbeat for a change?" In the hope that someone else would suggest a cheerful topic, she took a bite of her sandwich and chewed it thoroughly. It tasted terrible. No one else spoke up. "For example," she went on, "I always enjoy a good toxicology lecture. Common poisons under your kitchen sink. That kind of thing."

"Been done," said Jim "We had that guy last spring. You weren't there."

"Well, what about finding an agent, getting published, and so on?" Sonya suggested. "Quite a few of the people who come to meetings are interested in that. Hadley and

Felicity, what about you two? You could do that one. And maybe you'll be allowed to talk about your murder by then, Felicity."

"Yeah, we heard," said Jim.

"Well, that's settled," Sonya said. "January. Hadley and Felicity. Finding an agent and getting published. I think we've done excellent work today."

"There's dessert," Janice said. "And coffee. And my treasurer's report is here if anyone wants to see it."

All five board members headed to the kitchen, where they left their dirty plates next to the sink. Janice moved the sandwich fixings from the table and put out plates of cake, already sliced, a large bowl of cream-colored pudding, serving dishes, and silverware. Felicity, who hadn't finished the dreadful half sandwich, took a serving of cake and helped herself to a cup of coffee. Noticing an open case of the canned prescription cat food that Janice was always talking about, Felicity mulled over the possibility that the stuff tasted better than what Janice served at meetings.

Instead of returning to the living room, people hung around in the kitchen. To Felicity's embarrassment, Sonya mentioned a blurb that Felicity had written for the first book in a new cat mystery series, and, with Janice standing nearby, Felicity was unable to silence Sonya.

"Speaking of which," Felicity said, "someone was asking me about Isabelle Hotchkiss. She's notorious for being really nasty to people who want blurbs, you know."

"All via her agent," Janice said.

"Janice got a horrible response from her," Sonya said. "Vicious."

"Does anyone know who Isabelle Hotchkiss really is?" Felicity asked.

"No," Sonya said, "and if you want my opinion, it's a good thing that we don't have to meet her. She's mean enough to everyone on paper. I hate to think what she'd be like in person."

"Speaking of in person," said Janice, "I am just dying to go to Malice Domestic. It'll be my first conference, and I can hardly wait to meet everyone. I've signed up already. With luck, I'll get on a panel. My book will be out in April, and Malice is in May."

"Good timing for you," Jim said.

Janice looked pleased. "Are you going? You're not going, are you? It's strictly cozies. Felicity, are you going? Sonya is."

"I don't know," Felicity said. "I might. It doesn't make economic sense to go to all the mystery conferences every year. They're very expensive. Plane fare, hotels, registration, meals."

"Promotion always makes sense," Janice said. "You have to spend money to make money. I have someone designing my Web site, and I'm doing postcards, and, besides Malice, I'm going to Bouchercon and Left Coast Crime, at a minimum."

Hadley caught Felicity's eye and shrugged his shoulders.

"Janice, postcards are a waste of money," Jim advised. "Ask Ronald. Ask any bookseller. They get those postcards about new books all the time, and they throw them right in the trash. Hell, I get them, and I don't even look at them."

"Well, some people do," Janice said.

"These efforts are probably more important for newbies than they are for established authors," Sonya said. "Janice, we'll all be interested to hear about your experience."

There was a finality about Sonya's statement that ended not only the discussion of book promotion but the meeting as well. Everyone thanked Janice, who said that Dorothy-L enjoyed visitors and had loved having company. So far as Felicity could see, the cat hadn't moved from the position on the couch she'd occupied when Felicity had arrived. Still, what harm did it do if Janice attributed human emotions to the cat?

Once outdoors, Felicity said good-bye to Sonya and Jim. As Hadley walked with her to her car, he said, "It's useless to talk to Janice, but she's throwing money away."

"Maybe she got an astronomical advance," Felicity said.

"For a paperback original? Her advance won't cover what she's already planning on spending."

"I thought it was supposed to be a hardcover. Or a hard-soft deal."

"Nope."

"Someone needs to talk to her. Although Sonya probably has. Or has tried, anyway. Promotion doesn't need to cost what Janice is planning to spend. Or look at Isabelle Hotchkiss. Whoever she is. She's never done any promotion that I know of, and it doesn't seem to have done her sales any harm."

"Yeah, but Janice isn't Isabelle Hotchkiss."

"I know," said Felicity. "I know."

THIRTY-ONE

Edith is a mentally healthy cat: Her love of order is just that, a love, and does not constitute an obsessive-compulsive neurosis. For example, she happily tolerates a messy physical environment and was thus content to live in Quinlan Coates's slovenly apartment. Now, late on Sunday evening, she has no objection to the bottles of shampoo and conditioner, the can of shaving gel, and the disposable razor that Felicity has left at the edge of the bathtub. Edith does, however, expect her fellow creatures to be where they belong when they belong there. In particular, a person who goes to bed at night is supposed to remain there, thus leaving cats free to enjoy bathtubs undisturbed. The occasional quiet trip to the bathroom is permitted, but these prolonged visits are unacceptable, especially, as in this case, when marked by fits of groaning and gagging so loud and annoying as to suggest that the person is afflicted with a hairball the size of a litter box that she can't manage to bring up.

Edith's discontent begins at the tip of her tail. She flicks the tip with a sharp movement that travels to the base, radiates up her spine, and reaches her head, where it makes her ears flatten and puts a sour expression on her face. Abandoning the bathtub, she runs out to the hallway and is halfway down the steep, uncarpeted stairs when she is assaulted by Brigitte, the spirit of chaos, who has been lurking in the hope of a good ambush. Just as Edith is on the verge of trouncing the fluffy little aggressor, large feet stumble into the fray, thus ending it, and both cats vanish.

THIRTY-TWO

Felicity's years in the classroom had made her an expert on the minor illnesses transmitted to teachers by young children. On Sunday evening, she responded with a sort of negative nostalgia to the first wave of nausea, but within a half hour, she had decided that the cause of her acute suffering was not, after all, a stomach virus; rather, it was something she had eaten. Staggering back to bed, she felt an enraged sense of the unfairness of her plight: She hadn't touched the pudding, which had looked revoltingly like glue. The image triggered yet another bout of misery. After once again stumbling back to bed, she curled up on her side and worried about Uncle Bob's hidden money and the evil possibility that the hundred-dollar bill she'd put in the MSPCA donation box could be traced back to her. Had

anyone noticed her as she'd slid the bill into the slot? Her
thoughts then turned to Detective Dave Valentine and the
fool she'd made of herself by distorting the facts of Uncle
Bob and Aunt Thelma's fatal accident, which had been no
accident at all, but Uncle Bob's fault.

She eventually realized that the nausea was abating. Her
great need now was to avoid dehydration. Ginger ale just
might stay down. She dragged herself out of bed and put on
a heavy robe, but once in the hallway, couldn't find the light
switch and decided to make do with the light from her open
bedroom door. Weak and lightheaded, she clung to the banister. Consequently, when her right foot landed on fur instead of wood, she lost her balance for only a moment and
was surprised to discover that the presence of the cats was
comforting; she was sick, but at least she wasn't sick and
alone in this big house. By the time she reached the kitchen,
Edith was perched on top of the refrigerator. Felicity
thought of opening a can of food for her, but the prospect of
smelling one of those vile kitty dinners was unbearable. Ignoring Edith, she poured herself a half glass of ginger ale
from a large bottle, stirred out the bubbles, and took a trial
sip. Yes, she was ready for liquids. Carrying the glass and
the bottle back upstairs, she realized that she was too dizzy
to walk a straight line; the bottle, the half-filled glass, and
her faltering gait probably made her look like a drunk.

Collapsing in bed, she left the reading light on, but felt
too ill to read and, in particular, didn't feel like reading any
of the Isabelle Hotchkiss books that she'd stacked on her
night table. Chilled and weak, she lay in bed hoping that the
cats would show up to keep her company, but Edith would
probably be too shy to jump on the bed while Felicity was in
it, and Brigitte was obviously playing with something in the

bathroom. Through the open door, Felicity heard the soft sound of an object being batted here and there. She idly wondered what Brigitte had stolen. A tube of mascara? A lipstick? As Felicity was about to drift off, Brigitte sailed onto the bed. In her mouth was the disposable blue plastic razor that Felicity had left on the rim of the tub. Felicity's experience as a cat owner, consisting as it did of copyright ownership, failed to generate alarm about injury to Brigitte and consequent vet bills. Instead of seizing the razor, she lazily watched Brigitte tote it around and noticed that the blue razor and the cat's blue-gray fur and amber eyes made a pretty combination of colors. It then occurred to her that if she were living in a cat mystery featuring someone other than Prissy LaChatte, Brigitte's choice of the razor would represent a message about solving the murder. The famous Cat Who, Koko, didn't knock random books off shelves; rather, he made meaningful choices, albeit choices that Jim Qwilleran was often slow to interpret. Did anyone in the Coates case have a name connected to *razor*? Alas, there were no Shavers, Beards, Beardsleys, or Sharps, nor was there anyone who shared a name with any of the well-known brands of razors. Furthermore, Coates hadn't had his throat cut. A pun? *Raiser*? Nothing had been lifted, had it? *Razor*. Occam's razor, the simplest-is-best principle of logic that required shaving away concepts or elements that weren't needed. Was murder an example?

As Felicity's eyes were about to close, her gaze wandered to the stack of Isabelle Hotchkiss books. Who was she? And what was her link to Quinlan Coates's cats? Occam's razor: Start with Quinlan Coates and his cats, Edith and Brigitte. Trim off unnecessary elements: Shave away hypothetical friends of Quinlan Coates, throw out relatives of his who could be mystery writers, discard the weird woman in the police sketch, and what simple explanation remained? Occam's razor: Quinlan Coates *was* Isabelle Hotchkiss.

Too exhausted and sick to pursue the revelation, Felicity fell asleep. She needed to recover her strength. She had work to do.

THIRTY-THREE

On Monday morning, Felicity substituted tea for her usual coffee and ate nothing for breakfast except a slice of toast thinly spread with Dundee marmalade. She felt a little weak, but was no longer acutely ill. As she was drinking her second cup of tea, the phone rang, and Sonya Bogosian informed her that she was fortunate.

"Janice," said Sonya, "has by far the worst case. Hadley went to the Brigham and Women's Emergency Room and got treated and sent home. Jim's still sick, but he's toughing it out, and the best that can be said for me is that I've stopped throwing up. But Janice got very dehydrated. She fainted, and her downstairs neighbors heard her hit the floor and came running up, and one of them drove her to the hospital. Janice had them call me. She's going to be all right, but she's too sick to talk to anyone yet. She's on I.V. fluids."

Felicity silently congratulated herself on having eaten only a few bites of the half sandwich she'd made for herself at the board meeting. She'd also had the sense to keep herself hydrated. "Janice probably ate the leftovers for dinner," she said. "Sometimes the severity depends on how much you've consumed."

"What business did she have eating the leftovers? That food belonged to Witness!"

Felicity was far more interested in her Hotchkiss-Coates revelation than she was in Janice's possible consumption of contaminated food that had rightfully belonged to other people. "Sonya," she said impatiently, "do you honestly wish you'd taken your share home?"

"Well, no, of course not. Anyway, what I want to know is exactly what you ate. Last night when I was so sick, I promised myself that I'd find out what happened. The mayonnaise strikes me as a likely culprit."

"Actually, commercial mayonnaise is a very unlikely source of food poisoning. I was going to use it in a book one time, but I read up on it and decided not to. I just threw suspicion on the mayonnaise instead of actually implicating it. And I used homemade mayonnaise, made with raw eggs. That's the only kind of mayonnaise that's likely to make anyone sick."

"That was hardly homemade mayonnaise we had yesterday. I can't imagine that Janice made it herself. Did you have any?"

"A little. I had a ham sandwich. Well, half of one. With mayonnaise, lettuce, cheese, and tomatoes. But it wasn't very good. I didn't finish it. Oh, and I had some cake."

"Can tomatoes cause food poisoning?"

"Anything can if it's handled by someone with dirty hands."

"You didn't have any pudding?"

"No. It looked disgusting. Speaking of which, Sonya, I'm on the mend, and I'd rather not have a relapse. Do you think we could—"

"Felicity, this discussion is necessary! Admittedly, it would be more useful to all of us if we'd been given some kind of *real* poison and especially if one of us hadn't gotten sick at all, like in that Dorothy Sayers book. Which one is it? Where the murderer builds up his own tolerance for arsenic and then puts arsenic in something he eats himself and feeds to his victim?"

"An omelet," Felicity said. "But I can't imagine that Janice fed us arsenic."

Sounding disappointed, Sonya said, "Still, if we had to be poisoned, it would've been better to experience the effects of one of the classic poisons instead of this ordinary bug, whatever it is."

"Sonya, if we'd had one of the classic poisons, we'd all be dead!" Felicity's mind, however, was on titles: *The Hotchkiss Identity,* maybe. Or *Coates of Many Colors.*

"There is that," Sonya said. "In any case, we should never have been poisoned at all, and I want to know how it happened."

"We weren't deliberately poisoned. We just ate something that made us sick."

"Where did that food come from? That's what I want to know. It's some deli Janice likes. She knows people there. That's why we get a special deal. A discount. And I can't ask her because she can't talk to anyone yet. I thought you might remember the name of the place."

"It's in Jamaica Plain. Tony's? I think that's it. Tony's Deli. It should be on the receipts."

"Janice has the receipts. She's our treasurer."

"Maybe you should wait until she's well enough to talk."

"Wait? I am not waiting! You know, it's easy for you to take this incident casually, Felicity. You got off lightly. The rest of us are very ill. In fact, I'm going back to bed right now."

With that announcement, the conversation ended. Felicity felt well enough to follow her usual morning routine of making her bed, tidying the kitchen, and taking a shower. Brigitte having abandoned the disposable razor in the upstairs hallway, Felicity had returned it to the bathtub and used it to shave her legs. Maybe she should preserve it in some honorable fashion. It deserved to be bronzed. Quinlan Coates had owned many cat mysteries, including some of her own, some by Lilian Jackson Braun, Shirley Rousseau Murphy, Rita Mae Brown, and other successful contributors to the genre. But he had owned the entire opus of Isabelle Hotchkiss. He had been genuinely crazy about cats. As an academic, especially an academic who had started to write mysteries a dozen years earlier, he might well have chosen to use a pseudonym for any series, but it would have been one thing to be identified as the author of sophisticated academic puzzles or existentialist novels of suspense, and quite another to be recognized as the man behind the pen of Isabelle Hotchkiss and her talking cats. Yes, it all fit! And those venomous responses for which Isabelle Hotchkiss was notorious? The horrid letters in which she'd refused to blurb books? Exactly the sort of nastiness to be expected in the world of academe. Or, at any rate, in the world of academe as portrayed in mystery fiction. Felicity was so overjoyed at the prospect of conveying her brilliant insight to Detective Dave Valentine that after shaving her legs, she washed her hair with a perfumed shampoo she saved for special occasions and scrubbed with a body gel scented with the same fragrance.

Stepping out of the tub, she wrapped herself in a giant towel and practiced her opening line: "The intended victim," she proclaimed, "was not Quinlan Coates. The intended victim was Quinlan Coates *as Isabelle Hotchkiss!*"

So stunned would Dave Valentine be by this remarkable feat of detection that he'd overlook Felicity's minor misrepresentation of the manner of Uncle Bob and Aunt Thelma's death or perhaps reinterpret it as a sign of family loyalty carried to excess. Anyway, now that the truth about Coates and Hotchkiss had been revealed to her by her supersleuth cat, she, Felicity Pride, with the assistance of Detective Dave Valentine, would rapidly solve the murder. Having done so, she would finally be at liberty to put her very own real murder to work in promoting her books. The thought brought with it a new realization, namely, that since Quinlan Coates had been Isabelle Hotchkiss, then Isabelle Hotchkiss had perished with him. Ding, dong! By comparison with Felicity, Dorothy had felt indifferent to the news that the Wicked Witch was dead. No more Hotchkiss, no more Kitty Katlikoff, no more Olaf and Lambie Pie! Ding, dong, they were all dead!

There remained the question of who had killed them. The murder hadn't yet been solved; it had been recast. Best to think it out before calling Dave Valentine. Who killed Isabelle Hotchkiss? Someone who knew that she was Quinlan Coates. Supposedly, no one knew. Who could have known? William Coates, Quinlan's son, just might have known, but if, in Oedipal fashion, he'd murdered his father, wouldn't he have put on a show of grief at the funeral? Wouldn't he have made a to-do of claiming Edith and Brigitte as his legacy instead of complaining that his father preferred cats to his son? Who else? Hotchkiss's agent and editor might have known, but neither would have killed so prolific an author and thus so reliable a source of income.

Then there was Ronald: Wasn't it odd that Ronald, who knew everything about books and authors, knew nothing about Isabelle Hotchkiss? But Ronald *was* odd. Good friend though he was, he was peculiar indeed. Looking back to her signing at Newbright Books on the evening of the murder, Felicity vividly remembered that Ronald had appeared while she'd been talking with the fans who had lingered. In fact, he had appeared during a discussion of Isabelle Hotchkiss. Where had he been before that? Ronald doted on his cats, George and Ira, whose vet was someone at Angell, where, on the afternoon of his death, Coates had picked up Edith after her donation of blood. Ronald could have murdered Coates before Felicity arrived at Newbright Books. He could have driven the body—and Edith, of course—to Felicity's house during her talk and signing. But why? Ronald was Felicity's best friend. Was he friend enough to have killed her competition? And his own. Ronald was, after all, beginning to write a cat mystery.

Well, Felicity was Ronald's friend, too, and a loyal one. If she told Detective Dave Valentine that Quinlan Coates had been Isabelle Hotchkiss, he'd follow the same line of thought that had led her to Ronald Gershwin. Therefore, she could not tell him. Not yet.

THIRTY-FOUR

"Felicity, there is something you *must* do for Witness." Sonya's voice vibrated in Felicity's ear. She was sorry she'd answered the phone. "You are the only able-bodied member of the board, and this poisoning needs to be investigated immediately."

"Sonya, what happened was unfortunate, but I don't see the urgency."

"Naturally not! You had a light case of this horrible thing. The rest of us are prostate."

"Don't you mean *prostrate?*"

"I always mix them up. It's my sensitivity to all things verbal. The connections. Words to words. And what does it matter, anyway? The point is that the matter has to be investigated, and you're the only one in a position to do it. I checked the phone book, and there's a Tony's Deli in Jamaica Plain, just the way you remembered. Now, what you need to do is to go there and find out what's what."

"We know what's what. What's what is that Janice bought food there that made us sick."

"Yes, but when did she buy it? On Sunday? Saturday? Or a week before we ate it, in which case we can't report the deli, can we? Anything goes bad in a week. And we aren't positive that this Tony's is the same place. You know, Felicity, it's a very serious matter to report a restaurant. If the deli is blameless, we could be sued. And Jamaica Plain is in Boston, and all the violations of restaurant codes are posted on that Web site, what's it called?"

"The Mayor's Food Court. But what's posted there are reports by the city inspectors. It doesn't list complaints from customers who say the food made them sick. But I do get the point. If Janice bought the food on Sunday morning, then we probably should call the city and have the place inspected. And if this Tony's in Jamaica Plain isn't where she bought the food, we obviously shouldn't report it. I agree."

"It won't take you any time," Sonya said. "Just buzz down there and ask a few questions. It's not as if you had to do all that much for Witness most of the time, you know. But in a crisis like this, I'm glad you're coming through."

Before hanging up, Sonya gave Felicity the address of Tony's Deli, which was on Centre Street, a main thoroughfare of Jamaica Plain. As Felicity knew from having dined in the area three or four times with Ronald, there were dozens of eateries on Centre Street, many of them storefront establishments serving ethnic food that Ronald liked and Felicity didn't. Before leaving on what she saw as a quick errand, Felicity checked on the cats, who were sitting close together at the end of her bed. Edith was grooming Brigitte's ears. The cats were such dear friends! When she'd accidentally stepped on one or both of them last night, the cause of the scrambling and hissing that followed had been her foot rather than any animosity between Edith and Brigitte.

A half hour later, having encountered no traffic on Route 9, Felicity was driving Aunt Thelma's Honda along Centre Street in search of Tony's Deli. She passed a restaurant that Ronald had misrepresented to her as specializing in seafood, as it had, in a way, but the place had been Asian and the seafood cooked with dark sauces that Felicity had found unfamiliar and far too strong for her taste. Spotting the Tony's Deli sign above a storefront, she parked on the street, locked her car, and approached the store, which looked nothing whatever like her idea of a delicatessen. A deli, in her view, was an informal restaurant with a big case of takeout food. The best delis were Jewish and sold half-sour pickles, bagels with cream cheese and lox, pastrami, and fat sandwiches. From the outside, Tony's didn't look like a restaurant at all. Piled in the big windows were bottles, cans, and little packages with labels in some foreign language and, indeed, in some foreign alphabet.

Tentatively opening the door, Felicity saw a grocery store packed with what were obviously Russian foods. A pale-faced woman behind a small cash register nodded to her, and she nodded back. Mystified, Felicity wandered to the rear of the store, where there was, a long refrigerated glass case with takeout food, but not at all the kind of food Janice had served on Sunday or at any of the Witness meetings. Despite a thick brown coating, the piles of whole, flattened chickens looked nauseatingly like naked birds. Potatoes abounded: thick, fried patties, mounds of potato salad containing unidentifiable objects and bits of grayish-green leaves. Many of the vegetables were marinating in clear liquids. The cheese looked like provolone, but a tiny label identified it as yogurt cheese, something Janice had certainly never provided. A second refrigerated case contained whole dried fish, some large, some small, all with eyes that Felicity avoided meeting and mummified skin that reminded her of the foot exhibited by the forensic expert at the Witness meeting. Although the refrigerated cases and the rest of the store looked clean, a musty scent permeated the air, and Felicity was eager to leave.

On her way out, she paused at the cash register to speak with the pale woman. "A friend of mine shops here, I think," she said. "Janice Mattingly."

The woman was expressionless.

"Janice?" Felicity prompted. "I thought she was a friend of someone here?"

"No." Even the single syllable was heavily accented.

Embarrassed, Felicity said, "Could I have a half pound of yogurt cheese?"

While she waited for the woman to get the cheese, she reflected that people like her must wander in by mistake all the time. The shopkeeper must be used to customers who didn't belong and who bought strange foods they didn't want. Why had the proprietors chosen such a misleading name? Why wasn't the place called Boris's Groceries or Natasha's Russian Takeout? Feeling mildly victimized, Felicity paid for her cheese and left. As she drove home, she promised herself that if she ended up making a trip to the correct Tony's Deli, the one Janice patronized, she wouldn't buy anything at all.

By the time Felicity got home, she was feeling remarkably healthy and made herself a cup of tea and a small Russian-yogurt-cheese sandwich on white bread. The cheese was bland enough to be from Scotland and made an excellent food for invalids. Fortified, she called Sonya to report on her investigation.

"I'm sorry to disappoint you," she told Sonya, "but it was the wrong Tony's Deli. This one is Russian, and it's a little grocery store with takeout."

"Felicity, it certainly is *not* the wrong one! After I talked to you, I dug through a box that was handed over to me when I started as president of Witness, and I came across some old receipts. They're from Tony's Deli." Sonya had been the president of Witness for only a year. Her predecessor had moved to Oregon.

"Well, it must be another Tony's Deli, Sonya! This one sold pickled vegetables and whole dried fish. There were no cold cuts, no ham, none of the food we had at Janice's, and the woman there had never heard of her. It was the wrong Tony's Deli."

"On Centre Street in Jamaica Plain."

"That's where I went. I have just come back. Sonya, I'm telling you, it's a Russian shop where the woman at the cash register had never heard of Janice. The food we ate couldn't possibly have come from there. And we have never had food like that at any Witness meeting. Sonya, it was weird food! And everything we have is ordinary American food. It couldn't possibly have come from that place."

Sonya was silent for a moment. When she spoke, her voice was ominous. "Oh, Felicity, this is terrible. It is simply terrible. The food wasn't from Tony's Deli, but the receipts are. How do you suppose Janice got hold of the receipts?"

"What do they look like?"

"Oh, I see. They're rubber stamped. They're from those receipt pads you can buy at any stationery store. Staples. Anywhere. With the Tony's Deli name and address rubber-stamped on."

"Where do you suppose she's been getting the food?"

"I have no idea. Some place that charged her less than we've been reimbursing her. Maybe it's food that restaurants were throwing out. No wonder we got sick!"

"Maybe she got it from the school where she teaches," Felicity said. "It tasted a lot like school cafeteria food. She might've bribed someone in the kitchen. What a pitiful little scam! The poor thing."

"Poor thing? She could have killed us all!"

"She didn't. And she has by far the worst case of food poisoning."

"And you had by far the lightest. It's easy for you to call her a poor thing. What she is, is a thief! What on earth are we going to do?"

"What can we do while she's in the hospital?"

"Hold a board meeting that she won't be able to attend. Hash everything out. Decide what to do."

"Sonya, you and Jim and Hadley are too sick for a meeting."

"Well, Jim and Hadley will just have to pull themselves together. Have you ever read their books? Those hard-boiled detectives are always getting drunk, and they never sleep, and they don't eat properly, and then they get shot or stabbed, and they keep right on going, so Jim and Hadley can just put their bodies where their books are, so to speak."

"What about you? You're not well enough, either, are you?"

"That's no problem," said Sonya. "We'll meet at my house."

THIRTY-FIVE

To Felicity's great annoyance, the phone rang almost as soon as she had hung up. What must it be like to be the sort of fabulously successful author who can afford to rent an office away from home? Or who has the self-confidence not to answer even when Caller ID displays the name of one's mother?

"Felicity," said Mary, "I've been thinking about your Aunt Thelma."

"She wasn't exclusively *mine*," Felicity snapped. "She was *your* sister-in-law." Feeling guilty, she said, "And what were you thinking about her?" Felicity and Angie suspected that Mary was having transient ischemic attacks, ministrokes that sometimes thickened her speech and, in Angie's view, accounted for a tendency to harp on topics that, in Felicity's view, she'd been harping on forever. Still, a person experiencing TIAs deserved consideration, even a person who happened to be one's own mother.

"Well, I'll tell you," said Mary. "I was wondering if you'd happened to come across any of the jewelry she stole from my mother. There was a gold chain. And an opal ring. She weaseled it out of the undertaker, you know."

"I've heard."

"Those things were rightfully mine."

"I'm sure they were. But I have no idea what happened to them. I never saw them on Aunt Thelma, and they certainly aren't here."

"How's your murder? I haven't seen anything in the papers. Are you sure you didn't imagine it?"

"Mother, you did see something in the paper. And I did not imagine it."

"You're very high-strung, you know. You always were. Angie, now she was the easy one. Did I tell you she sent me a beautiful flower arrangement? I kept it going for weeks."

"That was for Mother's Day. It was six months ago."

"There's nothing stingy about your sister. Fresh flowers are very dear. It's a shame she ever married that Italian. She was such a pretty girl, and he was so short and dark. They made a very unattractive couple."

"That was the least of their problems. Among other things, he beat her."

"I've never believed that story of hers."

In desperation, Felicity said, "The doorbell's ringing. I have to run."

"I don't hear it."

"It's very quiet. Uncle Bob paid extra for it. It's the quietest doorbell I've ever heard. I'll call you soon. Bye!"

Feeling more done in by her mother than by the food poisoning, Felicity allowed herself to skip her time with Prissy LaChatte and to take a nap instead. When she went upstairs, both cats were asleep on her bed, Edith on the pillow that had formerly been Felicity's, and Brigitte toward the center, almost touching Edith. Although their extraordinary eye color was hidden, they were remarkably beautiful, especially as a pair. Their coats were an identical blue-gray, Edith's thick and short, Brigitte's long and flowing, and they had somehow contrived to fall asleep in the same curled-up pose, as if a photographer had positioned them to maximum advantage. Reminding herself that this was, after all, her bed, Felicity nonetheless sensed herself to be an intruder and took care to undress silently and to slip under the covers without disturbing the bed's self-proclaimed owners.

When she awoke two hours later, Edith was on one side of her head, Brigitte on the other. Could they have mistaken her head for a third cat? She stirred, and Brigitte suddenly ran across the comforter to pounce on Felicity's feet, and to her amazement, Felicity heard herself laugh aloud. What if she were deliberately to wiggle her toes? She did. And Brigitte again pounced. Neglected, Edith butted her large, solid head against Felicity's and drew another laugh. Attached though Felicity was to Prissy's Morris and Tabitha, she knew that neither had ever given her this silly, even childish, sensation of simple pleasure. Furthermore, although Morris and Tabitha had the convenient habit of making no demands on Felicity until she booted up her notebook computer, once she awakened them, they were quite demanding in the sense that they relied on Felicity to create and animate them; without Felicity's effort, they simply didn't come to life. Brigitte and Edith, in contrast, lived their own lives even when Felicity was asleep; because they existed apart from her, she didn't have to perform the work of making them up. It seemed to Felicity that she had had a minor revelation: She finally understood what people meant in characterizing cats as *independent*.

After washing her face and getting dressed, Felicity wandered downstairs to find a message from Sonya on her answering machine. Jim and Hadley, whose sleuths pursued bad guys despite bullet and knife wounds, were so depleted by upset stomachs that they refused to leave home. Consequently, Sonya had arranged for the board, minus Janice, of course, to hold a meeting online in a private chat room. Sonya had e-mailed the instructions for finding and entering this room, and she expected Felicity to be there at seven o'clock. Without fail! Felicity groaned. Sonya had chronic difficulty in distinguishing between minor obligations to the regional branch of a small writers' organization and patriotic duties to the Land of the Free. And this chat room! Felicity's computer literacy allowed her to create, save, move, copy, print, and delete files. She was fluent in the sending and receiving of e-mail messages. She searched the Web and shopped online. She had entered online chat rooms only three times, when she had been the guest visitor to cyberspace associations of mystery fans who had asked her questions about her books. Each time, she had found the experience unsettling. As she was typing her answer to one question, another would appear on the screen, and then another. By the time her replies had been posted, they'd had nothing to do with the immediately preceding questions. In her own eyes, she had ended up looking as if she were incapable of holding a normal conversation.

Although Sonya, Jim, and Hadley were fellow writers and not fans, she had no desire to make a fool of herself with them, either; on the contrary, she wanted them to see her as a computer whiz and chat room adept. Consequently, she planned to be at her computer by six-thirty to study the instructions Sonya was sending on how to enter this imaginary room. In preparation for a meeting with people who wouldn't see her and wouldn't have cared how she looked, anyway, she took a shower, did her hair and makeup, and put on tailored pants and a good sweater. Although she now felt healthy, she ate a bland dinner of French toast and applesauce. Then, to avoid prolonged exposure to the fishy odor of canned cat food, she moved the cats' water and food bowls to the bottom of the staircase that ran from the kitchen, past the back door that lead to the garage, and down to the large, open family room on the ground floor, which bore no resemblance to a cellar or basement. It had sliding glass doors she had never opened, comfortable-looking chairs and couches on which she had never sat, and a giant-screen television she had never turned on. The sight of all this previously unused space inspired her to move the cat litter and a supply of cat toys down there as well. The cats didn't sleep in the guest room anymore, and, of course, they were more than guests. When she'd finished carrying the cats' belongings two flights down, from the second floor to the ground floor, she felt an obligation to inform Brigitte and Edith of their change of address, but had almost no idea of how to go about communicating with them. On inspiration, she opened a can of some disgusting giblet concoction that Edith liked, and spooned it into a bowl that she carried to the family room. When she returned to the kitchen, Edith was standing on all fours on the table, the edge of which she was affectionately rubbing with her mouth. Looking Felicity in the eye, she uttered a soft, solitary meow.

"Your food is downstairs," said Felicity. "I have moved it." *I am learning to talk to cats,* she thought. It did not occur to her that Edith was soliciting the affection she was lavishing on the edge of the kitchen table.

At six-thirty, she sat at the computer in Uncle Bob's study, where she read Sonya's e-mailed instructions, easily followed them, and found herself waiting for the other board members to show up, as they finally did. Felicity pictured them in her mind, Sonya with her Scandinavian blondeness and her loose cotton garments; Jim with his Chinese-African-American coloring and features, looking like a grown-up version of a child in a UNICEF poster; and Hadley, probably pale and unshaven after his illness.

After a few preliminary postings that established everyone's presence and awareness of the purpose of the meeting, Sonya wrote: "Let's begin by stating that Janice did not intend to poison us. The poisoning we have suffered was accidental. It is, however, the occasion for our discovery of certain irregularities in Janice's billing Witness for money she claimed to have spent."

Felicity, feeling that details were required, wrote: "Janice claimed that the food she supplied for Witness meetings came from Tony's Deli in Jamaica Plain. I went there this morning. It is a Russian grocery store. The food Janice billed us for couldn't have come from there, and the store employee there had never heard of her."

"But I have old receipts with the name of Tony's Deli stamped on them," Sonya added. "Witness has been reimbursing Janice for money she didn't spend there."

"Food isn't the only thing we've been reimbursing her

for," Hadley wrote. "There are newsletter costs, photocopying, office supplies, drinks."

Jim posted a question: "She teaches school. Does anyone know where?"

"Boston," Sonya replied.

"Does the school have a cafeteria?" Jim asked. "Think about the food she's been serving us. Cold cuts, iceberg lettuce, sliced tomatoes. All that could've come from a school lunchroom."

"Those stale rolls," Hadley added. "You're onto something, Jim."

"The pudding," Felicity wrote. "I wondered the same thing. On Sunday, she was talking about all the conferences she was going to. I wondered how she thought she could afford all the promotion she was planning."

"Now we know," Sonya wrote. "By stealing from us!"

"Not stealing," Jim wrote. "Petty pilfering. There's no reason to be punitive."

Felicity agreed but wrote: "Teachers are paid quite decently. They make more money than writers do. But she already collects autographed first editions, and she'll have big expenses if she plans to go to all the conferences, and she also has a sick cat."

"She dotes on that cat," Hadley wrote. "Ugly thing."

"The cat eats special food," Felicity explained, "and the vet bills must be substantial."

"Means, motive, and opportunity," Sonya wrote.

"It isn't murder," Hadley wrote. "It's a sad little scam. It needs to be handled quietly. Look at all she's done for Witness."

Sonya was incensed. "All? Look at all she's stolen from us!"

"She didn't mean to steal," Hadley argued. "She probably

thought she was entitled. And she was ambitious. She wanted to go to conferences and be a star. Felicity, she wanted to be *you*."

"What a thrill!" Felicity posted. Then, remembering that she might be taken seriously, added a smiley face. "And let's remember that she made herself so sick that she had to go to the hospital. Sonya, if punishment is in order, Janice has been punished."

"We still have to do something," Sonya wrote.

"She can't stay on the board," Hadley agreed. "And no more handling money."

"Do we ask her to return what she took?" Jim asked.

"We don't know how much it was," Hadley answered. "Let's give her the benefit of the doubt. She was temporarily deranged. She deserves sympathy. We'll discreetly ask her to resign. And that's that."

"Who will?" Sonya asked. "Do we have a board meeting and spring it on her?"

The other three members vetoed the idea.

"It's a sad event," Jim wrote. "It needs to be handled privately."

"Are you volunteering?" Sonya asked.

"No," he replied. "Felicity could do it. Sonya, you're too worked up about it."

"I can't," Felicity wrote. "She asked me to blurb her book, and I didn't. She must have hard feelings about that."

"You can write a wonderful review of her book," Sonya wrote. "To compensate. Tell her that you've finally gotten around to reading the manuscript, and you love it, and you're going to publish a rave review."

"I don't write reviews," Felicity wrote.

"This will be the first," Hadley responded. "You love the

book so much that you're breaking your silence. Tell her you owe her an apology for not doing the blurb."

Felicity slammed her fist on the desk next to the computer. These chat rooms were worse than she'd realized. "There's probably still time to do a blurb. But I don't want to," she posted. "I don't want to confront her."

"Neither does anyone else," Sonya replied, "but you are the best qualified. I'm sure you will do an excellent job. All you have to do is explain what we've discovered and ask for her resignation. It's big of us to let it go at that. Janice will understand that we could press charges. She'll be relieved. She'll be grateful to you."

"Thanks, Felicity," Jim wrote. "Let us know how it goes."

Hadley and Sonya joined him in offering thanks.

After posting a good-bye, Felicity exited the chat room. As she left the computer, the realization crossed her mind that Prissy LaChatte was immune to other people's efforts to manipulate or exploit her. Prissy was nobody's fool! In the present case, Prissy would either refuse responsibility for confronting the malefactor, or she'd find a way to turn the situation to her own advantage. Felicity was not Prissy LaChatte. In effect, she had already agreed to deal with Janice, and she could think of no way to derive any benefit from what was bound to be an unpleasant confrontation. On the contrary, she was stuck with the job of firing the newsletter editor who'd been eager to write up the story of Felicity's very own cat-related murder. Damn! If only it were possible to shrink herself into near-invisibility, slip into her notebook computer through one of those mysterious ports she never otherwise used, infiltrate the files of her new book, slither out again, and, thanks to the miracles of technology and imagination, emerge as Prissy LaChatte! Prissy would make quick work of Janice Mattingly and her trivial misdeeds. Prissy would then solve the murder of Quinlan Coates, a.k.a. Isabelle Hotchkiss. Well, so would Felicity Pride!

THIRTY-SIX

Edith, the most placid of creatures, has about had it with Brigitte. Has no one ever told that little fiend to let sleeping cats lie? At two-thirty in the morning of Tuesday, November 11, Edith is curled up on the pillow that she defines as hers on the sumptuously large bed that she also defines as hers, and she has been asleep and would like to return to sleep, but Brigitte is sorely trying her almost endless patience.

What is especially infuriating about Brigitte is that she has her uses. In particular, the human inhabitant of this cushy and indulgent new abode is deficient in such interspecies basics as patting and stroking, and Edith must thus rely on Brigitte, who, when she is in an affectionate mood, snuggles sweetly, engages in mutual grooming, and otherwise compensates for the human being's incompetence. In Edith's view, Brigitte suffers from a warping of personality seldom observed in her species. Healthy cats are content to eat and sleep; they are almost incapable of boredom. Brigitte, however, is easily bored. What's more, she is afflicted with an abnormal amount of energy, and the excess is misdirected, usually at Edith. Tonight, for example, whenever Edith drifts into the delightful hypnagogic state that precedes (or should precede) sleep itself, Brigitte sneaks up and pounces. Edith has already given the fluffy little pest a few lessons in the hazards of sinking her teeth into the flesh of a big, strong cat. Brigitte should have learned the first time! Is it going to be necessary to trounce her yet again? Edith hopes not. Almost twice Brigitte's size, she is no bully. But Brigitte is starting to provoke her beyond endurance. Never try the patience of a patient cat!

THIRTY-SEVEN

How hard it was to play the role of Prissy LaChatte when other characters refused to stay in character! As Felicity's best friend in a mystery series, Ronald should have done his part by staying up late, creating dramatic scenes, and requiring Felicity to go zooming off into the night to save him from himself. Although he was permitted to be a suspect in the murder, he should have aroused the suspicions of the police rather than Felicity's own suspicions. As it was, Ronald stayed at home on most evenings. He read books and listened to Glenn Gould. So far as Felicity knew, the police had no interest in him; she alone understood the depth of his eccentricity, and she alone had a hunch that he'd known the identity of Isabelle Hotchkiss. Viewed as a continuing character in the series, Ronald was, in brief, a rotten best friend.

Then there was Dave Valentine, whose detective work should have consisted primarily of calling Felicity, visiting her to discuss theories and suspects, and insisting that she accompany him to assist in interviewing witnesses because they'd be far more forthcoming with her than with him. What had he actually done? Not much. Furthermore, his romance with Felicity should have flourished. By now, he should at least have invited her out to lunch, if not to dinner. In reality, the romance had barely sprouted before her stupid lie about Uncle Bob's accident had caused it to wilt and perish.

This wretched subplot about Janice's little scam was unsatisfactory, too. According to Felicity's literary intuition, it was developing out of its proper sequence. Instead of asserting itself now, it should wait until after the solution to the murder; it belonged in the denouement. What was it doing here?

These dissatisfactions troubled Felicity when she awoke on Tuesday morning. Having wrestled with characters, plots, and subplots before, she was not, however, discouraged. Rather, she vowed to make it plain to all characters, events, themes, and developments that whether they liked it or not, this story was going to be author driven; any elements that disagreed would suffer permanent deletion. At ten o'clock, she set to work rewriting reality by calling Detective Dave Valentine. Her true purpose was to rectify his failure to stay in incessant communication with her. At first, she'd thought of using her observations of William Coates as an excuse to call Valentine; in her books, the dullard police might have overlooked the significance of William's hostility to his father and his rivalry with his father's cats. On reflection, she had realized that there was no need for a trumped-up excuse; she had an all-too-real reason to call. She made a fresh cup of coffee and settled herself at the kitchen table with the phone.

Reaching Valentine, she said, "This is Felicity Pride, and I owe you an apology. I should have been perfectly straightforward about how my aunt and uncle died."

"Family loyalty," Valentine said.

"My uncle wasn't really an alcoholic, you know. He was in the liquor business."

"I know."

"Why is it that Scots don't object to those signs and ads? If there were Irish liquor stores with signs and ads covered with stereotyped pictures of leprechauns and the Blarney Stone, there'd be protests. Or Italian liquor stores with pictures of Mafia hit men. But all those caricatures of Highlanders? And no one minds?"

"Maybe some of us do," Valentine said.

"Maybe we do. Anyway, Uncle Bob wasn't an alcoholic. He was just in the liquor business his whole life. Since I'm making a full confession, I should tell you that he got his start during Prohibition. That's something of a family secret."

"Prohibition ended in nineteen thirty-three," Valentine said.

"So it did."

"He must've been an awfully young bootlegger."

"I hadn't put that together. I guess he was. Maybe he was earning his college tuition. As I said, it's a family secret. My mother just told me about it the other day. By the time I knew him, he was perfectly reputable." This topic was making Felicity nervous. Except to verify that no one had entered or tried to enter her house on the evening when Coates's body had been left in her vestibule, the police hadn't searched her house, and there was no reason why they should search it now. Bob and Thelma certainly weren't murder suspects; they had died months before Coates's slaying. Therefore, no matter what the source of the stashed money, the police had no reason to look for the fireproof box. Felicity's apprehension about discussing Bob and Thelma was pure paranoia. Well, it was impure paranoia. What had possessed her to slip that hundred-dollar bill into the donation box at Angell?

"As I was saying," she continued, "he wasn't an alcoholic."

"But he did drink and drive."

"Obviously," said Felicity. "Obviously, he did drink and drive. I should have told you about the accident the first time we discussed it. About his death and Aunt Thelma's. I feel like a fool. So, please accept my apology."

"Accepted," said Valentine. "Have you remembered anything that might help us out? Come across any letters? E-mail? Anything?"

"Nothing. I'm sorry. Not a thing. But I did wonder about William Coates. You probably did, too."

"In what way?"

"At the funeral, I told him that I had his father's cats, and he was very hostile. Not just about Edith and Brigitte, but about his father. He thinks that his father cared more about the cats than he did about his son. Quinlan Coates didn't leave his money to a cat shelter, did he? Or to—"

"His entire estate goes to Angell Memorial Hospital."

"Animal Medical Center. It's changed its name. Not that it matters. Well, no wonder his son is so hostile to him!" In her excitement, Felicity gripped the phone with one hand, and with the other, made a fist and shook it wildly in the air. At last, her very own detective was confiding information about the victim! At last, she and her detective were discussing a suspect!

"Quinlan Coates had planned it all out years ago. Planned giving. Angell saved the life of some cat of his a long time ago."

"William Coates can't have been happy to be disinherited." Felicity was on the verge of saying that if Uncle Bob had left his money to a veterinary hospital instead of her, she'd have been furious, but the statement would have raised the best-avoided topics of Uncle Bob's money and donations to Angell. "Did William Coates know in advance? If so, motive could go either way, you know. If he didn't know, then his motive could've been to inherit, and if he did know, then his motive could've been revenge against his father for—"

Valentine laughed. "Ideas for your next book, huh?"

"My next book is about mercury poisoning," she said with dignity. "And it has nothing to do with fathers and sons. Or I don't think it does. It doesn't yet."

To Felicity's disappointment, Valentine ended the conversation there. She hung up with a mild sense of insult. He had not taken her seriously! On the other hand, she had made him laugh, and that was something, wasn't it? It was a start. Maybe the dead romance could be nursed back to life and made to blossom after all.

On to the exoneration—or exculpation?—of her unsatisfactory best friend, Ronald Gershwin. She called Newbright Books and reached Ronald, who, as if to illustrate his deficiencies as a series character, said that he was busy. Could he call her back? As usual, he made it sound as if his busyness consisted not of restocking his shelves, advising customers about books, and taking their money, but of passing along state secrets. Ronald did, of course, blab confidential information, but he gossiped about authors, agents, editors, and book deals; his knowledge of espionage came exclusively from his reading of spy novels. Still, he indulged in breaches of confidentiality. So, if he'd known the truth about Isabelle Hotchkiss, why hadn't he tattled to Felicity?

"Are you free for dinner?" she asked.

"Thursday," he said.

"Thursday it is."

The phone went dead. Normal human beings didn't just hang up on friends! At a minimum, they said good-bye. Preferably, they made excuses for ending conversations and then said good-bye.

"Therefore," Felicity said to the cats, who were lingering in the kitchen, "Ronald is not a normal human being. Are you normal feline beings? Should I use the phrase about Morris and Tabitha? Or will the critics scratch out my eyes for being cutesy? And if so, will it be because my mother leads a secret life as an anonymous reviewer of mysteries, especially mine?"

Emboldened by her success in thus conversing with Edith and Brigitte, Felicity bent over Edith, who was rubbing against a table leg, and touched the top of Edith's big head. It would be a good idea, wouldn't it, to have Prissy speak to Morris and Tabitha more often than had been her habit. Also, Morris and Tabitha were perhaps hungry for affection. Prissy must remember to pat them frequently.

Felicity again sat at the table and placed a phone call, this one to Janice Mattingly, who answered immediately in a surprisingly robust voice. "I was dehydrated," she explained. "Once they got fluids and electrolytes and whatever back into me, I felt pretty much okay. I got home last night.

The stress of worrying about Dorothy-L was starting to make me sick, so the hospital let me leave. I kept thinking about what could happen to her with me gone. The neighbors know better than to let her out, but who knows? Anything could've happened, and she is so attached to me. And I wasn't sure they'd give her the medication when they were supposed to, and maybe she wouldn't swallow her pills for them, or she'd spit out her pills, and they wouldn't notice."

Felicity waited silently as Janice continued to voice her fears about the cat for another few minutes. When Janice paused for breath, Felicity said, "Well, I'm glad you're doing so well. The rest of us are, too."

"I can't imagine what happened. Tony's is very, very clean. Spotless. And I bought that food on Saturday afternoon. I have to wonder whether we didn't all have a stomach virus, something that was transmitted very quickly. I did notice that Jim looked a little under the weather. Did you notice?"

Eager to postpone the confrontation, Felicity said, "I didn't notice that, but maybe he did. Anyway, we've all recovered. But the reason I called, besides wanting to know how you were doing, is that I've finally had time to read your book."

She let the silence hang. Having published numerous books herself, she was familiar with the sensations an author experiences when someone says, "I read your book," and then fails to add, "And I loved it" or "It was wonderful!" or even "It was interesting."

Finally, she said, "I owe you an apology for neglecting you. And your book. I was just overwhelmed with work. Anyway, now that I've read it, I wonder whether we could get together to talk about how I can help you to promote it.

I thought you might to come and have dinner with me. But maybe you're not well enough yet."

"I'm well enough." Janice said. "I can't eat much, but who cares? I'm practically back to normal. Tonight?"

"Let's keep it early. Six-thirty? Do you need directions?"

"No, I've been there for board meetings, remember? And when Sonya and I dropped you off after the funeral."

"Of course," said Felicity. "After the funeral."

THIRTY-EIGHT

Out of consideration for Janice's traumatized digestive system as well as her own, Felicity planned a bland meal of roast chicken, steamed rice, and green beans, the ingredients for which she had on hand. She then turned to planning the Prissy LaChatte mystery to be written after the one now in progress. The motive and the opportunity for the murder were marinating to her satisfaction, but the means she'd chosen, mercury poisoning, was proving troublesome, and if she substituted some other toxin, it might prove incompatible with the motive and the opportunity.

She had originally been drawn to mercury in part because of its ready availability. It was in old-fashioned glass thermometers, fluorescent light bulbs, thermostat probes in gas ranges, and dental amalgam. Felicity preferred not to make the murderer a dentist, but perhaps the villain could remove the fillings from his own teeth. So, mercury was ubiquitous. But what kind of mercury? The elemental mercury in fever thermometers was far less toxic than she had hoped; contrary to a widely quoted claim, the one-half or one gram of mercury found in a glass thermometer was not enough to contaminate a twenty-acre lake. Damn!

What she needed was the kind of soluble mercury that descended to the earth in rain and was converted to methylmercury, which ended up in fish and, eventually, in the bodies of people who ate fish, especially big ocean species like tuna and swordfish. How many tuna sandwiches would the murderer have to feed to the victim to achieve a fatal result? And what did mercury taste like, anyway? She wasn't eager to experiment on herself. But the ideal form was dimethlymercury, which didn't pose the literary risk of leaving the victim stricken but alive; a drop or two on the skin was deadly. Unfortunately, the compound was used only in chemical analyses and wasn't sitting around where her murderer or any of her red herrings could get hold of it. Furthermore, it was so dangerous that it would be difficult for her to do in the victim while keeping the murderer alive for Prissy to bring to justice. Damn, damn, damn!

When Janice arrived at six-thirty, Felicity was setting the kitchen table and still fretting about the technical challenges posed by mercury. The rotten stuff! Well, at least she wasn't making tuna or swordfish for dinner. She had taken a short break from the irksome toxin problem to glance through the manuscript of Janice's book, *Tailspin*. The protagonist was a man in his fifties. A journalist, he had ruined a successful career by drinking and was now a teetotaler. His two Abyssinian cats were not named Koko and Yum Yum; they were called Louis and Murphy.

She knew that Janice had arrived before the doorbell rang. The luxury vehicles driven by the residents of Newton Park were almost silent. Hearing a noisy engine and the shotgun sound of backfiring, she looked out the window and saw that Janice was making the mistake of parking her mud-colored clunker with its wheels on the Trotskys' lawn. Consequently, she hurried out the back door and down the driveway while waving a hand to get Janice's attention.

Opening her car door, Janice stepped out and returned the wave. "I'm so glad to see you, too, Felicity!"

Felicity made a quick recovery. "I'm glad you're well enough to be here. Maybe you could move your car to my driveway?" Lowering her voice, she said, "The man who lives in that house has some silly notion that the street is his property."

Janice returned to the driver's seat and, after struggling to start her car, moved it as Felicity had requested. As Felicity headed toward the back door, Janice said, "Is this where you found the body?"

"No. The body was at the front door."

"Could we go that way? It's terribly important, I think, to view real crime scenes."

"There's nothing to view. Everything has been cleaned up. And I don't have the key to the front door with me."

"Maybe later? Atmosphere is crucial, isn't it?"

"You're welcome to soak it up whenever you want, but let's go in this way."

When the two women had climbed the half flight of stairs to the kitchen, Felicity took a good look at Janice and realized that she was still showing the effects of the food poisoning. Her chalky-white complexion was even paler than usual, and her crimson lipstick looked like blood applied with a brush. Her hair was lank, there were dark circles under her eyes, and her eyelids drooped.

"Let me take your coat. Have a seat," said Felicity. "You must be exhausted."

Janice hung her purse, a large handwoven sack, on the back of a chair and removed a red woolen cloak embroidered with colorful stick figures. Underneath she wore chino pants and a thick greenish-yellow sweater that smelled vaguely of animals. Goats? Felicity wondered. Or some more exotic species? Yak or llama, perhaps.

"I'm still a little bit weak." Janice seated herself at the table.

"A drink? Scotch? Wine? Or maybe you're not ready for that yet. Ginger ale? Spring water?"

"Ginger ale would be good. With the bubbles stirred out, please."

As Felicity was pouring ginger ale for herself and her guest, Brigitte flitted into the room, scampered to the table, and jumped onto it.

"What a beautiful pussycat!" Janice exclaimed. "Here, Miss Pussycat!" She smacked her lips and tapped her fingernails on the tabletop. Brigitte moved toward her. "What gorgeous eyes she has. Golden! Felicity, this cat is to die for. And she's young. She really is just a little baby kitten, isn't she? Aren't you lucky! Dorothy-L is fourteen, which isn't all that terribly old for a cat these days, but it isn't young. I've practically forgotten what it's like to have a young, healthy kitty like this one."

Brigitte, having moved toward Janice, sauntered to the opposite end of the table, where she sat on her haunches next to a dinner plate and fixed her amber eyes on the new-comer.

Addressing her, Janice cooed, "Aren't you a lucky baby girl to be allowed on the table! Not all kitty cats are so spoiled, you know." As Felicity handed her a glass of ginger ale and seated herself at the table, Janice returned to her normal tone of voice. "Felicity, was Morris allowed on tables? Your own Morris, I mean, not the one you write about, not that there's all that much difference, is there!"

"Morris was allowed everywhere." Felicity did not add that there was even less difference between her own Morris and the fictional one than Janice might suppose. "My other cat, Edith, is quite shy. She may show up, or she may not. She's young, too. She's four. Brigitte, this one, is two." In the hope of gently leading the conversation toward Janice's pilfering by way of one of her possible motives, she said, "And they are both healthy. Robustly so. Up-to-date on their shots, everything. In fact, Edith is a blood donor at Angell. She gets all her shots free. Free exams, blood work, everything. A bag of cat food when she donates. Dorothy-L must be costing you a fortune. All the medicine. And you're thinking about some new treatment for her. And she has to eat special cat food, doesn't she? That can't be cheap."

A startled expression crossed Janice's face. Felicity attributed it to her own indelicacy in having spoken so directly about money. Still, the topic of money was the only reason she'd invited Janice to dinner.

"But, of course, you have an advance and a book coming out," Felicity said. "A wonderful book!"

"Thank you."

"And you have such extensive plans to promote it. I'm very lazy about that myself. And the expense! Maybe it's my

Scottish heritage, but I can't see spending all that money unless I'm sure it's worth it."

"Oh, it is worth it!"

"Not always. It's important to be selective, not just to throw money randomly at any promotion at all. But I do understand the temptations. I really do. Mystery writing is a tough business. All writing is. It's very competitive."

"Fiercely."

"On the other hand, there's a tradition in mystery writing of supporting one another. Look at all our organizations. Take the two of us. We both belong to Sisters in Crime and Witness and some other organizations, too. But those cost money. The dues for Witness are fairly low, but some of the other groups? And it adds up when you join everything."

"It does," Janice said stiffly. "Then there are clothes. I need new clothes. And my car. I can't go around driving that junk heap."

Distracted from her goal, Felicity said, "Who cares what you drive? How many of your readers are going to see your car?"

"You never know. Image is terribly important. It's essential. When your readers meet you, they don't want to just meet some ordinary old person, do they? They want to meet a *star*."

"I wouldn't say that," said Felicity, who cultivated a rich picture of her readership and took care to present herself in stellar fashion. "If anything, your readers want to meet your protagonist. Or they expect to."

"My protagonist is a man," said Janice, "so they can't honestly expect me to be him."

"What matters for you," said Felicity, "is your sense of having to be a star."

"But my hair is awful. I've been thinking about going blonde. Could I ask you who does your hair?"

"Her name is Naomi. But I have to warn you—"

"Oh, I know! She must be hideously expensive. Cheap hair color looks so . . . cheap, doesn't it? But money is no object."

"Money is always an object," said Felicity.

THIRTY-NINE

Seconds after informing Janice that money was always an object, Felicity reminded herself that time, too, was always an object, especially her own time, and that she shouldn't waste too much of it on this business of Janice's scam. Having intended to serve an early dinner, she had cooked the rice, which was keeping warm in Aunt Thelma's new rice steamer. A small roasted chicken with no seasoning except salt was in the oven, and the green beans, which she'd blanched, needed only to finish cooking in a little butter. She now rose and began to heat the green beans.

"A drop of wine with dinner?" she offered.

"Well, a little tiny bit, I guess. You know, if you eat raw oysters, you're supposed to drink white wine with them. It minimizes your chances of getting hepatitis."

"We're not having oysters on the half shell, I'm afraid. Just roast chicken." It occurred to Felicity that the meal she'd prepared was so unexciting as to be almost Scottish. Her maternal grandmother had often served chicken. She had prepared it by boiling it in gallons of plain water for many hours. "But we can still have white wine."

"Actually, chicken is crawling with bacteria."

The bottle in the refrigerator was a white burgundy. As Felicity opened and poured it, she found herself thinking that it was a shame to waste it on Janice. She should have saved it for Ronald, who would have appreciated it. Even Ronald would not have referred to its germicidal properties. When she had served the food and taken a seat, she didn't bother to raise her glass. Janice hadn't waited for her, but was already sipping the wine while stroking Brigitte. At the sight and smell of the roast chicken, which Felicity had arranged on a small platter, Brigitte abandoned Janice to poke a curious nose into the food. Without consulting Felicity, Janice picked her up and placed her on the floor. "There are limits," she said.

Felicity had intended to delay the confrontation until the end of the meal, but she was annoyed to have Janice take it upon herself to remove Brigitte from the table. Had Felicity been a guest at someone else's house, she'd have been disgusted by the presence of a cat on the dinner table and nauseated by the thought of eating food that a cat had already sampled. This, however, was not someone else's house, and if anyone were to set limits on Brigitte, she herself, and not Janice, should do it. "There's something we need to discuss," she said.

"My book! I am so happy that you like it."

"Actually, it's something else." Felicity kept her eyes on

the chicken she was cutting. Instead of describing her visit to Tony's Deli and going on to accuse Janice of fraud, she spoke obliquely. "I went to Jamaica Plain this morning." She ate a bit of chicken. "And before I say more, I want you to know that I understand your motives and that I sympathize."

"Empathize."

Empathize? Felicity did not question the correction aloud. In fact, enjoying as she did a high opinion of her own communication skills, she disregarded the possibility that she and Janice were talking about two entirely different matters. In Felicity's view, her own mastery of verbal expression usually eliminated the risk that she would be misunderstood or would misinterpret the blundering efforts of others. Janice, she decided, failed to comprehend the distinction between sympathy and empathy. "I *do* understand," she said magnanimously.

"Of course you do. You of all people!"

If Felicity's conscience had been clear, she would probably have realized that she and Janice were speaking at cross-purposes. As it was, Felicity bristled. She was no thief! Keeping Uncle Bob's cash didn't count. She had inherited the house and its contents. Therefore, she had inherited the fireproof box. "It's ironic that you are the person who ended up suffering most," she said, with the intention of making a delicate reference to the severity of Janice's food poisoning. Glancing at the white meat that Janice was devouring, she added, "Look, it'll be best for everyone if you'll make a clean breast of things."

Janice said, "I don't know how you figured it out. Like take the cat food. How'd you know about that?"

Cat food? In softening Janice up for the confrontation about her pilfering, Felicity had mentioned free cat food as one of the perks of Edith's serving as a blood donor at Angell. Felicity also remembered having gone on to say that Dorothy-L must be costing Janice a fortune. Hinting at the economic motives for Janice's fraud, Felicity had acknowledged the cost of a possible new treatment as well as the need to pay for the cat's medicine and special food. By comparison with the veterinary procedure and the prescription drugs, the special cat food must be a minor expense; Janice had certainly picked an odd example.

Even so, Felicity answered Janice's question. "When we were at your house on Sunday, Dorothy-L's food was in your kitchen."

"But how did you make the connection?" The wine or perhaps the conversation had brought color to Janice's face. Her cheeks had round red spots. Something, perhaps the wine, had given her an appetite. She dug her fork into the rice and bent her head to shovel the food into her mouth. Again without swallowing properly, she said, "I found out by a fluke. How did you find out?"

Baffled, Felicity asked, "How did you?"

"You remember that horrible letter I got? I sent *her* my book and asked for a blurb, and I got simply the most awful letter. Sonya read it, and so did some other people, and they said it was the most vicious thing they'd ever seen. I know it by heart. 'This person cannot write and should not try.' And then there was, 'In a market glutted with cat mysteries and, indeed, with mysteries, this book does not stand a chance of success.'"

"That really is vicious." Felicity refilled both glasses and sipped from her own. Her heart was pounding, but determined to show nothing, she concentrated on keeping her face expressionless.

"So, about three months ago, actually, on the first Monday in August, it must've been, I was at Angell to pick up a case of Dorothy-L's prescription food. I always buy it by the case because I'm always scared I'll run out, and her digestive system just will not tolerate regular cat food, so I can't just go to the store and grab what's there. It really isn't clear what's causing all her digestive problems. Whatever it is, it's separate from her thyroid disorder, but it does make me wonder about the radioactive iodide treatment, you know, whether she could tolerate that." Janice took a break to eat voraciously. "Anyway, you know how they keep a lot of dog and cat food in the lobby?"

"Yes," said Felicity, who didn't trust herself to say more.

"Well, the kind I needed wasn't there, and someone went to look for it for me, but I knew it would take a while. Angell is the best place, but it isn't necessarily the fastest. And there's no place to sit in the lobby, so I went into that sort of corridor beyond it and took a seat on one of the benches, and I got to talking with this man who was waiting there, too."

"Yes," said Felicity.

"And his cat was a blood donor. He was picking her up. He told me all about how she gave blood, how he brought her in four times a year, the first Monday of the month every three months. Like, this was the first Monday in August. He showed me a picture of her and of his other cat, and he told me they were Chartreux. They really are gorgeous. You could tell he was crazy about them. And I told him about Dorothy-L. Anyway, I didn't tell him about *Tailspin,* but I just asked him if he ever read cat mysteries. And you know what he said?"

"I have no idea."

"He said, 'Most of those people can't write and shouldn't

try.' Just like that! So then he asked me if I'd ever read Isabelle Hotchkiss. Naturally, I said yes. And he said that he didn't know why anyone else bothered writing cat mysteries because the market was glutted with them and with mysteries in general, and most new mysteries didn't stand a chance. So, I knew."

"The same phrases as the ones in the horrible letter."

"But I didn't say a thing! I mean, I just made normal conversation, and then they brought out Dorothy-L's food. So, as I was sort of saying good-bye, I introduced myself, and he more or less had to do the same thing. And he said his name was Quinlan Coates. There's another piece of luck. I mean, the first was that we were at Angell at the same time and got to talking. And the second was that he had an unusual name."

"So it must've been easy to find out more about him." Feeling the need for strength, Felicity tried to fortify herself by eating, but she had to take small bites. Her mouth and throat were dry.

"I used all those Web sites. Once I knew where he lived and where his office was, I hung around, so I knew what kind of car he drove, his license plate, where he parked his car, all that stuff."

"In a way, you stalked him." In her anxiety, Felicity lost control of her accent and heard herself say "stawked," but Janice seemed not to notice the lapse.

"It was very interesting. You know how real private investigators always say how boring it is to keep someone under surveillance? Well, that part of it really was boring. But it was interesting to do it myself, if you know what I mean. I'm already using it in the book I'm writing now. And in terms of planning, that part was pretty easy, too, because I knew when he was going back to Angell for his cat to give blood. Every three months, the first Monday, so that made it November third, which was perfect, of course, because it was after daylight savings ended."

"What if he'd picked up his cat early?"

"I'd have had to wait for February, which I might've had to do anyway if he'd parked right near the entrance. But he didn't. The way it worked was that I took the T to Angell, which was very inconvenient. Public transportation isn't what it should be. Anyway, I did, and I hung around on South Huntington Avenue, waiting at bus stops and stuff, until I saw his car. I watched where he parked, and then I went in the main entrance and got a case of Dorothy-L's food and waited in line to pay for it. Coates had to wait in line, too, to let them know he was there for his cat and to do the paperwork. So, it was easy to strike up a conversation, remind him that we'd met there before, ask about his cats, and so on. And I said I'd love to meet the one he was picking up, Edith, because I'd never seen a Chartreux before. Just pictures."

"He was probably flattered."

"Oh, he was! He told me all about Chartreux cats, Carthusian monks raising them, all this stuff, until they brought out his cat. So, I gushed over her. She really is beautiful, by the way. And we sort of naturally left together. I told him my car was at the far end of the parking lot, and we just kind of walked together, with him carrying the cat in her carrier and me carrying the case of cat food, until we got to his car. I made sure I kept talking. I was telling him all about the radioactive iodide treatment that I was thinking about for Dorothy-L, and I didn't give him a chance to interrupt me. So, he went ahead and unlocked his car and opened the back door, and he kind of bent over to pick up the carrier."

"And?"

"And I whacked him over the head with the case of cat food. That hasn't been done before, has it? You haven't used it, I know, and it isn't in Isabelle Hotchkiss or Lilian Jackson Braun, as far as I can remember. I don't *think* it's been used before."

Felicity refilled both wine glasses. "I don't think so, either."

"Do you mind if I have seconds? This is really good."

"Please, help yourself."

Janice served herself more chicken, rice, and green beans, and ate hungrily before resuming her narrative. "He was heavier than I expected. *Dead weight* really means dead weight, not that he was probably dead yet, but he was a skinny little guy, very short and bony, and I'm stronger than I look, so I managed to shove him into the backseat with the cat carrier. He'd dropped his car keys. So I took them and drove the car a few blocks away, not that anyone would've noticed anything at Angell. I mean, the advantage of Angell is that all anyone notices is animals. Even if there'd been people walking by, they'd have been paying attention to their dogs or thinking about their sick animals in the hospital. But I didn't want to stay there too long. So, I drove over near Jamaica Pond, which is no distance, and I pulled over. I used duct tape that I'd brought with me on his nose and mouth, and just to be safe, I sealed his head in some plastic from the dry cleaner, which I'd also brought along. It's hard when you've read a lot of mysteries. The possibilities are endless, and there's always the question of what's reliable and what isn't."

Eager to maintain the role of sympathetic listener, Felicity said, "And then you drove to my house. You knew I'd be at Newbright, I guess. Janice, I understand why you were angry at me. You had every right to be. I should have known what a wonderful book you'd write, and I should've found the time to read it and blurb it. But, of course, I wasn't thrown off my work. Most people would've been, I guess, and that would've made two down."

"Room at the top. But you were sort of incidental. The real competition was Isabelle Hotchkiss."

"For both of us." In an effort to maintain the appearance of normality, Felicity forced herself to eat a little chicken. "In that sense, you did me a favor."

"God moves in a mysterious way," Janice said. "Like, take the cat. Edith. I thought that would freak you out. I mean, if you'd wanted a cat all these years, you'd've had a cat, and you didn't. So, I thought maybe you'd hate being stuck with the cat. Only you weren't. Anyone who lets a cat get on the table and eat off plates really is a cat lover."

"Brigitte doesn't exactly eat off plates. Not really. She just likes to see how food smells. But tell me something. How did you move the body to my vestibule?"

"Not easily! I parked in your driveway. This neighborhood is totally deserted, you know? I'd checked it out. No one walks around or anything. What's wrong with these people? Anyway, I parked there, and I dragged him, which was not, believe me, easy. But I did it. People get superhuman strength in a crisis, you know? Like those mothers who lift cars that their kids are trapped under. And then I carried up the cat in her carrier, and that was that. Oh, except that I returned his car to the spot behind his building where he always parked. And I walked home from there. It was a long walk, but that was the way. And on the way home, I found a dumpster behind a store and threw out the raincoat and the gloves I was wearing. It was a wet night, remember?"

Felicity took a token sip of wine. "Yes, I do remember. It was foggy."

In one of her books, the resolute and resourceful Prissy LaChatte wouldn't have been blathering about the weather. Rather, Prissy would have decided that the time had come to talk the murderer into surrendering herself to the police. Did real murderers ever turn themselves in? Could they be talked into it? Felicity felt sick to her stomach. She lacked the persuasive powers of Prissy LaChatte. Furthermore, the woman seated at her table was not a creature of her imagination, but a ruthless, ambitious killer who had no reason to confess to the police and go to jail. In fiction, amateur sleuths convinced murderers to give themselves up. In real life, murderers murdered again. Still, having been in comparable situations many times in fiction and never before in real life, Felicity did what Prissy would have done.

"Janice," she said, "just think! Once people know about all this, *Tailspin* will make the *Times* bestseller list. And stay there forever! The public will be *so* curious about you."

Janice rose, reached into the big woolly purse that she'd hung on her chair, and pulled out a small handgun. Pointing it at Felicity, she said, "Curiosity killed the—" She let seconds pass. "Finish it, Felicity!"

"Cat," said Felicity. Edith and Brigitte! No, not the cats!

"Cat *writer*," said Janice. "In this case, curiosity killed the cat writer."

FORTY

Out of the corner of her eye, Felicity saw that Edith was standing awkwardly in the doorway that led from the front hall to the kitchen. The big cat wore a puzzled expression, as if she'd just awakened from a trance and had no idea where she was or how she'd arrived there. Felicity broke into a sweat. Hack mystery writers had a phrase for the trick of injecting a thrill into a story by placing a pet at risk: *pet jeop*. Was Edith in jeopardy? The combination of the gun and the cat terrified Felicity and filled her with a deep, raw sense of protectiveness. Always beautiful, Edith was somehow more extraordinary than ever, her dense coat a more vivid shade of blue-gray, her eyes a richer amber. Despite her powerful build, she looked heartbreakingly vulnerable.

But Janice loved cats.

Didn't she?

"Sonya knows you're here," Felicity said. "So do Jim and Hadley. They discovered the little game you've been playing with the receipts from Tony's Deli and all the rest. They asked me to speak to you about it. They knew you were coming to dinner. Janice, please! I am totally sympathetic to everything you've done. All of us have to promote our books, and I know what that costs. And Isabelle Hotchkiss was competition for me, too."

Janice's face had regained its pallor. She was, if anything, paler than usual, and the hand holding the gun trembled. Her other hand rested lightly on the back of a chair. It occurred to Felicity that for a person recovering from serious food poisoning, Janice had eaten more than was wise. Also, she had drunk quite a lot of wine.

"Please let me help you," Felicity said. "I happen to have a great deal of cash on hand. A *great* deal. More than a hundred and twenty thousand dollars. Enough for you to go anywhere you want. You can disappear."

"You're lying," Janice said.

"I'm not lying. The uncle who left me this house was a very wealthy man. He left a great deal of cash."

"You like bloodless endings. I've noticed that."

"My readers don't like gore. Neither do I. Janice, neither do you! And there doesn't have to be any. I'll show you the money." With pain in her Scottish heart, she said, "I'll give it to you. I'll give you all of it."

"Where is it?"

"Upstairs. It's in a fireproof box behind a headboard in one of the guest rooms. The key is right here in a drawer. Look, you don't have much choice. If you shoot me, the police will find out you were here. Sonya and Jim and Hadley will all say so. Your car is in my driveway. Your fingerprints are all over the door, the table, the silverware, the chair. You'd never be sure of wiping off all of them. There'd be trace evidence. Janice, all you have to do is go away! I'll tell the board that you never turned up for dinner. You can mysteriously disappear."

"What about *Tailspin*? What about my whole career? What about Dorothy-L?"

"Tell your agent where you are. No one else needs to know. Isabelle Hotchkiss was a woman of mystery, and it didn't do her sales any harm. Quinlan Coates's lawyer probably knew his secret. His accountant must have. His agent. You can do it! Think of all this cash as a grant to launch your career. Dorothy-L can go with you. There are good veterinarians everywhere. And don't worry about this little local fuss with Witness. I'll settle that. If I make a generous donation, no one will care about the details." Inspiration struck. "Janice, just think! If you want to, you can stay in Boston! No one will ever guess. The money will tide you over until your royalties start pouring in. You can stay in Boston, but you can quit your day job! You'll never have to enter a classroom again!"

Janice's face brightened. Her shoulders relaxed, and the hand holding the gun stopped shaking. "Let me see the money," she said. "You go first."

"I'm going to open the drawer and get the key." With Janice almost pressing against her, Felicity did just that.

As she headed toward the front hall, Edith turned tail and fled across the slate floor toward the stairs. By the time Felicity reached the staircase, Edith was nowhere in sight.

Where was Brigitte? She'd left the kitchen a while ago. Where had she gone?

Felicity began to ascend the stairs. "As I said, the money's in a box behind the bed."

Janice said, "You're still going to help with my book, right?"

"Of course! I'll be delighted. I'll send the blurb to your editor. I'll review it, too. Here we are."

Felicity dropped to her knees, lifted the bed skirt, and was happy to find that Edith was not under the bed. She rose, reached behind the headboard, removed the fireproof box, and set it on the comforter. She unlocked and opened the box, gave Janice a chance to watch as she thumbed through the stacks of bills, and asked, as if offering to send leftovers home with her guest, "Do you want to take the box? Or I can give you a bag."

"Just give me the box. Are you sure it's a hundred and twenty thousand?"

"It's a hundred and twenty thousand five hundred fifty-five dollars. Most of it's in hundred-dollar bills."

"This would be easier if it was thousand-dollar bills."

"The largest U.S. denomination is one hundred."

"Really?"

"Yes, really." *And you've been teaching school?* "Janice, the box is quite heavy."

Nancy Drew would have managed to use the metal box as a weapon. And Prissy LaChatte? She'd never have allowed a murderer to pull a gun on her in the first place. Or she hadn't yet, anyway. Mercury poisoning would be a big bother. Maybe a nice, simple gunshot would be a better choice. Felicity usually avoided guns, mainly because she knew almost nothing about them. They couldn't be much worse than mercury, could they? The one in Janice's right hand wasn't difficult. Even Felicity recognized it as a revolver. What she knew about revolvers was that they were reliable: If you squeezed the trigger, a revolver fired a bullet.

FORTY-ONE

Edith recognizes the scent of unwashed llama. To Edith, Janice reeks of hunger, cold, and fear. In search of safety, the heavy-footed Edith runs upstairs to the bed she now prefers, the big one that offers warmth and companionship, the prime spot in this new household. So trusting is she of this secure place that instead of hiding under the bed, she hops up and settles on her usual pillow, where she rests undisturbed until Brigitte races into the room and onto the bed. With the unmistakable air of a cat looking for trouble, Brigitte sidles up to Edith and pinches the thick flesh at the base of Edith's big skull.

Edith flattens her ears against her head. Her eyes glow with suppressed rage. Still, she refrains from striking. Determined to awaken the wild ancestral feline that sleeps beneath Edith's infuriating air of civilization, her tedious contentment, her dull placidity, Brigitte withdraws to the foot of bed. Her eyes closed, her body relaxed, she pauses to enjoy a few moments of meditation. After taking two deep, full, cleansing breaths, she conjures the image of herself in her very own special place of perfect safety, and once she sees the place vividly with her inner eye, she relishes the sounds and smells of the place, its feel beneath her paws, and the tranquility of spirit with which it blesses her. After benefiting from her sojourn in the imaginary place, Brigitte says good-bye to it, gradually opens her eyes, and slowly returns to the foot of what was formerly Felicity's bed. The remarkable feature of Brigitte's imaginary place is that it is almost identical to the real pillow still occupied by Edith. The only difference between the real place and the imaginary one is this: Where Edith is, there Brigitte belongs.

Relaxed and refreshed, strong and self-confident, Brigitte eases forward, crouches, and springs on Edith, who rouses herself, hisses at Brigitte, and, propelled by her mighty hindquarters, jumps off the bed and zooms into the hallway and toward the stairs. Brigitte follows in close pursuit. Little and fast, she is a sports car to Edith's limousine, a sports car that catches up to the limo, trails it, edges forward, and smashes into its side, determined to force it off the road.

FORTY-TWO

"I'll manage," said Janice. "I'm stronger than I look, remember? Just close the box. Don't lock it. Now, move over there." She gestured to the opposite side of the bed. When Felicity had complied, Janice bent over a little, wrapped her left hand and forearm around the metal box, and lifted it to rest on her hip. "Let's go. You first. Walk slowly."

Felicity obediently moved to the door and into the hall-way, where she scanned for the cats. Janice had done nothing to threaten them. She hadn't aimed the revolver at either of them, hadn't spoken about taking them hostage, hadn't done a thing, really. Then again, she hadn't said outright that she'd shoot Felicity before making off with the money, had she? She hadn't needed to. Was she simply going to depart, leaving Felicity free to tell the whole story to the police? Did she expect Felicity to make so preposterous an assumption? Apparently so. Felicity knew better. Maybe Janice would kill her here in her own house, or maybe she'd force Felicity into a car, either her own clunker or Aunt Thelma's Honda, and then commit her second murder somewhere else. Near Jamaica Pond? In the parking lot at Angell? What did it matter! This house would be her best choice, Felicity thought. Perhaps Janice would stage a suicide. She'd fire her weapon point-blank at Felicity's heart. Or head? She'd wrap her victim's hand around the gun to leave prints. A good forensics expert would spot the ruse, but by then, Felicity would be dead. And Edith and Brigitte? Brigitte was so annoyingly interested in *everything*. It would be just like her to get in Janice's way. And both cats were so hideously vulnerable. Edith was big and solid, like an old-fashioned doorstop, but against a malevolent human being, she'd be defenseless. Where were they? Edith had probably taken refuge under the bed that had once been exclusively Felicity's. Where was Brigitte?

As Felicity moved toward the top of the staircase, with Janice right behind her, she experienced a sudden revelation: To her astonishment, she was more worried about Edith and Brigitte than she was about herself. Although a revolver was aimed at her back, her own fifty-three years were not passing before her eyes; rather, she was gripped by images of creatures who had just entered her life.

She prayed silently. "Dear God, You are on the verge of letting Janice Mattingly kill me. Why You should thus have botched the plot of a cozy mystery is Your business and not mine, but I can't refrain from pointing out that unless You've been publishing under an assumed name—if so, what is it?—I have more experience in these matters than You do, and it's my professional opinion, and that of other published mystery writers, that the amateur sleuth, namely, me, is supposed to survive to the end of the book, and that the murderer is supposed to get caught. Readers like to see order restored and justice done. If Your sales are lousy, You'll have only Yourself to blame. Anyway, I don't have time to critique Your efforts in full because, as You can see for Yourself, I'm about to die and would consequently like to put in a few last words. First, if there's one thing readers hate, it's the death of animals, so You would be ill advised to kill Edith and Brigitte. Second, on the subject of my immortal soul, in writing Your review, please ignore everything my mother has to say about me. She is wrong. I *am* capable of love. In particular, I love Edith and Brigitte. Love counts for something, doesn't it? If not, it should. Respectfully yours, Felicity Pride".

Felicity rested her right hand on the banister and began to descend the stairs. A scrap of her award-winning Latin came to her: *Facilis descensus Averno.* Virgil. *The Aeneid.* Easy is the descent to Hades. Ha! Her own route to the underworld was steep and uncarpeted. Why hadn't Uncle Bob hired an architect instead of buying a house from a developer! Money. Always, money.

"Slow down," Janice ordered her.

Only three steps from the top, Felicity paused. In the stillness of the big house, the sound of Janice's footstep was unnaturally loud. Then, breaking the silence, came a hiss, a quick snarl, and the familiar and uncatlike pounding of Edith's paws, followed immediately by a melee of sounds and sights as Edith rocketed down the stairs with Brigitte in close pursuit while, simultaneously, the metal box banged its way down after the cats, the revolver clattered after it, and Janice, tripped by the cats, lurched into Felicity's left shoulder, lost her balance, and, with a short, hideous scream, plunged down the steep, hard steps to the slate floor of the hallway. Felicity, who had no recollection of saving herself, found that she was huddled against the wall near the top of the staircase, still only three steps down, with her derriere planted on the wooden tread and both hands locked on the banister. Her eyes were on Janice Mattingly, whose motionless body lay below, face down on the gray slate. Near the door to the vestibule was the fireproof box. Close to it was the revolver.

The cats again broke the stillness. Brigitte, truly possessed of little cat feet, darted lightly up the stairs and past Felicity. The little cat's fluffy coat showed damp patches. With the unmistakable air of a victor, Edith strolled into the hallway from the direction of the kitchen, calmly seated herself on her haunches, casually bent her head to lick her front paws, and, with a glance up at Felicity, uttered her tiny meow, a single high-pitched note that Felicity somehow found reassuring.

With the brittle composure induced by emergencies, Felicity pulled herself to her feet, carefully descended the stairs, and stepped around the bundle of ugly greenish-yellow sweater, chinos, and dark hair that was Janice, who lay only a few yards from the spot in the vestibule where she had dumped the body of Quinlan Coates. Janice, however, might still be alive. Perhaps she was unconscious. Perhaps she'd merely had the wind knocked out of her. Felicity made for the revolver. Ever the mystery writer, she pulled the cuff of her right sleeve over her hand before touching the weapon. Knowing almost nothing about firearms, she was unable to identify the safety, but assumed that there was one. On or off? Why couldn't murderers use poison! Slowly and cautiously, she carried the revolver to the kitchen, opened a cabinet, and hid the weapon behind six bottles of single malt scotch. Then she called 911. She needed the police, she said. And an ambulance. And please tell Detective Dave Valentine!

After completing the call, she returned to the hallway, where Uncle Bob's shabby old fireproof box lay on the slate floor by the door. As Felicity had already worked out in detail worthy of the Scot she was, the cash in that box represented the sale of a great many books. The cover price of *Felines in Felony* was $22.95. She received a ten percent royalty, that is, $2.295 per book, of which fifteen percent went to her agent, Irene, leaving the author $1.95075 for each hardcover sale. Uncle Bob's cash, $120, 555.00, thus represented the sale of 61,799.307 copies of the hardcover edition of *Felines*. Even with the publicity she'd get now that she'd be allowed to grant interviews about her very own murder, she'd never sell anything close to sixty thousand copies. Furthermore, her calculations about book sales excluded the state and federal taxes she'd have to pay on her royalty income. Uncle Bob's cash was tax free. Felicity walked briskly to the fireproof box, lifted it with both hands, walked around the motionless Janice, climbed the stairs, and put the box back in its hiding place, which is to say, back where it belonged.

She returned to the hallway. As she had just reminded God, she was not a heartless person. In learning to love Edith and Brigitte, she had proven herself capable of love. She was also capable of decency to her fellow human beings. To her credit, she regretted never having learned CPR. She did summon the courage to lift the layer of lanky dark hair that covered Janice's face. One eye was visible. It was open and had a frozen, flat look. Felicity quickly let go of the hair. She had been wrong to touch the body at all.

FORTY-THREE

Alerted by an anonymous caller, a major Boston television station sent a crew to Newton Park. The media arrived only moments after the police and the emergency medical vehicles. In the powerful lights, night became day. Because the corpse lay inside Felicity's house, her abode became an official crime scene. In her interviews with Detective Dave Valentine and with the reporters sent by Boston television stations, radio stations, and newspapers, she modestly gave all the credit for solving the murder of Quinlan Coates to her beautiful Chartreux cats, Edith and Brigitte.

In describing Janice Mattingly's fatal fall, Felicity said nothing of the cats' role. Janice, she maintained, had intended to hold Edith and Brigitte hostage until morning, when Felicity was supposed to go to her bank, withdraw a large amount of cash, and give it to Janice, who, she said, had never specified the amount. Intending to incarcerate Edith and Brigitte in their cat carrier until Felicity had paid up, Janice had forced Felicity upstairs at gunpoint in search of the cats. After failing to find them there, she was on her way back downstairs, just behind Felicity, when she tripped and fell. Yes, the stairs were steep and uncarpeted, and the floor at the bottom was made of slate. Yes, Janice Mattingly had been recovering from acute food poisoning. Against Felicity's advice, she had consumed a considerable quantity of wine. And, yes, the entire story of Quinlan Coates's murder and its solution certainly did bear a remarkable resemblance to what one found in Felicity's own books. The latest, by the way, was called *Felines in Felony*. It was available wherever books were sold.

Trace evidence recovered from Quinlan Coates's body and from his car supported the account of the murder that Janice had given to Felicity. She had left no fingerprints, but an eyelash found on Coates's clothing matched hers, and his car had contained several hairs from her head. The revolver had belonged to Janice Mattingly's late father.

"So," Felicity said to Dave Valentine on Friday evening when the two were seated at dinner in her dining room, "there are still a few things I don't understand. For instance, who was that weird-looking woman in the sketch you showed me?"

Valentine had invited her out to dinner. They had agreed that a Scottish restaurant would be appropriate and had gone on to agree about why there was no such thing outside Scotland. Who really wanted spaghetti that had been boiled for thirty minutes and, for a special treat, topped with the contents of a bottle of ketchup? And cold ketchup at that.

Their grandmothers had served the dish often. It was as Scottish as haggis. There being no Scottish restaurants in Greater Boston, Felicity had insisted that Valentine come to her house for broiled Scottish salmon. In reading up on mercury poisoning, Felicity had discovered that farm-raised salmon contained dangerous amounts of mercury, but she found it impossible to believe that a product of Scotland was unsafe. Also, although one of her complaints about Scottish food was the repetitiousness of the menus, it did not occur to her that she herself served salmon rather frequently.

"The sketch," said Valentine. "Well, you remember the funeral? How devoted Coates was to his wife?"

"Dora. He never got over her death."

"In a way, he did. Dora Coates wrote the first Isabelle Hotchkiss book. When she died, he finished the book she'd been writing. When we went to his apartment, we found a room he kept locked. He had a computer in it, the usual stuff. And he also had women's clothing. And a wig."

"Good lord!"

"Not so good. It set us off in the wrong direction, look-ing for contacts he might've made wearing the wig and the dresses. But it seems like he never wore them outside that room."

"He became his wife. He kept her alive. Or by becoming Isabelle Hotchkiss, he became his wife. I wonder why she wrote under a pseudonym. I mean, he was the academic."

"Sexism? From *you*? She was a professor of English."

"So you knew all along that Coates was Isabelle Hotchkiss, but you were led astray. More potatoes?"

Dave Valentine was a hearty eater. Felicity liked a man with a good appetite. She especially liked a caber-tossing Scot with a hearty appetite who wore his kilt to the Highland

Games and had had the sense not to wear it tonight to have dinner with her. The former represented laudable Scottish chauvinism, whereas the latter would have suggested unpardonable eccentricity. As he was concentrating on his third helping of potatoes, Felicity said, "I have to tell you that I'm glad that you didn't go after my friend Ronald Gershwin. He can be quite odd, but he's harmless, and he's very bright. He went to Harvard."

"Like your uncle," said Valentine with a strange little smile.

"Like Uncle Bob," said Felicity. "What's wrong with that?"

"I don't know if I should tell you this or not, but your uncle's dead, so what does it matter? Felicity, he didn't go to Harvard."

"Yes, he did."

"If he did, he escaped Harvard's notice. They've never heard of him."

"You're joking. You're not joking. You investigated my dead uncle?"

"Not a lot."

"The liar! What an idiot I've been! Anyone can buy Harvard chairs and lamps and knickknacks! I can hardly wait to tell my mother. It'll give her something better to think about than what she calls 'my' murder. With the strong implication that I committed it."

"She got the profession right—mystery writer."

"Poor Janice. She was a horrible writer. And so ambitious. So sad." She paused for a sip of wine. "But her cat is going to be okay. Ronald has adopted her. One other thing. This is about my neighbor, that obnoxious Trotsky. The Russian publisher." Felicity continued to harbor the suspicion that he had pirated her books.

"He isn't a publisher."

"Yes, he is."

"Not a book publisher. He publishes software."

"Software? Computer software?"

"What other kind is there?"

"None," said Felicity in disappointment. "He doesn't publish books, too?"

"No. Software. What were you going to say about him?"

She had to think for a moment. "Oh, yes. This neighborhood is practically empty. But, he goes crazy when anyone goes near his lawn. So, when Janice drove Quinlan Coates's body here and dragged it all the way to my vestibule, why didn't he notice? Or maybe he did."

"He was out. Actually, his wife was still at work, and he was down the street."

"Down the street from here?"

"You've got a neighbor named Loretta."

"Loretta the organizer. She runs our condo association."

"That's where he was."

"With Loretta? What was he doing there?" Felicity belatedly remembered Loretta's two children by two different fathers. "Oh," she said. "Oh!"

"Yes, oh," Valentine said flatly. "Oh."

Brigitte wandered into the dining room and leaped onto the table. Janice Mattingly had been one thing; Dave Valentine was quite another. "Off! Get off right now!" Felicity scolded.

Brigitte ignored her. Dave Valentine gently picked up the dainty cat and placed her on the floor. Edith wandered in. He patted her.

"My hero cats," said Felicity. "The *Globe* and the *Herald* both called them that."

"Those stories are going to sell a lot of books for you."

"I hope so. I feel motivated to write these days. I have a lot to say."

She told the truth. Now that she knew something about cats, she was eager to write about them. She would, of course, always be grateful to her very own late Morris, but she was also grateful to Edith and Brigitte.

As it happened, Felicity's cats were indirectly responsible for solving her final mystery, which was, of course, the puzzle of how Uncle Bob had acquired cash worth the sale of 61,799.307 books. While savoring newspaper accounts of her role in solving the murder of Quinlan Coates, she had also scanned the papers for a report of a counterfeit or stolen hundred-dollar bill left in the donation box at Angell. She had found nothing. The bills certainly looked genuine and probably were. Who had paid the sums recorded in the notebook? And why?

On the Sunday afternoon following her Friday night dinner with Dave Valentine and their Saturday night together at the movies, Felicity, who was feeling increasingly at one with Prissy LaChatte, broiled a large piece of Scottish salmon for Edith and Brigitte. Prissy regularly cooked for Morris and Tabitha, but always remembered to set a timer. Felicity, however, burned the salmon and thus dirtied the oven of Aunt Thelma's expensive range. In search of instructions for persuading the self-cleaning oven to clean itself, she found the three-ring binder that contained the manuals and warranties for the many new appliances in the house. In leafing through it, she came upon a collection of receipts and acknowledgments of delivery signed and dated by Aunt Thelma. The names of the months were written in the same script that appeared in the little notebook. The numbers, too, were identical. It hadn't been Uncle Bob who had recorded those deposits. It had been his wife, Aunt Thelma, the same Thelma who had persuaded the undertaker to give her jewelry from her mother-in-law's body, the same Thelma to whom Bob had doled out the weekly house-keeping money in cash. For decades, Aunt Thelma had skimmed off her share to amass a private fund. The money was thus Felicity's to spend. On Edith and Brigitte.